DEADLY DOLLARS!

Quint scowled at Latigo a moment, then laughed as if wishing him good luck was a waste of time and breath. He pretended to look at the crowd, then lunged in, swinging the flat of his hand with its armament of ridged silver dollars. This time, Latigo was ready. He spun out of reach. Quint fanned the air with his open-handed blow. The silver dollars went rolling through the dust.

Latigo paid no heed. "I've done my damndest to get you off my back, Quint," he said through his teeth. "But you won't."

"How'd they ever let a halfbreed in a white man's army?" Quint taunted. "Suckled by a goddamn squaw . . ."

What happened next was too fast for most eyes to follow. . . .

TRACKDOWN

by

Dean Owen

FAWCETT POPULAR LIBRARY • NEW YORK

Based on LATIGO, the cartoon strip by Stan Lynde.

TRACKDOWN

Published by Fawcett Popular Library, a unit of CBS Publications, the Consumer Publishing Division of CBS Inc.

ISBN: 0-449-04644-9

Printed in the United States of America

First Fawcett Popular Library printing: March 1981

10 9 8 7 6 5 4 3 2 1

1 Devastation, seen through the drizzly haze of an April daybreak, presented Sergeant Burley Quint with a dilemma.

"Why couldn't they have left a tree?" he bellowed, his great neck swelling. "Just *one* goddamn tree!"

This roar of displeasure dried the mouths of his troopers. Because he was known to backhand the nearest face within reach when enraged, they edged their horses away from his dun.

In the furious cannonade of the previous late afternoon, before cavalry clashed, attacking guns had ripped to shreds what had been a pleasant slope of trees. What Union guns had failed to destroy was leveled by the cannon of retreating Confederates.

Corporal Jeff Crowder, a slender veteran with graying beard, gestured at stumps and shattered tree limbs.

"Not a tree that'll take the weight of a man, Burley," Crowder told the sergeant. He was one of the few not over-awed by the giant Quint. "Hell, why not turn the poor bastard loose."

Quint was outraged. "Me give up a chance to hang a *lootenant?* You know how I feel about them. Every damn one . . ." Quint glanced at his men to note any reaction to his expression of such hatred, but they had learned to show no interest in anything he might say. They were looking at the battlefield, deserted save for their small outfit and the prisoner. Lumps of dead among ruptured cannon and overturned supply wagons attracted vultures.

Crowder argued quietly with Quint, then shrugged off the attempt as futile. He knew that Quint's hatred of all officers, blue or gray, would soon claim another life on this bloodied strip of land.

Crowder turned to their prisoner, erect on a weary battle horse. "Sorry, it's gotta be this way Reb."

"Ah thank you for taking mah part, Corporal," Duke Sateen said in his soft drawl. Damned if he'd show fear to these troopers who had blundered onto him, just as the

5

opposing forces had blundered into each other yesterday. "May ah say again, that ah am not a spy."

"You won't be sayin' it for long," Quint interrupted. He absently fashioned a noose while glaring at the denuded landscape.

"Ah am Duke Sateen of Colonel Mosby's command and as a prisoner of war have certain rights . . ."

"Mosby left you behind to spy on us!" Quint's yellow-brown eyes were shot with triumph. "You got no rights!"

"As you can see, Sergeant, mah horse has a saber slash on the foreleg. Ah did not wish to press him in such condition, so ah hid out all night . . ."

"You bein' with Mosby is enough for me." Quint glowered. "You bastards always chewin' away at Grant's coattails."

"And one time we nearly got coat and all," Sateen reminded, but no one was listening. His cynical smile deepened in memory of a day at Warrenton Junction when they had been pursuing Union cavalry across the railroad tracks. And at a time when General Grant's train was due to arrive from Washington. Had they arrived five minutes earlier, the general would have been their prisoner. And Lincoln, hard pressed to fill the gap, might have chosen a lesser man as replacement. A most certain advantage for the battling South. But Grant as usual had his luck.

Sateen, in the tattered uniform of a Confederate cavalry officer, sat his saddle with apparent indifference, though his hands were bound behind his back. His handsome, cynical features were darkened by a downswept mustache and a beard that was usually neatly trimmed. Lately he'd been without scissors.

His mounted captors couldn't understand the smile he managed to keep in place. With the exception of Quint and his corporal, they were youngsters, mud-splattered from spring rains that had helped cleanse the air of the stench of yesterday's battle.

They rode a quarter of a mile trying to find a tree. A house burned to the ground, a flattened barn, but no suitable hanging tree.

How ominously quiet, Duke Sateen thought, looking up at the sky. His eardrums still throbbed from the sounds of yesterday's battle, the spit and roar of cannon, yellow-red muzzle flash, hiss and whine of big shells, men whimpering in mortal agony. Most hideous were the sounds of downed

6

war horses. Sateen's mount had suffered only slightly, but the wound had led to his capture.

After the Union forces had swept on in pursuit, Sateen hid himself and the lame horse in a deep gully. Not hidden too well as it turned out.

Quint reined in and took out his frustration on the troopers. He bellowed and they kept out of his way. A broken nose among recruits in Sergeant Quint's outfit was common as chiggers.

Even when passive, Quint's broad features were flushed. Now they were scarlet. His face was rectangular, mostly jaw, scant forehead. He was built on the grand proportions of a solid oak cabinet that could crash through flooring if tipped over.

"Corporal Crowder, go find us a goddamn tree!" Quint roared. "That's an order!"

Crowder knuckled his graying beard, judged Quint's fiery mood, then decided to risk one final appeal for leniency. "You oughta see Cap'n Cantrell before you go ahead with this, Burley."

Quint showed large teeth. "Mebby the Rebs shot off his head yesterday," he said in a low, tense voice. Mention of the captain worsened Quint's mood. A captain soon to be promoted to major, according to rumor. Hell, no wonder the war dragged on, if the army was fool enough to make an officer out of a man whose mother was a squaw.

While Crowder rode ahead to look for a tree, the prisoner spoke.

"Ah think you should listen to me, Sergeant," but Quint ignored him. Sateen drew a deep sigh. He had hoped that by daybreak the blue bellies would be gone in pursuit of the enemy. Most were. It was ironical that this ragtag remnant of cavalry had flushed him out. Sateen believed in luck. This day he'd drawn no aces. Eleven enlisted men, one corporal and a sergeant added up to thirteen. Unlucky thirteen.

"Me belly's rumblin', Sarge," spoke up one of the gaunt young cavalrymen. "Let's shoot him an' be done with it."

"You don't shoot a spy. You hang him."

"We ain't had no breakfast . . ."

"After we hang him, we'll forage," Quint muttered, glaring at a battlefield now ominously stilled. Nothing moved but Crowder in the distance. Quint's dun grunted under its load of two hundred and forty pounds.

A faint shout reached them.

"Crowder's found us a tree limb," said one of the troopers jubilantly. "Now we can get the job done an' eat."

Lashings cut deeper into the prisoner's wrists now that his limping horse was pushed to a fast walk. He thought irrelevantly of the blood from his wrists staining what had once been an immaculate butternut tunic. Sateen cocked an eye at the lone tree that was to be the site of his execution. All the limbs but one had been shot away. In the faint light of the overcast morning, it looked like a beckoning one-armed woman.

Quint reined in at the base of the tree. "What the hell's so funny, Lootenant?"

"Had ah the power, Sergeant, ah would prefer charges against the artilleryman who failed to shoot away that remaining tree limb."

"We'd have found another one for you," Quint said, his good humor partially restored. He tossed the rope over the limb, the noose dangling.

"How long's it take to hang a man, Sarge?" the complaining young trooper asked anxiously.

"I hope this'un takes a little longer. I ain't never hung a lootenant before. It'll be a pleasure."

The young trooper was interested in food. "Reckon soon's it's over with we kin find us some aigs?"

"Rebs likely cleaned the country of eggs," Quint said.

"*Our* country, Sergeant," Sateen reminded.

"Then sing *Dixie* when I lift your boot heels four feet off the ground." Quint dropped the noose over Sateen's neck and jerked it tight. A nervous titter broke from some of the young throats. Other troopers were pale. It was one thing to get used to seeing a man reduced to bloodied bits by the terrible shrapnel, or run through with saber or bayonet. But the deliberate killing they were about to witness chilled their empty stomachs.

One of them retched. Quint seemed amused.

Corporal Crowder gently massaged his beard while he addressed Sateen. "You're takin' all this mighty calm."

"Last night ah held a pat hand. This mawnin' it appears ah didn't have the right cards after all."

"You a card player?"

"Some."

"I like a game," Quint chimed in amiably.

"Ah'll make a bargain with you, Sergeant."

"Bargain for what?" Quint demanded suspiciously.

"We cut for high card. Your neck or mine."

More nervous laughter dribbled from the young cavalry-men. There was some knee slapping.

Crowder winced at the bad joke. "Lieutenant, I wish you'd yell or scream. Or wet your britches like some of 'em do. Instead, you sit there with that damnable smile on your face."

"Mah luck ran out. Simple as that."

Quint was suddenly all business. "I'm s'posed to asked if you got any last words."

"Take care of mah horse, if you will. He's a good one. That wound will heal in a week or so."

Sateen turned his face to the sky. Clouds had thickened so that even a final view of the sun was to be denied. To take his mind off the jolting drop from the back of his horse, he thought of the women he had known. Their scented images reeled through his mind. He felt again their warm limbs, heard their laughter. He remembered the rustle of impatient Melinda's petticoats as she scampered up the staircase ahead of him to open the bedroom door. Dorene's mouth, Ellen's slim and elegant legs. The wonderment in his young eyes when first he beheld the naked loveliness of a woman. What was her name? He had forgotten.

A pity.

Sergeant Quint said jovially, "You know any prayers, Reb, you best make it quick. You got about five seconds to live."

Sateen's bearded lips curled. "Ah've nothin' against the Almighty if such there be. But ah'd find it tedious prayin' to a deity who created Yankee scum like you."

"That's the last insult you'll be throwin', Reb! Corporal, when I give the word, swat his hoss."

Crowder nodded. "A good drop will snap his neck. Reckon he deserves that much . . . to go quick. . . ."

"Sergeant!" An authoritative shout cut through the still-ness. Men twisted in their saddles to look around. "Hold up there, Sergeant!" The same voice, nearer now.

"That goddamn Cantrell!" Quint raged, but softly.

A tall, dark man wearing the blue of a Union cavalry captain, galloped toward them. Quint snapped a hand to his pistol, but Crowder hissed a warning. "Don't be a fool, Bur-ley. Shoot him an' you'll be the next to hang!"

Cole Cantrell spurred toward them over a rise of ruined

ground, and reined in. A glowering Quint was the last man to salute.

Captain Cantrell jerked a thumb at the condemned. "What are you up to, Sergeant? Who is this man?"

Quint choked down his anger. "One of Mosby's murderin' devils. We was about to make a *good* rebel outa him." Quint, at attention in the saddle, forced a smile. Despite their recent strained relationship, the captain might unbend enough to appreciate battlefield humor.

Cole Cantrell's mouth hardened. "We execute no prisoners in my command."

Quint was silent.

Captain Cantrell was staring at the prisoner. "When you seemed about to die, you actually smiled."

"Thinkin' of somethin' pleasant, ah was, Captain. A lady."

A livid Quint obeyed Cantrell's order to remove the noose from the prisoner's neck. Cole saw blood on the wrists.

"Who tied this man?" he demanded.

"I done it." Quint failed to keep the snarl out of his voice.

"It isn't a time to neglect military courtesy, Sergeant. Will you repeat what you just said . . . and properly?"

"I done it . . . *sir.*" A muscle twitched in Quint's cheek.

"No need to tie a man as if you were trussing a hog for the butcher," Cole snapped. Then he steadied his frayed nerves. Yesterday's battle had erupted suddenly. It was much worse than those that are planned.

Sateen spoke. "Ah am grateful for your timely arrival, Captain. Ah had no real wish to be hanged."

"An understandable reluctance," Cole agreed. "You did serve with Mosby?"

"Ah had that honor, Captain."

"If the dead could speak, they wouldn't consider it an honor. Who are you?"

"Lieutenant Gaylord Sateen . . ."

"Calls himself Duke," Corporal Crowder put in.

"A nickname," Sateen explained. Cole nodded. He had his own, Latigo, from boyhood.

"Feelings against Mosby's raiders run high here in Sixth Corps," Cole said.

"We have been troublesome," Sateen admitted, smiling.

"A little more than troublesome."

"Ah hold no ill feelings. Yankee blue bellies are merely men, after all, just like us. And mankind in general must surely be one of the Almighty's greatest failures."

10

Cole almost laughed. After four years of carnage the ex-Mosby raider just might be right.

Cole looked at the sergeant and made up his mind to see that the man was transferred. This wasn't their first run-in. Let some other company have the blessing of Quint's meaty fists, Cole thought sourly. He outlined in crisp tones what he wanted done.

"He's your prisoner, Sergeant," Cole finished. "A *live* prisoner. Do I make myself clear?"

"That you do, Cap'n. Anything else . . . sir?"

Cole made him repeat the orders so there would be no misunderstanding. He glanced again at the prisoner, then rode away.

Yesterday afternoon had been explosive. Most of the night he had been with pursuing cavalry. Shortly before dawn he doubled back. He was expected at field headquarters.

During the night the clouds spilled rain. There were some who claimed God drew a curtain because He was sickened by the sight of such earthly madness as had taken place yesterday in a stretch of spring woods. Cole was heartily sick of it himself.

Some claimed it would soon end, the madness. But he wondered if stubborn pride would allow such luxury within his lifetime. . . .

When the captain had ridden away, one of the young troopers let out a whoop of joy. "Mebby now we can fill our bellies!"

They rode slowly back the way they had come. Corporal Crowder swung in beside Sateen. "Glad your neck wasn't stretched, Lieutenant."

"Ah share the sentiments." Sateen looked around at the captain who was just dipping from sight in a hollow where all that remained of farm structures was a privy. "Ah never want to forget your captain," Sateen said. "May ah ask details?"

Crowder lowered his voice so that Quint, riding stiffly in the lead, couldn't overhear. "Cap'n Cole Cantrell. Half-Irish, half-Indian. An' all man."

"Ah certainly can attest to that, Corporal."

"One of the best officers Phil Sheridan has. It's on account of men like him that you Rebs are losin' this war."

"Ah can say nothing against the man who quite literally yanked me from the clutches of the hangman. But ah believe that your havin' more men, money an' supplies is by far the greater factor."

11

After Sateen had been turned over to a supply outfit returning north with empty wagons, Burley Quint spoke to Crowder. "One day I'll kill that captain son of a bitch. Damn war won't last forever. An' when he shucks outa that uniform . . ." Quint slapped one of the meaty fists into the palm of a hand.

"Wouldn't mess with him if I was you, Burley," Crowder said as they walked to the cook fire.

"Made me look like a fool in front of my men." Quint flung himself down on the damp ground. "Somethin' I'll never forget."

"You got hate comin' out your ears, Burley."

"I burn with it."

Crowder plucked a blade of grass that plunging cavalry and rampaging fieldpieces had somehow missed. He put it between his neat white teeth. "Got no love for officers, but Cantrell's one of the best."

"One of the worst." By then the sun was a pale orb directly overhead in the clouds. All they had been able to forage was a piglet that a small girl had been hiding as a pet. She wept when it was taken away. Fortunes of war. Stewed with black-eyed peas it stretched far enough to give each man a full plate.

"Why's Cantrell one of the worst?" Crowder wanted to know.

"Half-breed."

"What's him bein' half Indian got to do with it?"

"When I was little, I learned to hate twice. Once for half-breeds. Once for army officers."

Crowder lounged on the damp ground, using a twig to pick boiled pork from his teeth. "Go ahead, Burley, tell me your sorry tale."

Quint failed to note the faint sarcasm. "My great-aunt, she run off an' married with a Cherokee. Gran'pa never let her come home. Not even for a visit . . . never. An' she was his favorite, too. But he ended up hatin' her insides."

"Just 'cause she married a Cherokee?" Crowder shook his head in disbelief.

"Gran'pa had strong feelin's." Quint looked at Crowder so there would be no mistake when he said, "Gran'pa passed 'em on to me."

"Seems like he sure done that, Burley." Across the way three gunners were trying to replace a broken wheel on a fieldpiece. Buzzards squawked and beat the air with black

12

wings. Tree limbs usually used as perches had been blown to pieces by cannon.

Crowder was interested in the basis for Quint's hatred. He asked if the Cherokee in question had been not only Indian but also an army officer.

"Hell no," Quint said.

"Then why the hate for officers?"

"That Cherokee bastard's got nothin' to do with army."

"I don't see the connection . . ."

"It was back when we was fightin' the Mexes in forty-seven."

"The Mexican War, you mean."

"My Uncle Settle, he come home with whip scars on his back. A drunken lootenant took a bullwhip to him. When Uncle Settle knocked him down, they jailed him, by gad. He was never right in the head when they finally let him out. I tell you, Jeff, he had them scars till the day we buried him."

"Your gran'pa filled you fulla hate like some folks fill a keg with molasses."

Quint's mouth tightened. "I swore that in this war I'd find me a cap'n or a lootenant or mebby even a general. Up in front of me when the bullets was flyin'. I'd watch my chance an' blow out the back of his head." Quint grinned and awaited Crowder's approval.

"You come close to hangin' yourself a lootenant this mornin'," was all the corporal could think to say.

"That goddamn Cantrell buttin' in."

"Glad he did. I kinda like that Reb."

Quint glowered and thrust out his empty plate. "Fill it up, Corporal."

"Kettle's empty . . ."

"Scrape the kettle!"

Crowder groaned and got to his feet, wondering why badgering Quint had been so important. He always paid for it.

He scraped up a few morsels of food, handed the plate to Quint, then changed the subject to that hoped-for day when the war ended. "What you figure to do, Burley?"

"Got me a cousin out West. Runs a freight line. Might work for him. Likely will."

"Mebby I'll go out that way myself. Got no chains on my legs." Crowder hugged his knees and watched a burial detail dig a trench for the dead. He thought of his own loss back in '58. A bridegroom at twenty-five, a widower a year later. He lost not only his wife, but the unborn child too. His first ties

13

since were with the man next to him. Mean and unpredictable as he might be, Burley Quint provided an anchor.

"I'll get you a job drivin' mules," Quint said. And the matter was settled.

2

Two Union couriers swept past Cole Cantrell at full gallop, dispatch bags bumping at each long stride taken by their sweated horses. He watched them disappear into a long dip of land. Then they emerged on the far side, not slackening their furious pace.

"Wonder what's up," Cole said aloud, and spurred his big black horse into a lope.

Minutes later Cole dismounted at the command post and turned his horse over to a trooper. The animals ridden by the couriers were being rubbed down, and the couriers were hurrying toward cook fires for what would probably be their first meal in many miles.

Cole pondered the reason for the urgency while he straightened his uniform, brushed off dust and tried to make himself presentable.

He approached a small house on a rise of ground. One of the front windows was shattered. A corner of the porch overhang had been splintered, possibly by the same cannonball Cole could see lodged in the field stones of a fireplace chimney.

In what had once been a parlor, General Phil Sheridan stood behind a flat-topped desk, staring at a clutter of papers. A series of maps decorated the wall at his back.

When Sheridan did not look up, Cole said, "Captain Cantrell reporting, General. You sent for me, sir."

Sheridan finally took his eyes from a paper he had been studying. "Yes, Captain, I did." Sheridan smoothed his mustache; he seemed weary. "But for a reason that no longer exists."

"I . . . I don't understand, sir." Cole wondered at the suppressed excitement that now seemed about to erupt from the slim general at any second.

Sheridan waved Cole to a chair. Cole sat stiffly while Sheri-

14

dan poured whiskey into two tin cups. He leaned over and handed one cup to Cole.

"Thank you, sir," Cole said, wondering what was coming next.

"I just received word that General Lee surrendered at Appomattox Courthouse," Sheridan announced dramatically, his eyes dancing. "Lee turned over his sword to General Grant."

Cole sagged back in his chair. "Thank God."

Sheridan lifted his cup in salute to the victory. They both drank. "After all the blood," Sheridan said grimly, "all the pure living hell, the war is finally over."

"Times when I didn't think it would ever come, sir."

"We've won, Cole!" Sheridan emphasized it by smashing a fist on the desk top, scattering some of the papers. Cole started to retrieve those that had floated to the floor. Sheridan waved him back to his chair.

"No need now for battle plans or requisitions . . ." Sheridan broke off, grinning. "We've finally crushed the enemy."

"I . . . I understand, sir."

Sheridan regarded his junior officer gravely. "I thought you'd jump to your feet and shout when I told you the good news. You seem strangely subdued."

"I . . . I don't know what to say, General. I'm glad it's over, of course. But victory at what cost. It's hard for me to feel that *anybody* won this war."

"You're a sentimentalist, Cole. A good quality, especially in a peacetime army." Sheridan watched Cole from a corner of his eye. "We'll have a defeated South to handle, Cole. Not to mention that we'll be up against savage marauders out West. During the war we were unable to spare the men necessary to cope with their depredations. But now we can handle the situation." Sheridan broke off in faint embarrassment. "For a minute there I forgot you're part Indian."

"It's all right, sir . . ."

"I spoke of the illegal acts of some members of that race only. There are good Indians, after all."

Cole nodded, but was remembering that someone had recently referred to the only good Indian as being a dead one.

"You've been a fine officer, Cole," Sheridan went on after the awkward moment had passed. "I'm proud to have you in my command."

Cole thanked him. It was flattering to be commended by a general of Sheridan's stature. He knew what the general was

15

leading up to, however. Sheridan wouldn't like his decision. As Sheridan spoke about the need for experienced officers, Cole tried to frame a reply that wouldn't offend his superior.

"God knows what President Lincoln plans for the peacetime South," Sheridan continued solemnly. "Some say he favors amnesty. Which won't set well with a lot of people."

"He'll make a wise decision, sir. As he did with the Emancipation Proclamation."

"And as good officers we'll never question the judgment of our commander-in-chief."

"Of course not, sir." Cole finished his whiskey and tried to fully absorb the morning's startling news, no doubt brought by the fast-riding couriers. The gallant Lee had finally admitted defeat. A hard decision for a proud man, Cole well knew from what he had heard of the general. But in turning over his sword, Lee was saving lives. And at this point, what else mattered?

Sheridan cleared his throat. "Another drink, Cole?

"Thank you no, sir."

"I suppose I might as well get to the point," Sheridan said gravely, and Cole braced himself. "Have you considered making a career of the army?"

"Sir, I've thought about it, but . . ."

"As I said, we're going to need good men to help subdue the hostile western tribes."

"General, may I speak frankly?"

Sheridan looked disappointed. "Speak your mind, Cole."

"I've already had a bellyfull of killing enemies that more often than not I admired."

"There were many gallant men fighting for the Confederacy, I agree."

"I'd like to go home, General. I want to see my folks."

"You'll have time for a visit."

"More than a visit." Cole explained about land his father had taken up near the foothills of the Rockies. "Out there is a simple life, General. Right now I think I need that kind of life."

Sheridan turned to stare out a window at a wagon rumbling down a hill with a full load for the burial detail. The general frowned and turned away. "Yes, I can understand your feelings, Cole," he said after a reflective pause. "I suppose in many ways it's the life we all need right now."

"I hope my decision not to remain in the army hasn't offended you, sir."

"I'm disappointed, of course." Then Sheridan smiled. "Go

home to your parents. Find some of that tranquillity. In a lot of ways I envy you, Cole. Live the good life."

"I intend to sir."

Cole took his leave and stepped outside. News of surrender had spread. Men were shouting, slapping one another on the back.

In their exuberance some of them forgot to salute. Cole pretended not to notice. It was no time to demand military courtesy from men so long under stress. He rode away with a light heart. To see his parents again after four long years. To embrace his mother and savor the special dishes she would prepare for his homecoming. Join his father on a hunting trip into the Rockies. Or would there be work to do first at the ranch? He felt a surge of excitement. All he wanted was to get home, to breathe clean air untainted with the bite of cordite.

He was jolted back to reality when he saw directly ahead of him the stark remains of an oak tree with its single remaining limb that had been intended for a gibbit. At least on this morning of surrender he had spared one life.

He thought of the prisoner; the cynical smile. Cole guessed the man's age to be his own, mid-twenties. But it was hard to tell in these war years. Several times in his command he had had seventeen-year-olds who, after the horrors of battle, seemed forty.

The noose still dangled. Cole cut it down and left it coiled like a snake upon the damp, scarred ground. He rode on, thinking of the Confederate lieutenant. Had Duke Sateen been as scornful of death as he appeared to be? Or had fear frozen ever fiber into a bold facade of courage?

Cole speculated on what Sateen would do now that he had his life again and the war was over. Return to a ruined plantation? Or perhaps he came from a family of ship owners whose vessels had been bottled up in some harbor such as Mobile by the Union fleet.

He heard the thump of picks against soft ground, a scrape of shovels on stones. He did not look at the numerous burial parties now at work. In the light of surrender it made yesterday's battle all the more horrendous. What a waste that men had died only a few hours before the announcement of peace.

But would there be peace even now? Cole recalled Sheridan's words about "subduing hostile tribes." His parents in their isolation would never be involved in such troubles.

17

Untouchable in that sanctuary they had founded at the foot of the Rockies.

As for himself, he did not intend to bring harm to another human being as long as he lived, except in defense of his own life. And he would never allow himself to be placed in a position where that would be inevitable. He had had his fill of killing.

3 Claudius Max arrogantly swung his bulk from the step of the gold-trimmed black carriage even before it was completely halted. Ignoring the cringing coachman, he stared disdainfully at the paving stones he would have to cross to reach the Python Building. Since the war's end, New York traffic had become intolerable. Max was certain that in no part of the world was there a greater concentration of horse droppings than on Manhattan streets. Yesterday he had made an offhand remark to his top assistant, Lorne Payne, that if manure sold for a dollar a ton any man with ingenuity could corner the market and become a millionaire.

Payne threw back his handsome head and laughed heartily. Max weighed the laughter for sincerity, decided it was genuine and allowed himself a spare smile. What had attracted Max to Lorne Payne was a mutual interest in Roman history. Plus a keen mind essential in a captain of the Praetorian Guards, which Max considered Payne to be. Max wondered if Payne would be in the office across the busy street. Not this early. Probably not yet out of the silken sheets in the bed of some New York beauty. A true Roman, Lorne Payne. A time for war. A time for women.

Yesterday when Claudius Max had joked about cornering the Manhattan manure market, he had been in a reasonably good humor. A rarity these days. Several things had gone wrong lately, among them his marriage to Theodora. She was much younger, high-strung, opinionated. Whenever her antics became more than annoying he corrected the matter with the flat of his hand.

Other pressing matters that vexed him could not be dealt with so conveniently. Nor as excitingly, Max had to admit.

What he could not abide was failure. Defeat was a word

18

unknown to a true Caesar. He had his own empire to rule, Python, named for that deadliest of serpents which so easily squeezed the life from its prey.

He anticipated opposition; it was normal. And he relished the conquest of worthy opponents. What galled him most was some unworthy individual trying to block him, as was happening out West. Such a situation became a sliver under the skin, festering in time. It was festering now.

Max lurched away from his carriage. Rumbles of traffic muffled his coachman's plea to be allowed to locate the vehicle closer to the Python Building. Max plowed straight ahead, ignoring other pedestrians who were forced to step aside. Some who did not know the power represented by the figure in the sable-trimmed cloak cursed under their breaths.

"When will you require my services again, sir?" cried the coachman.

"Never!" Max thundered without looking at the hapless driver. Then he swept disdainfully across the street as if daring any team to run him down. Some drivers in their agitation started to curse him. But the small, darting eyes in the layers of fat seemed to freeze all profanity.

"Who is he?" shouted the driver of a delivery van, pointing his whip at the obese figure.

"Claudius Max!" yelled the driver of a dray loaded with pianos. "A nabob he is. One of the biggest men in New Yawk!"

"Big he is!" someone else shouted. "Wide as a stable gate!"

Max shrugged off the reference to his obesity; he was used to it. What nettled him on this black morning was the remark that he was only one of the most powerful men. He intended to be the *most* powerful man in New York, and in the whole reunited country, now that Lee had finally shown the good sense to give up his sword to Grant.

Thinking of Grant deepened his scowl. Grant the plodder, nibbling at the enemy and content with small victories. The South could have been crushed much sooner had Lincoln the foresight to seek advice from Claudius Max. It had cost the federal government one million dollars a day to fight the war. The Bankruptcy of the nation had been close.

Max climbed to the second floor of his building, his walking stick thumping on a marble staircase. He puffed from the exertion. In a darkly paneled anteroom with tall, brass-trimmed doors he spoke crisply to a balding man hunched over a desk.

19

"Akins, fire my driver. Hire another before noon."

"It shall be done immediately, Mr. Max," said Akins.

Claudius Max stormed down a long hallway, jowls quivering at each step. He glanced into a room where men at rows of desks were industriously copying figures into ledgers. Only the sounds of many scratching pens could be heard from the cavernous room. Max had determined long ago that females would never invade this domain. Despite the rantings of that Anthony woman. He made a face as if something sour had passed his lips. Even thinking about Susan B. Anthony's misguided attempts to better the lot of females always produced such a reaction. He believed in assigned roles for females, household chores, childbearing and bed. Only the latter interested him personally.

The tapping of the walking stick on the marble floor was a signal for a middle-aged man in a high collar and tight black suit to fling open a tall, carved door.

"Good morning, Mr. Max."

Max grunted a greeting, handed over his hat and stick, then strode into the large room that in some ways seemed more museum than office. He seated himself at a massive desk of cherry wood. He stared reverently at a bust of Julius Caesar at one end of the desk. A pudgy finger touched the majestic skull of marble.

A painting that depicted the fall of Carthage covered one wall: Roman Legions marching in dreaded phalanx to destroy the enemy with lance and sword.

Max's eyes flicked to a statue of Constantine. The sculptor had caught the emperor in an oration. Probably urging his legions to victory. A sword was more convincing, Max believed, than rhetoric.

Max focused his attention on his underling at the desk by the double doors. "Lackman, I trust you have a good report this morning. I'm sure you know what I mean."

Lackman's thin features were pinched, as if the high collar had suddenly constricted. "Things are proceeding as planned, Mr. Max."

"Proceeding as planned, you say." Max's voice was deceptively mild. On the upper rim of the hardwood frame of his chair, padded in rich leather, was carved the symbol of Rome's birth, Romulus and Remus in gold leaf, suckled by the she-wolf. "What I mean specifically, Lackman, is the status of our western business."

"As I said, it is . . . ah . . . proceeding, Mr. Max."

Max slammed a heavy fist on the desk top. Julius Ceasar in marble trembled. "Yesterday you said it was proceeding. Last week. Also last month. Proceeding *where?*"

"I have lengthy correspondence, sir."

"I've read copies of every letter, Lackman. Apparently they made as much impression on Badger Cantrell and his cohorts as a block of ice in a bonfire."

Lackman licked his lips. "Our emissaries have contacted each of the . . . ah . . . reluctant landowners."

"Contact is an interesting word, Lackman," Max said thinly. "Do you know how the mighty Caesar contacted a man who opposed him?"

"I rather suspect forcibly, Mr. Max."

Max's lips tightened against gleaming teeth. "Caesar would question a man. And if the answer was unfavorable all he had to do was lift a hand. Praetorian Guards quickly ended the so-called contact." Max crashed his fist against the desk and again the bust of Caesar trembled. "That's what I need, a Praetorian Guard. I thought I had one. Apparently not!"

"I feel we must move carefully in these turbulent times, Mr. Max," Lackman said in a strained voice. "Now that President Lincoln has been taken tragically and there is no firm hand at the helm . . ."

"Lincoln had the bad grace to allow himself to be assassinated, yes," Max interrupted. "An incorruptible fool. He could have died a rich man."

Max's gaze flicked to a mural beside one of the double doors of the Germanic tribes being subdued by Romans. "Our surveyors aren't going to be able to move fast enough on the northern route if we don't have action."

"Yes, I . . . ah . . . understand, but . . ."

"I may have to turn this matter over to Mr. Payne."

Lackman's jaw fell. He knew that failure meant dismissal. "I'm sure I can get our northern route proceeding as planned . . ."

"Proceeding," Max snorted. "The word annoys me. Don't use it again."

More to himself than to Lackman, he muttered, "Should have handled this myself, but I've had other things on my mind lately." Max scowled at Caesar, who scowled back from the desk top. Theodora had occupied his mind to the exclusion of some important business matters. She had thrown another tantrum. This he tolerated because in bed she could quiet the tremendous engine of his body. His only foolishness had been in giving her the protection of marriage. Her latest display of pique he quelled by flinging her across his knees. Silken drawers proved scant protection against the broad palm of his hand.

He would not put up with a fractious horse, nor with a peevish woman. Both needed discipline. For two days following the latest clash of their wills, Theodora's classic features reflected slight pain whenever seating herself. At night she seemed as exciting as ever, apparently not resenting the punishment given as if she were a naughty child. He sometimes wondered if she feared to be otherwise.

Thinking of Theodora had pulled his mind into channels other than business. He snapped back to the problem at hand. "Lackman, we must acquire that right of way, damn it!"

"Things are proceeding . . ." Lackman paled at his slip of the tongue. "I mean, sir, I am pushing things as fast as possible."

Claudius Max pulled a map of the area from his desk drawer. He studied it for a few moments, then said, "Our surveyors must have access within thirty days."

"That is understood, Mr. Max."

"Don't tell me you can't sway a few reluctant settlers, and that Badger Cantrell . . . Badger. What a name."

"He is a former trapper, sir, a mountain man as they refer to them out there. A stubborn breed, I must say. He refuses to sell . . ."

"Refuse? Refuse *me?*" Max seemed appalled. "I do not accept obstacles such as reluctant settlers. Eliminate them."

"El . . . el . . . eliminate them, sir?"

"If your hearing is bad, purchase an ear horn!"

Lackman laid his hand upon a neighboring chair, horsehair covered with black leather.

"Mr. Max, legally, we can't . . ."

"Legally!" Claudius Max roared. Lackman trembled.

"We've learned that these settlers have clear title to their land, Mr. Max. We are negotiating and some of them are beginning to bend . . ."

"I said eliminate them, Lackman! Which means removing them from the path of progress."

"It is illegal . . ."

"No Caesar permitted legality to impede the expansion of empire. They were the law. As *I* am the law!"

Had Lackman not needed his job to support a wife and six

22

children, he would have fled in terror from the vast room with its reminders of Roman glory. Instead he stood mute.

"Send my centurions against those vermin," Max snarled. "Do you understand, Lackman?"

"I . . . I understand, Mr. Max." Lackman sounded as if in pain.

"I will put up with delay no longer. I want those people destroyed if they refuse to bend to my will. Get the message to Creed out in Basin City. Relay my instructions. If he fails, it's his neck. As well as your own!"

Lackman made a stiff bow, then hurried away.

Max watched him slip quickly out one of the tall doors. A rabbit, Max thought in disgust. After the tirade he felt spent. He hadn't realized how thinking of Theodora had upset him. Well, the deed was done now and to hell with it.

Lorne Payne entered the office, jaunty in a light-brown suit. "I could hear you shouting from the street, Claudius."

"Better if my shouts could be heard out in Beaver Valley."

"Still a problem, eh?"

Payne removed his hat, placed his walking stick in a rack. "Lackman was scurrying down the stairs as if pursued by the devil himself. You'll frighten the poor man to death one of these days."

"At least he'll go quickly. A better death than for those who fail me . . . or cross me." Max held his smile but the hooded eyes were blue steel.

"You'll never have to worry about me either way, Claudius."

Max smiled. Payne was slender, with fine shoulders, an easy smile. He had cold nerve, was utterly ruthless. Max enjoyed allowing him certain liberties in the Python organization denied anyone else. It would be interesting to see in what direction Payne might bend those liberties.

Claudius Max spent the morning dictating letters to a male stenographer. Shortly before noon, Theodora stormed in, flinging both double doors wide so that they crashed back against the walls, not bothering to close them. Lackman, who had returned from the telegraph office by then, jumped up to do it for her.

She trailed rich perfume all the way to Max's desk. "At Braxton's they refused me further credit!"

"That means they're following my orders."

Theodora's delicate chin dropped. "But why?"

"Punishment." He stared coldly up into her face. "Or do you prefer the other kind?"

23

She flushed in embarrassment.

The stenographer hurried away. The door to the adjoining office swung open and Lorne Payne looked out. "Thought I heard a woman scream. . . ." He broke off as he saw the elegant young woman at Max's desk. She looked around, frowning in a superior way. Until now he had seen her only at a distance.

Max beckoned. "Come and meet my wife. A duty too long neglected." He introduced them.

Theodora offered her slim, gloved hand. "Claudius speaks of you so often."

"My *daring* young assistant," Claudius Max amended with a chuckle. His bright eyes assessed them together. Payne was tall. Theodora came to his chin.

"Daring only when it comes to business." Payne met Max's eyes.

Max scribbled a note, handed it to Theodora. "Your credit will be good at Braxton's."

"Thank you, Claudius." She dropped the paper into a small blue bag. "A pleasure meeting you, Mr. Payne." The extended hand again. This time it was gloveless. Payne's handclasp lingered over her warm fingers.

Max, plump hands folded across a mountainous belly, watched them from his chair. "Why not first names?" he suggested blandly. "Eventually you'll become good friends, I'm sure."

Payne's brows twitched ever so slightly. He released Theodora's hand.

"Bring Mr. Payne . . . I mean Lorne to the house for dinner some evening, Claudius," Theodora said in her bright voice.

"Speaking of home, I'll be there early. Punctually at three." And be in a receptive mood, his eyes seemed to warn.

"I understand, Claudius." She tried not to look embarrassed in case Payne understood the innuendo. Which, being a man of the world as Claudius was always saying, he undoubtedly did. At the Academy she and some classmates had once discussed the horrors of prostitution. How could a woman possibly sell herself into a bed? Theodora and the others had wondered. After marriage, she realized prostitution did not necessarily mean walking the streets or answering a door where a red light glowed.

4 White Elk reread the letter, which she did more than once each day. Her son was coming home. The Great Spirit, father of all men, had spared Cole. As she did after each reading of the letter, she squeezed her eyes shut and uttered an Indian prayer of thanksgiving. She opened them and looked out a west window of the modest house and to the towering Rockies. Higher peaks still wore their winter crowns although summer's warm breath was near.

White Elk was a handsome woman with a straight back. Not a thread of gray showed in the thick black hair. Her dark skin was firm, her smile radiant. She wore a belted cotton dress and moccasins.

Her only jewelry was a choker of beads, intricate silver work and two elk teeth worn in front as a pendant. A birthday present from Cole when he was fifteen. Made by an old Indian craftsman who assured him there was not another like it. And she knew it to be true.

She glanced at the letter again. Cole was bringing his horse home with him, rather than let someone else possibly mistreat such a gallant and faithful friend. She smiled wistfully. Cole was compassionate.

She poked a hen into the field stone fireplace for their supper. The puncheon floor was faintly damp from her recent mopping. There was a bedroom and a loft to the rear of the living room where Cole slept. His buckskins hung where he had left them. Her gaze flicked to the Indian rugs on the floor, the curtained windows. It had been an adjustment for husband and wife. He a mountain man, his only roof the wheeling stars. Hers had been the deerskin of a lodge. They had a good life together. She was grateful.

She watched her husband cramped in a chair cleaning his rifle. He disdained more modern weapons, preferring the old, the reliable, such as the Hawken rifle and his Navy Colt. As he used the cleaning rag he stole a glance at this woman he had married as a very young girl and who had borne them a son. He loved her as deeply now as he had the day her father, a Crow chief, proclaimed a wedding celebration. There were games and feats of horsemanship, with young Badger Cantrell competing with the best of the braves his own age. This was followed by a great feast of elk and buffalo hump and antelope.

Since coming West at fourteen with a party of trappers, Cantrell had been a friend to the Indian. Some of his fellow-trappers were not. Eventually he broke with these and went to live with his new brothers, the Cheyenne, the Arapahoe, the Sioux. But mostly it was the Crow. He learned to speak their language and to communicate with the other tribes by sign language.

Nearly a month had passed since they had received the letter from their son. Even more time might have elapsed before receipt of the letter had they not traveled fifteen miles to the Amber Creek Trading Post. The trading post was one oversize room of a residence owned by Si Lansing.

At the post Badger Cantrell drank beer and listened to the latest gossip concerning railroad surveyors said to be in Basin City.

"Due to the mule-headedness of certain settlers, they ain't workin' yet," was the way one man put it with a wink.

"Far as I'm concerned, they'll never work." Badger Cantrell's grin was tight through a beard as white as his hair. As usual he wore buckskins and moccasins.

It was that day that bald Si Lansing, who held mail for all the settlers, called out, "Letter for you Badger. Been here most a week. Was aimin' to send it down by somebody goin' your way."

Badger gave a whoop of joy when he recognized his son's handwriting on the envelope. He read welcome news. The war was over, which had been rumored for some weeks in this remote corner of the West. What was more important to Badger and his wife was Cole writing that he'd had enough of bloodshed to last a lifetime. He intended to spend a year with his parents, getting both feet on the ground, as he put it in his letter. After that he would seek a wife so as to make sure there were children to carry on the name, and with the best blood of two races, red and white, be a credit to their country.

"Grandchildren to spoil," said White Elk, her dark eyes shining.

"We better hurry home," Badger said, slipping the letter under his buckskin shirt. "This was written on the day of surrender."

White Elk agreed. "He could be home at any time."

"I would rather draw my own blood than not be there to welcome our son." Badger spoke in Crow.

Several men in the post, some with cups of frontier whiskey, openly admired White Elk. Even though her son was over twenty, her body was youthful. Badger was aware of the admiring glances. It made him feel proud that she was his wife.

Long days had slipped away and still their son had not returned home. To occupy his mind, Badger decided to clean his rifle. White Elk was at an east window, her slender body rigid.

"Your eyes will grow tired from so much looking, woman," he admonished. "Our son will come back soon. You staring out that wondow won't hurry him."

"Yes, my husband." Her eyes sparkled. "But I notice you fling open the front door at the slightest sound and search for him with your eyes."

He raised his white head from the Hawken rifle. Next to him oil and cleaning rags littered a small table. "I only go to the door to get a breath of fresh air." When he met her smile, he broke into laughter. Their most intimate thoughts were always conveyed in her language. Somehow it lent itself to their closeness better than English.

White Elk stirred the contents of a pot on the back of the new stove. Badger had freighted it in from Scalplock six months ago. Cole would be pleased with this modern addition, but she still preferred the fireplace where the hen was browning. Her eyes lifted to the loft. She had aired Cole's blankets, made his bed. Above his trunk she could see the war bow her father the chief had presented on Cole's twelfth birthday. Everything on the loft just as Cole had left it.

"How thankful we are that the white man's war is over," she said, her eyes misting.

"Our son has become a great warrior," Badger said proudly.

"Warrior he may be, but to me he will always be my little one." She spoke softly, more to herself than to Badger who was placing the cleaned rifle on wall pegs near the door.

Perhaps it was the sight of the rifle or the war bow that she had glanced at a moment ago that brought a freezing premonition. She stood so rigid that Badger looked alarmed.

"Woman, you're pale."

She put a hand to her brow, stared down at the intricate design on one of the Indian rugs. "I hope we are here to welcome our son."

"Course we'll be here. What do you mean?"

"Just a feeling . . . a strange feeling that came over me." Her smile was wan.

Badger had been around Indians long enough to know better than to ridicule a premonition. He knew that some of them seemed to communicate without sign language or the spoken word. And some could pry up the lid of tomorrow and see what lay ahead.

He looked anxiously at White Elk. "Has the feeling gone?"

"It is gone, my husband."

"You are still pale."

"I was thinking of your promise, yours and Cole's. That when it is time for me to leave this life for the land of shadows, I will be taken home to my people."

"I will go long before you as I am older. But you and Cole see that my body is placed on the scaffold so that it is nearer the stars. The ritual shall be a Crow ceremony. Chant their death song so that my ears may carry it to the far place where I will wait for you both."

White Elk smiled and went to him. "We have many happy years to spend in this life with our son. And do you think I would leave before I have seen the grandchildren Cole promised?"

She gave his beard an affectionate tug and turned quickly back to her stove. She did not want him to notice that although she smiled, her eyes were troubled.

It was the following day that their nearest neighbor, Del Brooks, who ranched a dozen miles to the east, sent a message by one of his hired hands.

"Sold out to the railroad," the hired hand announced, speaking with some difficulty through swollen lips.

Badger reacted strongly to the startling news. "Del Brooks sold out to the railroad?"

"Yep." The hired man stood in the doorway, half in shadow.

"Brooks promised he'd stick with me to the end."

"This here's the end."

White Elk called from inside the house to offer the messenger coffee and hot food. But the man declined. He was agitated and apparently in no mood to linger.

At first when Badger had seen the man alighting painfully from a horse in the yard, he thought the battered face was the result of a brawl. The man was noted for strong drink and quick trouble. But now Badger looked more closely at a purplish eye, a deep gash on the jaw.

"Railroad men did that to you?" he demanded coldly.

"Won't say. Boss give me an extry dollar to ride over here an' tell you he's quittin' the valley. So am I."

When the man fled on his weary horse, Badger cried, "Railroad!" He made it sound like an epithet. "Got a hunch Del looks worse'n his hired hand."

White Elk bit her lips as her grim husband buckled on his Navy Colt. "We must try and reason with the railroad people," she cautioned. "Del Brooks has a bad temper. Maybe he said something to anger them."

"Reason with scum?" Badger snorted. "You saw the face of that hired man. An' I never saw a fella more scared in my life."

"You are no longer a young man, Badger," she reminded. "Our son will be home any day. Put them off as best you can."

"Mebby Del Brooks run out, but there's others. I'll make the rounds an' spread the word that there'll be a meetin' at Amber Creek."

White Elk would not be left at home. She would go with him and have a social visit with Mrs. Lansing at the trading post while the men planned a defense of their lands.

Besides, she could keep one eye on Badger to see that he didn't rush headlong into something that might get him killed.

5 From the first, after Appomattox, Cole Cantrell realized peace would not come easily to a nation reunited. Already some politicians in Washington were scrambling to make inroads on the peace that had come at such a price. All that mattered to them were their own greedy interests. As he sweated out the weeks engaged in what he sometimes felt was a purposeless task for Colonel Malcolm Erskine, Cole heard rumors of former fighting men from both sides banding together for plunder. A madman's bullet had scratched from the world the revered name of Abraham Lincoln. Loss of his firm hand had spurred lesser men to wild ambition.

For Cole, the many delays encountered since Lee's surrender had been frustrating. As a favor to General Sheridan he had agreed to help Colonel Erskine straighten out records for the sixth corps.

One day when he had completed an inventory of usable supply wagons that could be sent to the South on a project of restoring a ravaged land, he happened to see a note on the colonel's desk. It mentioned that Sergeant Burley Quint was in detention on a charge of brutality of enlisted men. Cole was only surprised that the overbearing sergeant had not been brought up on charges before this.

Cole had written his parents concerning his delay on arriving home, but with uncertain mail service there was no telling how soon they could receive a letter in such a remote area. Or if it would be delivered at all. Cole's impatience and frustration deepened. He was about to confront Erskine and demand his release when he was called to the colonel's office. Colonel Erskine was a tall man with a beard, a weary smile. "It seems we have both discharged our obligations, Captain Cantrell." He shoved a paper across his desk. "Sign this and you are free to go."

Cole scratched his name. "May I ask, sir, why the sorting of papers these past weeks has been so vital to the U.S. Army? In other words, who in Washington decided I should remain in the service?"

"I receive orders. I pass these orders on to you." Erskine added a shrug to his weary smile. "As of this minute you are a civilian. That's all I can say."

"Thank you, Colonel," Cole said stiffly. All he cared about was starting the first leg of his long trip toward the Rockies. It was mid-June; the surrender had been in April.

One benefit of the delay was that Trooper had had a good rest. He had been newly shod and was ready for the long miles. As Cole rode out of camp, his back to the eastern horizon, he said loudly, "I am going home at last."

It was spoken in the Crow language. Sentries at the main gate looked at him in surprise. Then they sprang to attention and saluted.

Cole shook his head at them. "I don't rate a salute, men. I'm plain Cole Cantrell, not a captain."

"You'll allus be a captain to me, sir," said one of them at rigid attention.

"Good luck to you, sir," said another.

"And good luck to you men in our peacetime army," Cole offered. But he wondered just how much peace there would be.

With a wave of his hand, he put Trooper into a lope.

Even though it was weeks since the surrender, the roads were still filled with soldiers on their way home. Some coming north from the Deep South, New Orleans or Vicksburg or Sherman's command in Georgia. Some were in rags with ravaged faces. Others were half-drunk, itching for trouble.

It was late that first afternoon when Cole suddenly realized Trooper was beginning to limp. Dismounting, he inspected the right foreleg. One of the new shoes had worked loose already. He swore under his breath at the incompetence of a certain army farrier.

"Now that the war's over," he muttered, "nobody gives a damn."

For a few miles he had been aware of riders keeping pace with him. They were always some distance down the narrow road he traveled. He paid little attention. There was something more important on his mind, the loose horseshoe. A lame horse could turn into a cripple before too many miles.

At a crossroads the driver of a hay rig gave him directions to the nearest settlement. Cole thanked him and swung north along a road narrower and more deeply rutted than the one he had been on before.

The settlement was called Eaganville. Whoever Eagan was, Cole reflected looking around, he hadn't left much of a namesake. It consisted of a store, a church with a steeple that had been shot away in some forgotten episode of the war and a low-roofed tavern called the Oaks. What gladdened Cole's heart was the blacksmith shop. Outside under a big shed roof a farrier in a leather apron was shoeing a work horse.

Cole introduced himself and stated his problem. "I can do the job myself, if you're too busy," he said. "I'll pay you for the use of the tools."

The farrier cocked an eye, folded his thick arms and looked Cole over. "That an order?"

"You don't have to take orders from me . . ."

"Went in as a private an' come out as one," said the farrier, whose name was Ed Giggley. He spat. "After four years, it kinda gets to be a habit, salutin' an' doin' what an officer says."

Cole explained that he was no longer in the army.

Giggley pointed at Cole's clothing. "Then why you wearin' that there *yoo-nee-form?*"

Cole smiled. "Because it's the only clothes I've got."

"You could buy a suit."

Cole said he'd think about it. There was no use explaining that the money he carried, every spare dollar, was to go to his parents.

31

"Be through with this hoss in a minute," Giggley said, "then I'll do your job."

As he bent to finish the shoeing on the work horse, two small boys and a girl with a smudged cheek, came to stare up at Cole.

"Our pa was a general," said the freckled spokesman for the trio as he stared at Cole in his uniform.

"A general, well, well."

"He got kilt."

"I'm sorry to hear that."

Giggley clapped his large hands together. "You kids run off. Ain't no place for you to be playin'. Too dangerous, these hosses an' all. Told you that before."

The little girl stuck out her tongue, then scampered away with the two boys.

"Ol' Pete wasn't no general," the farrier explained solemnly as he picked up horseshoe nails. "Pete wrote fancy letters home. But he got kilt, all right. A lot of the boys from around here did. Some ain't been heard from for two years or more. Folks don't know whether they're alive or dead."

Cole said that for some reason during the war, mail pouches seemed to make good targets. "A lot of them blown to smithereens," he said. Not exactly a lie, only an exaggeration to ease the farrier's obvious worry over some of his neighbors. "That probably accounts for why you haven't heard. They'll be coming home. I just got out of the army myself."

"Whyn't you go down to the Oaks," Giggley suggested, pointing his hammer at the tavern down the road. "Have yourself a beer or somethin' stronger. I'll have your hoss ready to go in half an hour."

"A beer sounds good," Cole had to agree. "And thanks."

He was just turning away when a familiar voice put a chill across his shoulders.

"Damn if it ain't the cap'n. The same one that wouldn't let me hang that son of a bitch reb *lootenant*."

Cole turned to face Burley Quint. He was leaning against one of the uprights that supported the shed roof.

"War's over, Quint," Cole snapped. "Time to go home and forget it."

"They locked me up on account of you makin' charges."

"I had nothing to do with that."

Quint's large mouth shaped a nasty grin. "Busted me down to private, they did. Just turned me loose."

"I want no trouble from you, Quint."

32

Giggley was leading Trooper under the shed roof. He flashed Quint a nervous glance. Quint was even a bigger man than the farrier, who towered over most.

Cole thought of his pistol in Trooper's saddlebag. He took a quick step. Quint guessed his intention and sprang forward. Quint's fingers bit into the flesh of his upper arm. They felt like pincers.

Cole knocked the large hands aside. "Don't push this, Quint. I'm in no mood for it."

"Ho ho! No mood for it, says our cap'n." Quint threw back his head and bellowed with laughter.

Cole knew he had two chances, the pistol in the saddlebag, or the rifle in a boot. He delayed as three men rode up, leading Quint's horse. Two of them he remembered vaguely from the army. The third man was the bearded Jeff Crowder.

"You figure to be part of Quint's game, Corporal?" Cole demanded coldly. He realized suddenly that these were the men who had kept pace with him for the last hours. He should have investigated. Too late now.

Crowder said, "Cap'n, jobs are hard to come by. Burley knows the freight business. Might be we'll go all the way to Californy."

"Then get going, Crowder."

"Burley's gotta have his fun, reckon. I made noises enough down the road, talkin' loud. I thought you'd look around an' see us an' ride like hell."

"For one thing I had a lame horse."

"Wasn't no use tryin' to warn him, anyhow." Quint rubbed the broad palms of his hands together, laughing again. "Might's well bury him here as later."

Crowder looked at Cole's weaponless belt. "Was I an officer just outa the army," the bearded corporal said, "I'd sure as hell carry a gun. An' I sure as hell wouldn't be wearin' a uniform neither. That makes about as much sense as puttin' your fist in a bear's mouth. Figured you was smarter'n that, cap'n." Crowder wore an old shirt and homespun pants.

"You're right on both counts, Crowder," Cole admitted, edging toward the shed. "I'll get myself something else to wear. Should've known better, I guess. As for the gun . . ."

He sprang toward his horse under the shed. But he didn't even get fully under the shed roof. Somebody hurled an empty keg. It caught him at the back of the knees and sent him sprawling. He narrowly missed striking his head on the rim of the cooling tank. His hat sailed off

Roaring laughter beat against Cole's eardrums as he got his legs under him. It brought men running. Drawing those who had been to war and back and possessed nerves that still twitched for action. Others who hadn't gone to war needed a bloody spectacle to make up for their dull lives away from the fighting.

By now a double row of excited men blocked him from reaching his weapons. The fall had not only jarred him but skinned his right knee.

Quint taunted him. "Cap'n, suh, why don't you shout an order. I just might sprain my arm tryin' so hard to salute." Quint grinned with his big teeth at the growing crowd.

Ed Giggley said, "Wish I could help you, Cantrell. But I learned years back to keep outa the other man's fight. Looks like he aims to make one." The farrier jerked a thumb at the gloating ex-sergeant.

"He's bent on settlin' with you, Cap'n," Corporal Crowder put in.

Cole eyed Quint. "I've had a bellyful of fighting. Four years of it. I don't want to see your blood. I don't want to see my own. I'm giving you this chance to back off."

Quint's smile was ugly.

Cole looked around at the men who blocked him from his horse and the weapons. "If I've got to kick crotches and break noses, I'm going to get to my horse. I'm not going to waste my knuckles against Quint's stone skull."

Cole started for the line of men that blocked him. Trooper was now tethered under the shed, eyes rolling because of the excitement in the air. Some of the men backed off and gave Cole room when they saw the anger in his dark eyes, the thrust of his jaw.

Cole took half a dozen steps. A man with broomstick legs, with wrists no thicker, snatched up a horseshoe from a bench. He winked broadly at those onlookers who could guess his intention. Cole, trying to reach Trooper, failed to see the man's arm whip overhead. Perhaps it was the suddenly held breaths, the silence that first alerted Cole.

He was already twisting aside when the ex-corporal yelled, "Cap'n . . . *duck!*"

Cole wasn't quite in time. But he did manage to jerk his head aside so that the metal shoe only grazed his skull instead of cracking it. He glimpsed the culprit, arm still far forward. Cole's blurred vision settled on the man's narrow face with its grin frozen now to a grimace as he realized his

34

intended victim was not unconscious on the ground but quite able to do battle. Cole's quick surge of anger toward the man faded. He was one of the small ones whose only stature in life came from pleasing a giant, in this case Burley Quint.

While Cole's head began to clear, Quint got between him and Trooper. Quint continued his taunts, playing to the crowd. Hardly a man there would have given Cole Cantrell the chance of a splinter of ice in a hot tub against Quint. Cole knew well what was running through most of their minds. There was scant sympathy for an ex-captain. By now his head noises had diminished from clanging to a mere buzz. But he felt pain, a knife of it down his spine. He hadn't struck a blow and already he had a bad knee and a scraped place on his skull from the hurled horseshoe.

A sunbonneted woman of forty or so, attired in an old cotton dress, pried herself through the circle of men. She glared around at the onlookers.

"Haven't the lot of you had enough blood and pain in the war?" she snorted indignantly. "You oughta be ashamed of yourselves!" Then she beckoned to Cole. "Young man, you come with me an' I'll tend to your head. . . ."

"You'd best get away, ma'am," Cole warned.

"She'd best stay, Cap'n," chortled Burley Quint, "so's she can hide you behind her skirts." This brought on such a wave of laughter that some of the horses grew edgy.

"Emmy!" A bearded man wearing a narrow-brimmed town hat and carrying two squawking hens upside down by their feet, jerked his head at the woman. "You stay clear of this ruckus, hear? We got to git for home with these here two layin' hens I got from Toshby."

Emmy stood her ground for a moment. "They're pickin' on this captain, which ain't right," the wife complained.

"He likely had worse'n that in the war. Emmy, you take one of these here hens. An' keep your nose outa business that ain't no concern of yours."

He thrust a chicken into her hand. The hen beat its wings and made loud sounds of indignation at such handling. An onlooker playfully plucked some feathers which brought an even stronger reaction from the hen. Laughter again; this was better than a medicine show.

The husband finally got his outraged Emmy through the circle of men and to a wagon.

Burley Quint continued to play to his appreciative audience. "You hear what them chickens was sayin', Cap'n? They

35

was squawkin' loud an' clear that you're too yaller to fight. That about right, Cap'n suh?"

Each time he addressed Cole it brought on another wave of laughter and knee slapping. Cole gingerly felt the back of his head. He thought of the woman Emmy. Had she lost a son in the war, or perhaps a nephew? She seemed heartily sick as he of men trying to murder each other.

Finally he managed to stand erect without vertigo. The pain in his skull and knee had lessened. He drew a deep breath, knowing there was no way to avoid the trap Quint had set for him. He happened to turn his head and saw another woman, this one younger. She was on the seat of a farm wagon, staring wide-eyed at him over the heads of the crowd. Her unlined and rather attractive face was partially shaded by the brim of a man's hat sitting high on a mass of dark red hair. She was alone in the wagon. In the moment their eyes held, her lips slowly parted and he saw a neat row of teeth, the tip of a pink tongue. He wondered for an instant if she might protest as had Emmy.

There was a stillness settling over the town, a prelude to battle.

6

The farrier's voice roared into the silence. "You fellas keep the fight out in the street!" he shouted. "You get to rasslin' around inside an' you could bring down my overhang. It happened once before."

"Fight'll be over quick!" Quint yelled through cupped hands to the tall Giggley. "About five punches is all I'll need."

"A dozen you'll need," spoke up a thin-faced man in the growing crowd as he sized up Cole's build.

"Got me three dollars says I can do it in five." Quint dug the silver dollars from his pocket. One moment the broad frame was immobile, the eyes flicking about the crowd with a sly triumph. He suddenly bounded toward Cole, nimbly for so large a man. His palm, still holding the silver dollars under a locked thumb, swung open-handedly toward Cole's jaw. Cole's numbed brain failed to signal reflexes properly. Even though he did jerk up his chin a fraction of an inch, the silver dollars with all that muscle behind them slammed against his jawbone. A redness burst behind the eyeballs. His knees, already shaky from the sneak attack with the horseshoe, threatened to cave. He managed to straighten up. Quint dropped one of the dollars. He picked it up, stepped back and repositioned the three coins again in the palm of his hand. A murmur of anticipation swept the throng as they awaited another example of Quint's versatility.

"One blow down, four blows to go!" Quint chanted.

Cole backed swiftly. Without taking his eyes from Quint, he shucked out of his tunic. He tossed the coat into the crowd.

"Watch it for me, will you, Crowder?"

"Right here, Cap'n," the ex-corporal sang out, then added, "An' good luck."

Quint scowled at Crowder a moment, then laughed as if wishing Cole good luck was a waste of time. He pretended to look at the crowd, then lunged in, swinging the flat of his hand with its armament of ridged silver dollars. This time Cole was ready. He spun out of reach. Quint fanned the air with his open-handed blow. The silver dollars went rolling through the dust. A boy pounced on them and before anyone could lay a hand on him, ducked away. The small man who had hurled the horseshoe tried to grab the boy and received a solid kick in the shin. He let out a howl of pain.

Cole was paying no attention. "I've done my damnedest to get you to back off, Quint," he said through his teeth. "But you won't."

"How'd they ever let a half-breed in a white man's army?" Quint taunted. "Suckled by a goddamn squaw . . ."

What happened next was too fast for most eyes to follow. As Quint lumbered in for the kill, Cole feinted toward the cliff of jaw looming above. Two hard lefts dug into Quint's midsection. A sick look whitened Quint's face. He grabbed his stomach and gasped for breath.

As his head came down, Cole's uppercut caught him on the point of the jaw. Quint wavered, still fighting for the breath Cole's fists had smashed from his solar plexus.

Just as Cole was set to end it, someone flung a clod of dirt. It burst on the side of his head. Dirt particles stung his right eye. By the time Cole brushed aside the dirt, his eyes watering badly, Quint had recovered. Their bodies crashed together as they lunged. Quint's superior heft knocked Cole on his back. Before he could roll aside, Quint plopped down on him, butt first. For an agonizing instant Cole wondered if the tremendous weight had snapped both legs. But even as the

37

grim possibility roared across his mind, he was twisting aside. Quint snatched at his hair, missed.

"Goddamn injun!" Quint cried in frustration.

They regained their feet at the same time, yet Quint was still hunched. Cole's elbow crushed cartilage in Quint's large nose. This brought a bellow of pain. In his fury, Quint tried to seize Cole by the throat. They crashed to the ground, Quint again on top. Cole jackknifed his body. Lesser men in previous fights he had been able to hurl aside. This was like trying to dislodge a mountain. Quint teetered to one side, righted himself and tried to thumb Cole's eyeballs. Cole hammered the side of his fist at the nose streaming blood. A sob of pain and rage erupted. Quint fell over on his side, but sprang up, his eyes wild. He kicked viciously at the crotch of his opponent. Cole danced aside.

Although his right eye still watered, he could see out of it again. He slammed Quint on the side of the head, then struck again at the midsection, which diminished the bigger man's roundhouse swing. Quint's fist fanned empty air.

"Stand still, goddamn it!" he roared. His right forearm was bright with the blood he had tried to scrub away from his ruined nose.

"Get him, Cap'n!"

Cole thought it was Crowder's voice, but he couldn't be sure because of the lusty cries from onlookers. Others took up the cry. "Get him, Cap!"

"Keep outa his reach, Cantrell!" was the farrier's shouted advice.

Cole did stay out of reach of the futilely flailing fists. When Quint was in close, losing wind, Cole staggered him with solid smashes to each cheekbone. One was split. The other blow was high enough to include the lower rim of an eye.

"I'll kill you!" Quint roared. One eye was puffing up. The other was red with fury. Quint suddenly made a half turn, reaching down. From the back of one of his boots appeared a gleaming blade.

"Put up the knife!" someone yelled. "Fight fair. Look out, Cap!"

At this point Quint was past all reason. He lunged with the knife. Cole acted instinctively, remembering holds he had learned as a boy at the Crow camp. He allowed Quint to advance, but kept out of reach. He gauged the next vicious swipe with the knife point. When the knife missed its mark and Quint was half-turned, off balance, Cole sprang. Catch-

38

ing the thick wrist in both hands, he pulled the arm with its knife hard across his chest. The arm of any man but Quint's would have snapped from such pressure. But it did at least cause him to lose his grip on the knife. A man at the fringe of the yelling crowd kicked the weapon out of reach.

When Quint tried to knee Cole in the groin, the hold on the wrist was released. Cole hit him in the mouth. Quint grabbed him, locked up his left arm. Cole slugged away with the right, took a savage blow to the forehead. He tore free of Quint's grasp and spun away. Quint lumbered after him, roaring.

Cole caught him in the midriff. He skinned knuckles on the heavy jaw, was himself driven back on his heels. For a second his mind went blank. Then he closed in again, breathing hard, desperate now to finish it. Just out of reach was Quint's face, a mask of blood and torn flesh. Quint had enough respect for his adversary now to keep out of his way until he could measure him. But when he tried to close in again, Cole wasn't there. Quint's right eye was nearly swollen shut.

"Stand still an' fight like a white man!" Quint's voice cracked.

Cole laughed at him. Laughter was instantly contagious, sweeping through the crowd like a strong breeze. Quint saw Crowder holding Cole's blue coat. To his maddened brain the coat was a symbol of despised authority. Before Crowder could react, Quint snatched the coat away. He stomped down on one sleeve and heaved back with the other clutched in both hands. Weakened from months of battle in all kinds of weather, the cloth parted easily.

With a yell of triumph, Quint flung the ruined coat at Cole's face. "It's what I'll be doin' to *you!*" Quint screamed.

Cole clawed aside the coat, saw the bloodied giant bearing down. Any cleverness the big man might have possessed had been beaten out of him. No longer trying to guard face or midriff, he swung wildly at a bobbing and weaving target.

As Cole backed, his arms felt as if weighted with heavy chains. His breath was short and painful. He was hurting from the crown of his head to ankles. It had to end quickly, he knew, or it would end him.

A fist whipped by an inch from his chin. He struck swiftly, savagely at a target two inches above the broad belt buckle. A low sob burst from Quint. And as Quint sagged, Cole shifted his attack to the jaw. He struck hard with lefts and rights.

39

Quint's eyes crossed, and he staggered. He went back on his heels.

Cole was aware of a great roaring either from inside his own head or from the crowd. The din made it impossible to hear what Quint was trying to yell at him. But Cole read enough on the smashed lips to know that "son of a bitch" was part of it.

He slammed Quint's jaw with a sore fist. Quint shuddered, stood poised as a man would who is ready to leap from a high place into deep water. Then everything went out of the big body, the legs collapsed and the arms hung like ropes. Quint crashed face down into the street. It took only a moment for the dust around his face to begin to redden.

Cole weaved over to Trooper who was still tied under the shed roof. With numbed fingers he untied him, pulled himself into the saddle.

The farrier looked anxiously up at him. "I never fixed that loose shoe yet."

Cole barely heard him. He didn't intend to stay around Eaganville. Because the next man who tried to jump him he'd shoot. He disliked the possibility. But he'd had enough brutalizing for one day. For one lifetime, for that matter.

Crowder and two of the ex-troopers were crouched over Burley Quint, trying to revive him. Crowder glanced up at Cole, almost grinning.

"Quint wanted to wait till he had a crowd to watch you get whipped. . . ."

Cole didn't hear the rest of it. He didn't even look around. Even Burley Quint, a great bloodied hulk in the dust, was no joy to see.

The farrier called for him to come back. So did some of the others. But he kept going. Several small boys ran after him for a ways, gazing up at him in awe. Some of them would be handing down the story of that momentous brawl to their grandchildren.

Although no one realized it at the time, the legend of Cole Latigo Cantrell had put down its first roots.

7 The brain inside Cole Cantrell's throbbing skull still functioned enough to point him westward. His head began to clear, but with no diminishing of his pain. He rode slowly so as not to loosen further the bad shoe on Trooper's hoof. Each deep rut of the road he traveled was packed with dust. He had gone perhaps half a mile when his eye settled on a farmhouse of unpainted lumber. Apparently it was the last dwelling at this western edge of the settlement. Beyond it the flatlands stretched to purplish infinity. He had no idea of the time.

He reined in and studied the farmhouse and the yard, looking for signs of movement. All that moved were some chickens pecking the ground around the big farm wagon. He remembered vaguely the woman who had tried to coax him away from trouble. Her husband with the two squawking hens interfering. Emmy was her name. His gaze shifted to a large barn in a grove of oaks some distance from the house. A barn meant tools. Every farm had its own supply of horseshoe nails. His gaze sharpened as he looked for a dog. He saw none and decided to gamble. The nearest house toward the settlement was at least a hundred yards away and well screened by trees. He left the road and pointed Trooper toward the barn. A farmer at a house window could knock him out of the saddle with a rifle shot. But he had to take the gamble. He wouldn't get far if Trooper threw that shoe and came up lame.

In the barn, smelling of hay and manure and dust, was a milch cow. It mooed and chewed a cud noisily in the dusty stillness. He dismounted, closed the barn door to a crack that would give him some light. He limped to a workbench. On the walls hanging from nails were bits of harness. A plow was half-hidden by a stack of gunnysacks. Tools littered the worktable. He found pliers, a hammer and the precious horseshoe nails.

His fingers were so swollen it was hard to work, but Trooper was patient. Cole was refastening the shoe, correcting the sloppy workmanship of the army farrier when a faint rustling in the doorway brought him swinging around. A slender woman stood in the opening. She stared at him in silence that made him nervous.

41

"You startled me," he said lamely.

"I expect I did." Her voice was low, controlled. She wore a man's shirt and work pants, the bottoms rolled up. A big Remington rifle was slanted across rather full breasts. Cole noticed that the weapon was cocked.

He licked his lips. "I'm trespassing," he admitted. Then he explained about the shoe.

"I watched you at work," she said, no animosity, no fear in her voice.

"Why didn't you speak up?"

"I had to make up my mind if you meant me any harm."

"I don't, ma'am. None at all." He lowered Trooper's foreleg and stood holding nails and hammer. He guessed she could be thirty, possibly younger. It was hard to tell about farm women. She wore a wedding band. When she turned her head he had a better look at her in the waning sunlight. Somehow her face was familiar, the smooth skin, large eyes, the mass of dark red hair. Then he remembered that when he saw her in town she had been wearing a man's hat. He mentioned it.

"I was setting my wagon when that big bully picked a fight with you," she explained. "I watched long as I could, till it turned my stomach."

His bruised mouth grinned. "Kinda turned mine too, ma'am."

"I'd have put my rifle on him and made him back off. But if I did, the crowd would have followed you out of town like a pack of snarling dogs. You saw how they hooted when Emmy Monahan tried to get you away."

He nodded. "I remember. I'll pay you for the horseshoe nails and the use of your tools."

In the fading light of afternoon her hair took on a richness. Her eyes seemed brighter. It made her look younger. She ran her tongue over her lower lip as she studied him. He knew that in his present condition he could frighten children. Aside from the bruised features one leg of his blue uniform was ripped up the back. The other leg was out at the knee, stained with blood. His shirt was speckled with blood, his and Quint's. She seemed to make up her mind.

"Come in the house and I'll fix you a meal. My husband left a bottle of brandy. It'll ease the kinks in you."

He was suddenly cautious. "When will your husband be back?"

"Never, likely." She uttered a strange little laugh.

"You mean he's dead?"

"Maybe. He went to war three years ago. I've had one

42

letter. He's either dead or gone to South America. He was always talking about it."

"Dead, probably, sorry to say. No man would miss coming home to a handsome wife like you."

"You Irish by any chance?"

"Part."

"I thought I smelled blarney." She threw back her head, laughter gushing pleasantly from her soft, white throat. Then she let down the hammer of the rifle. "There's hay and oats in the bin." She pointed. "Leave your horse in here. So's nobody can see him." She turned, incongruously graceful in the too-big shirt, the baggy homespun trousers, the heavy work shoes. Then she looked around at him. "Come in by the back door," she advised, "not the front. Away from the road." Her large eyes rested significantly on his. "You understand?"

"I'll make sure nobody sees me. And I thank you for your kindness."

"Perhaps I'll be thanking you for yours," she said lightly, the corners of the full mouth faintly upturned. Then she left him.

It was nearly full dark by the time he fed and watered Trooper and reached the house. She hadn't lit any lamps. Water had been heated, however. She was filling a tin tub in the center of the kitchen floor.

She said, "Lye soap's the best I've got."

He tried to decide if she was bold or just unworldly. Hot soapy water would be a balm after the beating he had taken. He hesitated about pulling off his shirt. She smiled.

"When you finish your bath give a holler. "I'll come back. She left the kitchen, closing the door behind her.

When he had soaped and rinsed and was hunched, knees to chest, in the murky water, she knocked and opened the door before he could speak. She had changed into a long white dress, the hem brushing planks of the floor. An evident strain at the buttonholes made him guess that it had been a few pounds since she had worn it last.

"I've got arnica," she said solemnly. "Can you doctor yourself, or shall I?"

He hesitated. "I think I can manage. . . ."

"Likely there are places you can't reach very well. You've got abrasions and deep cuts that need tending." She made the decision for them both, hitched up the dress and knelt beside the tub.

"You speak well," he said as her soft warm fingers applied arnica to his hurts.

43

"I taught school for a year. Then I ran away with Tom. I was married in this dress. I wear it summers. Or I used to, rather. Before Tom went off to war he was usually looking somewheres else. So I got tired of trying to look nice for him."

"It's a pretty dress." And it was. He didn't know what else to say.

"Good thing it's pretty dark in here because I'd be embarrassed for you to see me blush. It's been so long since I've had a compliment."

"Men in this town must be blind not to notice you."

"They notice all right." Then she added bitterly, "They also know that Tom'd kill the man that looked at me for too long."

He squirmed a little at that. "I don't even know your name."

"It's Mallie." She spelled it for him.

"Mallie, I'm Cole Cantrell."

"I heard that bully say that your mother was a squaw."

"She's the daughter of a chief. She's royalty just as purple as any in England. A princess." He spoke more about his mother and her people, the Crow.

Mallie sat back on her heels. "Strange, but the only Indians I ever saw were sketches in school books. Mutilating settlers with tomahawks and scalp knives. You make it sound different, Cole." She sighed. "I've patched you best I can for now."

"My thanks." The water had cooled. He had goosebumps on the forearms as well as bruised places. It was an awkward moment. Should he climb out of the tub? Ask her to leave? Would that sound as if he were a schoolboy? It was a new experience. Another man's wife and raw hunger so evident in her voice, in the shining eyes.

She said, "Not much for supper. I'm too excited to think."

She stood up and looked down at him. Tired as he was he felt a quickening of pulse.

"White meat and beans," she said softly. "Suit you?"

"It'll be a banquet."

"Biscuits to help fill out the empty places. And I've got a cake left over. Go ahead, get dressed. You're embarrassed, I can tell." She smiled. "So am I." She left the kitchen.

They ate mostly in silence. And when he'd been warmed by brandy and by her soft blue eyes and was filled with food, he spoke tentatively because he still was not sure. "I can bed down in the barn."

"You're not a fool, no more than I am, Cole Cantrell. I'm a

44

human being and I've been three years without a man and sometimes I ache from it. Do I shock you?"

"No." But in a way she did.

"When I saw you stand up to that brutal man, saw you draw his blood, the ache was the worst. That's when I drove away. In the back of my head I said to myself, 'If there's anything to this business about gifts from the Lord, let him send me that man.' So I guess there is, after all."

A strange woman, he thought, bold in some ways, almost shy in others. "You shouldn't live here alone. At least have a dog."

"Old Rex died on me last month. I haven't had the heart to get another. Not yet. But I will."

After she had piled the dishes on the workbench, he stirred uneasily on his chair. Silence built between them until she wiped her hands, turned and looked into his face. She leaned down, both hands flat on the tabletop, eyes on a level with his own.

"You must be dead tired after that terrible fight," she said softly. "I'll light a lamp for you."

The bedroom was cramped with the bed and chest of drawers and small table and homemade rocking chair. She slipped from the room, closing the door. The lamp was turned low, the window covered.

He got out of what remained of his uniform and lay down on the bed, hearing the faint rustle of cornhusks that filled the mattress. No soft down for a mattress here. Down was probably sold. Or did she even have geese? He strained to hear any sound from her in another part of the house. There was only the faint brushing of a tree limb against the roof as the breeze freshened. As he waited tensely he wondered about her missing husband who had written only one letter in his three years of war. Killed in the first skirmish, perhaps, and the report of the incident lost when the battlefield records were blown to bits by cannon fire. Perhaps her husband had been a prisoner, spending the war in the horror of Libby Prison. Confederates at times were no better at maintaining records than the Union.

He heard the door squeak open. He lifted his head, saw the bright eyes, the curved lips. Her soft breath blew out the lamp. She pulled aside the heavy drapes from the open window. The image of her in a bulky nightdress vanished with instant darkness. Then the bunched garment, warmly scented of lavender, was flung lightly across his face. He clawed it aside. As his vision adjusted to the dimness, he saw her ample breasts, the sweet fullness of thighs, the darkness at her fork.

He started to roll aside to give her room in the narrow bed. But she shook her head. She had uncoiled the mass of hair so that it hung in a dark red wave that reached her back to the waist. His body, though bruised and cut and worn from strain, responded quickly.

"No, stay where you are, on your back," she whispered. "Don't move." She crawled on the bed, the mattress of cornhusks grinding under her weight. "I've dreamed of this."

She laughed, and the sound filled the small room now laced with moonlight from the open window. The sheer pleasure of her warmth encompassed his strong urge for her body.

No longer laughing, she leaned forward so that the tips of her fine breasts could brush his lips. What he did for her then evoked small shudderings and sighs. Then her response became more violent, more vocal.

"I really should worry that the neighbors might hear me," she whispered warmly down into his face as she rested a moment. The luminous eyes were near his own.

"I don't want you to get in trouble with your neighbors," he whispered back at her.

"Little I should care about them. I've done my share in three years." Her voice was bitter. "Living like a man, doing a man's work while Tom was off to war. And only one letter, one."

For her to speak of the husband at a time when their bodies were arched as one, embarrassed him for a moment.

"But if he's dead," Mallie continued, "than I guess he sacrificed more than I."

"Your husband will come home eventually."

"I don't think so."

He told her about seeing returning soldiers on the roads even though hostilities had ceased weeks ago.

She spoke again of Tom with thin anger. "Things were wrong between us for so long. Even before he went off to fight in the war."

"Why didn't you leave him?"

"Because it's something that isn't done. Not around here anyway."

He tried to console her. "No matter, you'll survive. You're a strong woman." A dog barked in the distance, followed by a

46

squawking of fowl. A fox in somebody's hen house, he thought. As I am the fox in Tom's.

"Survive I will, Cole. I can cope with anything by daylight. It's the nights that make the emptiness." She teased his mouth with her breasts again, then said, "Would you stay on and help me run this place?"

He told her of his own plans. "There'll be men coming back from the war for another year. If your husband isn't one of them another man will come along."

"Then we'll live for this night alone," she said wistfully.

"You talk a lot for a woman making love," he chided her.

"Know why I talked so much? Because I want my time with you to last. With Tom it seemed I could blink twice and everything was done. Then he was either snoring or off to milk the cow, depending on whether it was night or daybreak."

"Poor Tom should have paid more attention to you," Cole said lightly.

"I've learned to live from one dawn to the next. And this will be the best night of my life."

"Best for me since I came east for the war."

"At least you'll stay tomorrow . . . rest up from your terrible fight."

"Neighbors would see me."

"I'll do the chores. You stay in the house." She laughed and kissed him, then said, "And I won't take very long with the chores."

It was no more than an hour later, her head on his bare shoulder, that he heard someone come running into the yard. He tensed. A woman screeched, still at a run.

"Mallie, Mallie, git yourself up!"

Mallie had been coming out of a relaxed sleep, beginning to stir and whisper her wants to him. The voice brought her bounding to the window where she crouched below the sill because of her nakedness.

"Emmy, that you out there?" she called nervously.

Emmy's voice was shrill with important news. "Some of the boys says Tom's home!"

"Home . . . you said Tom's come home?" Mallie's voice faltered. She sat on her heels below the windowsill and glanced around at Cole. What he could see of her face seemed suddenly drained. He reached down for the gun he had placed on the floor beside the bed.

"Tom's down at the Oaks," Emmy went on. "Not dead like

you feared." Emmy yelled excitedly. And Cole was reminded of the noisy hens Emmy's husband had been holding by their feet that afternoon.

"Down at the Oaks," Mallie echoed dully.

"With the boys, his good friends. Ain't that wonderful?"

"The Oaks," Mallie finally said with a strangled laugh.

"Unlock the front door, Mallie, an' I'll tell you how they say Tom is lookin'."

"I . . . I can't. I . . . I shouldn't. I've got the grippe," Mallie covered quickly. "I wouldn't want to give it to you, Emmy."

Emmy sounded as if she was right outside the window now. "Poor Tom, comin' home to a sick wife. But then reckon he won't care much after he's soaked up all the whiskey they're buyin' him at the Oaks. . . ."

"I . . . I'll hitch up the wagon and go fetch him," Mallie said. Her voice shook.

"Best you do that, Mallie. Too bad if he fell off his hoss an' busted his poor neck after bein' gone for so long."

"Thank you, Emmy, for bringing me . . . the good news."

"You want I should bring you over some sassafrass? It's good for the fevers."

"I've got some. I'll brew me a cup right away . . . for my grippe."

Mallie crawled away from the window, her face a pale oval in the moon glow that lanced the room. Out in the yard Emmy's footsteps crunched off into the night.

"At the Oaks," Mallie said despondently. Then she laughed; it was filled with despair. "At the Oaks . . . his drinking cronies more important than a wife he hasn't seen in three years."

Cole let out a tight breath. "Thank God he didn't come home first."

She stared at the gun he had picked up from the floor. "Tom's not much of a husband. But I wouldn't want him dead."

"Or me dead," he said with irony. "Most I'd have done to him was hit him with my gun. After I was gone, you could have yelled that I was a burglar."

Her teeth gleamed as she started throwing on her clothes. "Burglars take," she said. "You gave. I won't forget this night, Cole. For the rest of my life I'll always remember it."

She insisted he take her husband's good suit to replace his ruined uniform. Tom deserved to lose it, she told him. But

48

Cole refused the offer. He did accept an old coat and a pair of work pants.

"Let me hitch up the team for you," he suggested. But she thought it unwise for him to linger. Some other well-meaning neighbor might bring her news of a husband home from the war, as Emmy had done, and not be so willing to accept a story of fevers.

"The Lord giveth, the Lord taketh away," Mallie whispered. "I asked Him to send me you. And now He's taking you away."

Between them was a final kiss, a touching of hands. Then he was riding away, keeping to pools of shadow under the trees.

For two days Cole kept one eye on his backtrail, in case Burley Quint recovered sufficiently to demand satisfaction because of the humiliating defeat at the hands of a smaller man. Thinking of his time with her, Cole hope Mallie had no more trouble. She deserved none. She was a remarkable woman.

8 Cole crossed the big river. To the north was an old camp site where he had come as a boy with his parents. That year Badger had many pelts which he intended to sell to the Vermillion Trading Company, one of the largest. It was the first trip Cole and his mother had made this far east, which some people referred to as civilization.

Cole remembered his young chest swelling with pride when one of the buyers remarked that the furs brought in by Badger Cantrell were not only of sufficient quantity to warrant a bonus, but also of superior quality.

The speaker was a tall man in his mid-twenties, slightly stooped, with a long, sad face. He wore half-moon eyeglasses in brass frames.

"I'm happy to make your acquaintance, Cantrell," the man told Cole's father. "My name's Samson." He gave a dry chuckle. "If you forget my name, just think of Delilah."

"Papa, is Delilah his wife?" Cole was eager for knowledge even at age six.

Both men laughed. Samson started to put out his hand for

Badger Cantrell to shake, but a portly man arrogantly called him aside.

"Ned, you're new out here," the man snapped. "so I'll not expect you to know all of our customs."

"I guess I don't understand, Mr. Lathrop," Samson said, blinking through his eyeglasses at Lathrop in fawn-colored suit, the garment much too fancy for a river fur camp.

"Cantrell's a squawman," Lathrop said in his loud and arrogant voice. "I wouldn't lower myself by offering to shake hands."

Cole remembered feeling nervous. His father had wandered over to the bales of furs.

"I don't see what being a squawman has to do with his value as a trapper," Samson said a little stiffly.

"Would you ask an Indian to sit down at your table?"

"If he was my friend I would."

Lathrop pursed the dainty mouth in a small round face. He looked exasperated. "You'll have to learn, Ned, that a white man doesn't sup with an Indian. Nor does he shake the hand of a squawman."

Ned Samson slid the brass-framed spectacles lower on his nose to examine the pompous shorter man. Then Samson gestured at the bull boats tied up, the various camps up and down the river bank. "I'll wager half the trappers here are squawmen," he ventured.

"Ned, you buy their furs. You bid them good day. Better yet, you don't carry on a conversation with them, aside from haggling over prices, which is part of the game."

"I prefer to look at each man as a human being, Mr. Lathrop."

"Were you South and owned slaves, I daresay you'd change your tune in a hurry."

Samson reddened. "Thank God I'm not South!"

Some trappers just beaching a bull boat nearby heard the voices and looked up on the bank where Lathrop and Samson were squared off. The trappers were in buckskins, dark from the splashings of river water. A sun that had lost its summer heat glinted off the river and the tossing boats, each made from the hide of a large bull and stretched and dried over willow frame. Small waves made by a stern-wheeler lapped a sandbar that within weeks would be iced.

Lathrop, his face drained of color, continued his tirade. "Worst of all, Ned, you allowed his woman to accompany him to this camp."

50

"What of it?" Samson demanded. "You do business with a man any way you can. You strike a bargain for the company. What the hell difference does it make if he brings his wife along?"

"No need to shout, Samson." Lathrop's chest swelled under the fawn skin coat. "This isn't the mountains, may I point out . . ."

"Of course it's not the mountains."

"Out there in the wilderness such conditions are tolerated out of necessity. But this is what passes for civilization. We didn't invite these trappers to come here. Our representatives out West could have transacted our business as well you know. But they came of their own free will to our river camp. Therefore, they abide by our rules. *My* rules, I might add."

Samson shot a baffled look in the direction of Cole's father, as if to convey that the policy was Lathrop's, not his.

"I guess I didn't understand how you felt about things," Samson said icily, turning back to Lathrop when Badger did not look up.

"I took you out of a mercantile because of your stated wish to learn the fur trade." A fine spray issued from Lathrop's prim mouth at each word. "Well, I've given you this chance."

"Which I appreciate, but . . ."

"However, you must remember that a squawman has abandoned his own race by marrying into one inferior." Lathrop's small eyes flicked to Cole who was standing beside a bale of beaver pelts, mouth agape.

"Next time, Samson," Lathrop continued, "insist that these women and their brats stay out of camp."

Lathrop gave Samson a friendly slap on the arm. "I'm glad I was able to set you straight, before you got in too deep with these people. You'll also thank me in time, Ned."

"I wonder," Cole heard Samson say.

Cole tried to keep his attention on furs being loaded on flat-bottomed river boats. Scurrying lines of men handling the heavy bales reminded him of ants.

Lathrop said, "Before you conclude your business with Cantrell, ask him to take his woman to his own camp."

"She's harming no one," Samson responded curtly.

Lathrop fought for patience. "Ned, I spent a year out West. I know how these people live. A squaw in a place like this is an open invitation. This one's a pretty woman as these dark-skinned ones go, which makes her even more of a threat. More than one man has had his throat slit by a trapper trying to outbid him for the affections of such a female."

"I feel that's sheer nonsense. . . ."

"How these people want to live in the mountains is their business," Lathrop continued, his eyes smouldering now. "But they don't bring their immoral ways to the Christian East." He stabbed a finger in Cole's direction. "That half-breed kid of theirs is a reminder of what an illicit union can produce."

Cole understood enough of it to be startled. It was the first time he had ever heard of himself referred to as a half-breed. And a moment later his heart was beating crazily as he realized that his father was about to make trouble.

Badger Cantrell had been busily adding up a column of figures during most of the discussion between Lathrop and his underling. He must have picked up an occasional word because Cole noticed his mouth through the beard begin to tighten. At last he deliberately put his stub of pencil and the list of figures into a pocket of his buckskin shirt. Just as casually he leaned down to pick up his Hawken rifle from where it rested against a bale of furs. He aimed it at Lathrop. The man paled, flung plump hands over his chest as if to block a bullet. His eyes were filled with terror.

"That's my *wife* you was talkin' about, mister." Badger Cantrell's tone was frigid.

Lathrop's chin sagged and his voice came out as a squeak. "I could have you flogged for threatening a white man."

Badger's teeth gleamed through his beard. "I wanted to show my wife an' my boy this part of a great river. Show 'em some of the land where I hail from. Show 'em some of my people. 'Stead of that . . . . in your case . . . I showed 'em scum."

"I . . . I resent that."

"You apologize to my wife, mister." Badger's finger stiffened against the trigger. "You hear me, mister?"

The order given so coolly had more impact than if it had been shouted. Lathrop understood a threat when he heard one. And no one nearby seemed inclined to take his part. They all stood stiffly, watching. Some shaded their eyes against the sun.

Lathrop was finally able to speak. "I . . . I . . . a . . . a . . . apologize to your wife."

Badger Cantrell lowered his rifle. "Now that's settled," he said, still in that deceptively mild tone, "I'll take my furs downriver. Even if I got to sell cheaper."

52

Ned Sampson jerked angrily on the nosepiece of his eyeglasses. "Lathrop, I'll find a job with another fur company. Even if I have to work cheaper."

Lathrop began to whine. "You can't quit me now. . . ."

"You lost yourself some prime pelts with your stupidity, Lathrop," Samson said angrily.

Lathrop wheeled about and stalked away, coattails sailing.

"Papa, that man called me a half-breed," Cole said.

But it was Samson who replied. "Son, remember this. We're all half-breeds. The only originals were Adam and Eve. If you can believe the Bible, that is. Come on, Mr. Cantrell, let's go find us another fur company."

They did find another company. Samson was unable to land a job with the outfit that gladly bought Badger Cantrell's furs, but he did connect later. Ned Samson wrote them at least once a year. When Cole was about twelve the letters stopped. Cole wondered what had happened to the man he considered a friend. . . .

As Trooper ate up the prairie miles, Cole remembered later occasions when his mixed blood had been discussed. For a time he attended the mission school up at Antelope. There some of the Indian boys resented that he was not a pure blood Crow as his mother was. The crisis even carried over for a time when he'd visit the Crow camp where his mother had been raised. One of the chiefs, Great Bear, settled the matter. He addressed the camp, his fierce eyes singling out the young.

"Twin Rivers," using Cole's Indian name, "is your brother. Remember that always. Your *brother!*"

Nothing more needed to be said. Great Bear's word was revered.

9 On that day when Cole was pushing ever westward, Badger Cantrell and his wife paid another visit to the trading post on Amber Creek. As had been their hope, they found another letter from their son. The envelope was wrinkled, smudged and apparently had suffered many delays in its journey across the wilderness. It was dated some weeks before. Cole wrote that he had been unable to leave the army as quickly as he had hoped. But within the week he would be on his way.

White Elk was overjoyed. Badger kept his emotions hidden.

But there was sobering news at the trading post to dampen their joy. There were rumors that a band of renegade Indians was about to go on the warpath. Badger was skeptical. The leaves had whispered no such possibility of violence.

"Indians are my friends," he told those men who gathered about him anxiously. "If there was goin' to be trouble, I'd be told."

"These ain't Crow, they're Cheyenne," spoke up bald Si Lansing.

"Who's spreadin' these stories?" Badger demanded, his bearded face tense.

"Dude sort of fella in here last week," Lansing recalled. "Claimed he'd heard the story over east of here."

To Badger Cantrell a dude these days meant one thing.

"Railroad's spreadin' them stories, sure as hell," Badger said later when he and White Elk were hurrying home.

"You tried to tell them, my husband," White Elk said soberly. "But they refused to listen."

Uppermost in Badger's mind was the homecoming of his son. Since Cole's first letter, their worry had deepened when he failed to arrive home as expected. Nor had there been further word until today. Turning in the saddle, he gestured at the granite spires of the Rockies and spoke of how he and his son might run trap lines as they had done when Cole was a boy. White Elk cautioned him.

"We must remember to let him do what he wishes, not what we wish. The war must have been terrible and it will take many moons for him to forget."

"As usual, you are right," Badger said in Crow. He rode for a mile across grass that was browning in spots. "Cole might like to join me and your people on a buffalo hunt," Badger said, his voice rising. "Cole loved the excitement and I'm sure not too old for it."

"Much too dangerous for a man your age, my husband."

Badger packed tobacco into the bowl of his Irish clay pipe. White Elk looked around at him, a placid smile on her lips. Badger was still a fine figure of a man, but he was apt to ignore his white hair and beard and the fact that his bones could easily snap. A wild charge after buffalo on a speeding pony was a game for the young, the daring.

"Mr. Max will do more for the West than his competitors," Creed said, as if reciting from rote.

"He already done a lot for my neighbor, Del Brooks," Bagder cut in.

Creed's brown eyes brightened. "Ah, so you've heard the good news. Yes, Mr. Brooks listened to our representatives and decided to sell. . . ."

"Beat the hell out of him first."

Creed managed to look mystified. "I don't understand."

"You personal sure as hell didn't beat either him or his hired man. That hired man coulda tied you in a bowknot. I had a maiden aunt that had bigger arms than you."

"I accept the jibe, Mr. Cantrell." Creed smiled with his crooked teeth. "I am prepared to offer you a draft for seven hundred dollars, drawn on a St. Louis bank. . . ."

"Not for seven thousand."

"Think about it, Cantrell. Seven hundred dollars. With money like that you and your squaw could rendezvous with your trapper friends and have yourselves a time."

"I don't rendezvous with trappers."

"I'm sure a squawman could find ways to spend that much money." Creed gestured at White Elk who stood rigid in the doorway of the unpainted house. "A mountain man shouldn't live under a roof. Neither should his squaw. Get out where you belong and live under the stars and forget trying to plow up the prairie. By the way, your squaw is a mighty attractive . . ."

"She's my *wife!*"

"Of course she is." Creed made a vague gesture as if to indicate he'd go alone with a lie if it pleased this buckskin-clad fool. "Why not introduce me to your wife and let me try and persuade her. . . ."

Creed took a step toward the house. Badger blocked him.

Creed said, "I'm sure she would be interested in seven hundred dollars. But it might be hard for a simple Indian mind to comprehend such wealth." Creed took another step, skirting Badger.

"Stay where you are!" Badger ordered and Creed halted, the facade of a genial businessman dropping momentarily to reveal the hard shell underneath.

Then Creed forced a smile and gestured at the man in the wagon. "Maybe Doak Lancer has an idea how this matter might be settled. . . ."

Badger said, "Got my hand on my Navy Colt, Creed. The

57

holster ain't tied down so all I got to do is swivel it. At my age I don't figure to try an' outdraw a younger man. So you tell this Lancer fella that if he even twitches on that wagon seat I'll blow a hole in him big enough for a mule's head."

Lancer, who had started to straighten up, froze. Then he relaxed and actually laughed. "You're one suspicious man, Cantrell."

"Been known to be," Badger said thinly. "Now you fellas git off my property."

Creed tried again. "Seven hundred dollars is a lot of money to people like you."

"Ain't near enough. Not for all these acres that mebby might be fit for cattle. When my boy gits home from the war, me an' him will make up our minds."

Creed looked at him for ten seconds, the tip of his tongue pressed between the crooked teeth. "A son?"

"A captain an' General Phil Sheridan's right-hand man." Badger was bragging a little, but Creed seemed impressed.

"Let me get in touch with Mr. Max and perhaps . . . just perhaps . . . he might be willing to raise the price so there will be money to share with your son."

Creed wheeled to the wagon, climbed in and spoke sharply to Lancer, who whipped up the team. Creed turned to give Badger a friendly wave of the hand.

But Badger stepped to the house for his Hawken just in case one of them decided to cut loose with that rifle on the floorboards. The Navy Colt was better suited for close shooting, but not distance. But the wagon kept going, swaying and lurching out past the barn and the corral.

"Mention of General Phil Sheridan," Creed muttered above the rattle of the wagon, "put a new light on it. I didn't even know there was a Cantrell son. An army captain. Jeezus, why didn't Mr. Max let me know?"

"Probably figured it wasn't necessary," Lancer said. "I could have handled the thing easily today."

"And I stopped for a good reason. Mr. Max has army friends in high places. I'd better telegraph and make sure about Cantrell's son being Sheridan's right-hand man."

"You believe everything that old coot said? I don't."

"Pays to be careful when handling Python business," Creed warned. "You'll realize that after you've been with us longer." He'd seen others come and go, some violently. "I'd rather spit in the eye of a grizzly bear than offend Claudius Max."

* * *

58

It was several days later that Badger learned from a drifter that the trading post at Amber Creek had mysteriously burned to the ground. Renegade Indians were suspected of burning him out, Si Lansing believed. Badger learned that Lansing would make no attempt to rebuild, but had fled the country with his family.

"Indians hell," Badger snapped when he heard the grim news. "It's the railroad."

But the frightened messenger wasn't so sure, or wouldn't admit it.

10

Cole's impatience to get home deepened. To take his mind off the monotous miles, he visualized his homecoming. His father in the doorway, familiar Irish clay pipe jutting from his lips, perhaps even a hint of moisture at the eyes which a gnarled hand would surreptitiously brush away.

"Son! By gad, my boy's come home at last!"

They would embrace in what the Mexicans called the *abrazo,* and pound each other on the back. Then Cole's mother would come flying from the house, her braids dancing. How would she be dressed? he wondered. Wearing a beaded blouse and skirt of deerskin? Or perhaps a cotton dress. She was a fine seamstress and could work magic with yard goods purchased at the Amber Creek trading post he would likely reach in two days. How often as a boy he had watched in fascination, while pretending to read a book of his father's, as her needle fairly flew over the cloth.

For his tenth birthday she had made him his first fine suit of buckskins. Something he would always cherish. Just before leaving for war he had taken it from his trunk in the loft and marveled at her handiwork.

As Cole pushed westward he was finally able to see the distant blur of mountains. He was watering Trooper at a springs where buffalo grass was thick and showed fresh tracks of horses, shod and unshod. He didn't think anything of it at the time.

He rode on, studying the mountains at the far edge of the prairie and calculated how long it would take him to reach Beaver Valley and home. But distances were deceptive in the clear air. He decided it might take two days, perhaps three. Anxious as he was to see his parents, he refused to push Trooper beyond his limits. The gallant horse was about done in after crossing what amounted to half a continent.

Rumors of trouble were in the air. But it couldn't concern his parents in isolated Beaver Valley. He rode on, rifle loose in its boot, keeping out of the way of marauders, white and red.

The few travelers he encountered didn't seem to know any details about "trouble." Only that there was supposed to be some.

The next time he saw fresh tracks of horses, shod and unshod, at a creek, he did not linger.

Cole made early camp and soon had a cook fire of buffalo chips glowing in the twilight. He prepared his evening meal.

He was staring thoughtfully at the yellow-blue flames when Trooper snorted. Cole picked up his Henry rifle. A man hailed him from some trees.

"Smelled your coffee," said a voice he failed to recognize. "You want company?"

"You alone?" Cole called.

"Yep. Been nawth for a spell. Headin' south now. Figure to see Santa Fe. Name o' Billings," said the man, riding from the cottonwoods on a mule.

"Light and eat with me," Cole offered when his keen eye detected no shadowy figures lurking in the clump of trees.

Cole introduced himself. They shook hands. Billings was slope-shoudered, wearing a worn shirt and pants. They talked about the war while Cole put on extra coffee and then shared the last of his antelope.

"I'll cut north to Amber Springs Trading Post," Cole said conversationally, "and pick up some things for my folks. My mother's got a sweet tooth. And they've got tobacco there that my father thinks is special. . . ."

"You won't buy nothin' there," Billings said, after slurping coffee from his own tin cup."

Cole experienced faint alarm. "What do you mean?"

"Fellas yesterday told me it was burned to the ground. Not a damn thing left. Fella that owned it cleared out with his family, so I heard."

"Si Lansing? How'd it burn down?"

"Fellas told me it was renegade injuns. . . ."

"What men told you that?" Cole demanded suspiciously.

Billings said he had encountered some riders to the north.

"Fellas claimed they'd been chased by a war party. Likely the same bunch that burned down the tradin' post."

"How do they know so much?"

"All I know is they acted scared. Said these injuns was Cheyenne. Told me to spread the word. So I'm spreadin' it, Cantrell."

"You are," Cole grunted.

That night a troubled Cole managed a little sleep while in a seated position. He leaned against a flat rock that jutted from prairie grass like an oversize thumb. Not that he mistrusted Billings, but this was tough country. Even tougher, it seemed, than when he had left it four years ago.

Cole didn't take time for breakfast. He quickly broke camp, leaving leftovers for Billings. If Billings could be believed and the trading post at Amber Springs had been burned out, then the trouble was getting dangerously close to home.

Badger Cantrell finished his breakfast and tamped tobacco into his Irish clay pipe. His lips were taut with worry as he stared out an east window into the bright morning. His eyes strained for signs of movement on the prairie. A faint breeze rustled the cottonwoods by the small barn. In contrast to the sunny morning, Badger's mood was bleak as a December day. The Amber Springs Trading Post was gone. Si Lansing had fled the country.

A sound of horses brought White Elk rushing to a window, hoping it might be Cole, possibly with friends. Her heart was stone as she saw five riders approaching at a walk. Their mounts and the way they rode caused her to cry out to Badger.

"What does it mean? White men on Indian ponies!"

"I'll damn soon find out, woman." Badger belted on the Navy Colt, took down the old Hawken rifle from the wall pegs. He flung open the door and stepped outside. The riders were in single file, abreast of the cottonwoods along Beaver Creek. This close he could see their emotionless faces. The stamp of men who lived by the gun was on them all. Their mounts were smaller than those that normally carried such large men. Stolen Indian ponies.

Badger walked ten feet from the house and halted. The only one of the five men he recognized was the readhead Doak Lancer.

Badger's mouth dried as they drew closer and he could see

61

that they wore moccasins instead of boots. Without turning his head, he hissed a warning to White Elk.

"Stay inside. Don't show yourself."

He tried not to transmit his alarm to her. All he could do now was bluff; one man against five.

The man Lancer hung back from the others. Possibly as a rear guard to give warning if someone approached.

"Far enough!" Badger sang out to the four who kept coming on at that slow walk. "You're trespassin'!"

A wide-shouldered man with a heavy black beard was in the lead. "Got a message for you, Cantrell," he shouted, not slackening his pace. He pressed on toward Badger who stood with his back to the house. A plume of cook smoke curled from a stone chimney into the clear sky.

Badger leveled the Hawken. "Far enough, I said. What's your message?"

"My name's Stark," said the black-bearded man, pulling up a paint pony that from its markings, Badger knew, was Cheyenne. Three of the men reined in a few yards behind Stark. Lancer sat his saddle down by the barn.

"Speak your piece, Stark," Badger said coldly. "Then you an' your friends clear out!"

"Tough old bastard, ain't you?" Stark said.

"Press me too far an' you'll find out, Mr. Railroad!"

"We've come to give you one last chance, Cantrell."

"I ain't sellin' out!"

Stark shrugged and looked around, exchanging grins with the three riders behind him. Down by the barn, Doak Lancer's freckled features were expressionless.

"Didn't say anything about buyin' you out, Cantrell," said Stark, facing him again. "We're long past that." Stark's voice whipped into the stillness. "Here's your message. Move out. You got ten minutes!"

"You're wastin' time, Stark. *You* move out! I won't tell you again!"

Stark had been slouched on his Indian pony, but at Badger's words he slowly straightened. "Yeah, I guess you are stayin' here at that, Cantrell. *Permanently!*"

Badger fired the Hawken rifle. But the bullet whistled harmless as Stark spun his pony aside. At the same instant a Colt swept from Stark's holster. It spat a faint blob of flame that was quickly washed out by sunlight.

Badger felt the smash of the slug in his left shoulder. Impact slammed him backward. He fell hard. When he tried to reach a sitting position, the redheaded Lancer, coming at a gallop now, shot him in the chest. Badger had a glimpse of the sky wheeling crazily. Then everything slipped into darkness.

White Elk screamed from behind the closed door, a keening heard above the reverberation of the gunshots against the house walls.

Still screaming in grief and defiance, White Elk lunged out the door brandishing a butcher knife with a long and glittering blade. Without breaking stride, she leaped over the body of her husband and tried desperately to reach the nearest of the mounted men.

One of them, Lewt, shouted a warning to the man White Elk was about to slash with her knife. "Cutter! The old she-bear's on the warpath!"

Cutter had his head turned, awaiting further orders from Stark who had danced his pony aside several feet. At the shouted warning, Cutter jerked away from the knife point the leaping woman had aimed at his face. He drew a Remington revolver and almost casually fired at the Indian woman. The bullet grazed her jawbone. She dropped to her knees, stunned. The blade of her knife caught sunlight as it fell to the trampled prairie grass.

"I'll finish her!" Doak Lancer announced, riding closer. He fired twice into the body of White Elk.

Dismounting, Stark dug the toe of his moccasin into White Elk's ribs. The body rolled loosely.

"Dead," he grunted, careful not to get her blood on his wool pants.

Ed Lewt looked at her with faint regret. He rubbed at a button nose, then gave a howl of laughter. A gold tooth gleamed in his mouth. "Handsome wench. Shoulda kept her alive for an hour an' had our fun."

"We ain't got an hour," Stark snapped. "Let's get to work."

"Yes, boss," Doak Lancer drawled and Stark shot him a sharp glance that was coolly met.

Stark said, "Creed told me to run things."

Ed Lewt unfastened lashings that held a war bow to his back and nocked an arrow to the string. With no show of emotion, he fired it into Badger Cantrell's chest, slightly below one of the reddened bullet wounds. Then he shot two arrows into the front of White Elk's cotton dress.

The stocky Bill Cutter with the scarred face also had a bow

which he used to shoot arrows at random, into the ground, a fence post, the bole of a cottonwood.

Al Dain, a large man with shoe button eyes in a pock-marked face, yanked White Elk's dress to her waist. He laughed and called to Ed Lewt.

"Hey, Ed, when they find her they'll think them dirty redskins had their fun anyhow."

"Good looker, damn if she wasn't," Lewt complained. "Shoulda took her along with us for a spell."

Al Dain entered the house. Fire tools were racked beside the fireplace where contents of an iron kettle simmered. Using an ash shovel, he scooped hot coals onto the flooring. In a few moments the dry wood began to smoke. Then a small yellowish flame blossomed.

Lancer appeared in the doorway with kerosene he'd found in the barn. "Get out of the way, Dain. This is quicker."

And it was. Flame burst, then raced across the flooring, up the walls to the loft. A small upper window exploded.

Down by the barn, Lewt was opening the corral gate. The three horses penned there pounded south toward the low line of hills that still wore spring greenery.

"Gimme a hand!" Stark yelled. He and Cutter pulled the two bodies out of reach of the flames now shooting out the doorway. Embers rained down on the barn roof, setting it afire.

Wherever the five men moved, moccasin tracks were left in the grass, in the dust. It took the combined strength of two men to snap one of the war bows. The two pieces were cast aside, giving the impression that a brave had discarded it as useless. A broken bow was no weapon for a warrior. Colored feathers, as if ripped from a headband, were scattered about. Also a torn piece of Indian legging. A war lance driven into the ground as if hurled from a raider pony at full gallop.

Stark ordered the bodies of the murder victims dragged even further from the flaming house. "We don't want 'em burned up."

Bill Cutter snatched up the butcher knife from the singed grass. Bending over, he drove the blade several times into White Elk's body. "She figured to put another scar on my face with that damn knife. A screamin' bitch. Them squaws are all the same!"

"This one ain't got a scream left in her," Al Dain observed. Firelight reddened his pockmarks. Smoke boiled into the sky.

Cutter straightened up with the dripping knife and said to

Stark, "You want me to take the old man like you said?"

"If you're too squeamish, I'll do it."

Cutter turned to Badger Cantrell's body, made several deep cuts, then added the final desecration by using the weapon as a scalp knife. He flung the gout of snowy hair into the grass. Stark ordered him to get rid of the knife. Cutter, shielding his face with a forearm to ward off the intense heat pouring from the house, tossed the knife through the doorway.

Stark's black eyes happened to fall on a beaded necklace that had been dislodged from White Elk's throat. A handsome trinket that might be useful sometime in bribing a reluctant female into his blankets. He jammed the necklace into a pocket of his black pants.

Doak Lancer returned from making a wide circle to see if there was any sign of movement on the horizon.

"Nobody's got curious about the smoke so far," he said, reining in.

As the five men got ready to ride, the roof of the burning house collapsed, sending up a geyser of sparks. House walls folded inward with a crash. The barn was already ruined. Half of the corral fence had been burned away, the rest singed and smoke-blackened.

Lancer stood some distance away, hands in hip pockets, watching the fire. Stark's lips curled. "I do the job good enough to suit you?"

"We're paid to pick trouble with others," Lancer said, his intense blue eyes on Stark's face, "not with each other."

Ed Lewt sidled close to Stark and spoke quietly out of the corner of his mouth. "Better not rile him, Sam."

"Big gun hand," Stark sneered, loud enough for Lancer to hear. "But not big enough to get this job done when he was over here the other day. Creed had to get us to finish what Lancer started."

Lancer only laughed. But there was a quality to the laughter that sent a cold flutter down Ed Lewt's backbone.

Dain and Cutter came stomping over to where Stark stood with Lewt.

Dain's small eyes were worried. "Wouldn't push that bastard was I you, Sam," he warned in a low voice.

"Creed's payin' him a full share. Wasn't for him we'd have that much more. All he done was stand around with his hands in his pockets."

"He finished off the woman," Cutter reminded.

65

Cutter felt the strain in his long arms from using the war bow. "Sam, you want him dead," he whispered above the crackle and spit of the dying fire, "speak up."

Stark turned it over in his mind as Lancer vaulted lightly onto the back of the pony he had captured. The hunting party of five Cheyenne braves, who had provided their mounts, lay buried some miles north. Stark debated Cutter's suggestion. But even with three men at his back, Stark wasn't all that confident about facing Doak Lancer. The man was an enigma. He spoke sparingly and always in a low voice. He seemed indifferent most of the time but Stark sensed those blue eyes were registering everything in a quick mind.

And the fact that he suddenly seemed to be a favorite of Creed's was also a deterrent to making a move.

No use jumping into a hole, Stark told himself, unless you knew how deep it was.

"Let's clear out," he said, then added to Lancer, "Guess we're all under kind of a strain. Didn't mean to shout at you like I done."

Lancer didn't smile or speak. He just sat that Indian pony, red hair sticking out from under his hat, the light-blue eyes drilling two holes in Stark's face. Stark started to boil, then checked his anger.

He fingered the Indian necklace in his pocket and consoled himself by imagining the female who would receive it as a present.

11

Never would Cole forget that first glimpse of the awesome smoke that boiled into the sky, turning the clouds to gray-black. At first he tried to tell himself it was a grass fire on the uplands some miles beyond his father's place. But it was the wrong color for a prairie fire. Besides, the smoke was closer than that. Too close. As he spurred toward the source of the smoke it seemed that every tendon was frozen, every artery drained. His stomach knotted like a clenched fist. After a mile or so the wind shifted so that he rode through a curtain of fine ash that whitened his shoulders and cavalry hat.

As he came over a rise of ground, he saw in the distance

timbers still burning, the house walls folded in on themselves. A child's house trampled by a giant's boot. He slowed the weary Trooper who snorted and rolled his eyes at the new scent. Death was in the air.

Cole sat perfectly still and stared at what might easily be mistaken for two bundles of clothing, tossed carelessly into the yard. He saw the buckskin shirt of one, charred from embers that had rained down. He rode closer, finding it hard to focus, for it was like a nightmare. Nearer now, he could see that in places the buckskin was darker than in others and not from the fire. Arrows protruded from the buckskin shirt. He tasted bile as he saw the raw meat crown of the head where the scalp had been lifted.

Nearby lay the other bundle, this with lifted dress, underclothing ripped away. The cotton dress like a pincushion for the six arrows that pierced flesh.

Cole's mouth opened to scream at the sky, a death chant learned at his mother's knee. But all that emerged from his throat was a faint cry, like that of an animal in pain. More a whimper than a cry of rage and anguish.

Numbly he flung himself from the saddle, going first to his mother. He fell to his knees, his mind spinning. He reached out, his eyes squeezed shut, and gently pulled down the torn and bloodied dress so that she was covered. He found a blue bead that looked as if it might have come from the necklace he had given her. He searched the grass for the necklace. It was gone.

All during the hellish years of war he had never felt the clutch of murder twist his heart as it did now. He had never really wanted to kill an enemy, but had done it only to win battles and eventually a war. He felt the poison of hate sweep through his body, sear his mind. Those who had done this terrible thing he would kill slowly. He would relish each scream of agony.

Gently he carried the limp body to the sparse shade of a tree singed from the heat. He brought his father and left them together, as they had been in life. Sight of such ravaged bodies might under ordinary circumstances empty his stomach. He was too far gone for that.

His father had been mutilated but Cole felt it had been done for effect, to shock whoever found the body. Cole was certain his father was already dead from the bullet in the left breast.

Moving as an automaton, he began to search the ground.

His eyes smarted from the smoke still drifting from the ruins of the house and barn. He ignored the arrows fired into the ground, the discarded legging, the war bow broken in two pieces. Instead he concentrated on the tracks left by the five marauders. Moccasin tracks, to be sure, but no Indian ever left such a splayed track. No light touch of foot as would be made by a warrior, but heavily pressed into dust and grass. Made by five big men. It all showed clearly in the tracks he read as easily as most men read a printed page.

Tracks less than two hours old.

Mounting up, he skirted the remains of the barn, the dead cow in the wreckage. He passed the wagon, a charred ruin.

For two miles he followed the tracks of the five riders, then came to a thicket where shod horses had been hidden. There the unshod ponies had been turned loose, stampeded southward. The new tracks of shod horses led west, toward the mountains.

He had been right. Shod horses meant white men.

He started to follow the trail. All that filled his mind for the moment was vengeance. Then he reined in, remembering a vow made to his mother when he was a boy.

"When my time comes take me home to my people. And your father . . . he is as much Crow as he is white. . . ."

A vow that could not be ignored.

Leaving the bodies where they were would draw predators.

He turned back, remembering that his mother had been a full blood, his father adopted into the tribe. After the important ritual of death, he would take the war trail. He had the rest of his life to track down the white savages who hoped to blame their murderous act on the Indian.

He had the rest of his life, and theirs.

Still numbed from shock, he hunted for a tool. In a shed only partially destroyed he found an ax, its blade still warm, the handle charred. But he was able to use it to cut two cottonwood poles. He trimmed them. A further search revealed an old cowhide set out to dry. He cut rawhide strips.

Reverently he wrapped the body of his mother in a blanket from his bedroll. The second blanket was for his father.

It was late afternoon before he finished making a travois out of the two cottonwood poles and the rawhide lashings. One end of it he fastened to his cavalry saddle. With the bodies of his parents lashed to the travois, he started in the direction of the Crow camp to the north. He walked beside his horse. His weight plus that of the two bodies on the travois would have been too much for a weary Trooper.

At a rise of ground he looked back. The wind had died and only a spiral of smoke marked the death scene. Again he experienced that shock of murderous rage.

"The rest of my life to hunt them down," he said through his teeth.

Sheer instinct kept him going. His eyes saw no mountains, no hills with grasses beginning to brown. No sky with giant clouds. At full dark he flung himself to the ground beside a creek.

The following mid-morning he surprised a band of deer in a grassy wooded valley. As their heads came up it crossed his dulled mind that he could use venison. All he'd had in his stomach since that night meal with the drifter Billings had been morning coffee and later a few chews of jerky. Instead of reaching for his rifle, he let the deer scamper away. He had no desire for food.

He pushed on, trudging the long miles, Trooper walking patiently at his side. The end poles of the dragging travois made twin tracks through grass and brush. Toward afternoon hunger pangs tried to edge past his numbness. He shrugged them off. Every fiber of his body seemed to have been seared in that blinding moment when he realized his parents were dead.

He skirted hills, crossed wild creeks.

"Four long years of killing," he muttered. "All that behind me for good. So I thought." The sound of his voice caused Trooper to turn his head and twitch his long, velvety ears.

Cole was thinking that east of the big river he had fought a war because of a country divided. Here in the West he was now committed to his own personal war. In the other war the enemy had been anonymous. Seldom did you see a face close up enough to read fear or determination to survive. If you did, then it became necessary to take a life in order to preserve your own.

The five men he would hunt down were also anonymous, at least for the present. But eventually he would know their faces well, every mole, every scar.

It had always been his code never to hunt an animal unless in need of food, never to push a horse to its limits, except in an extreme emergency. To try and avoid trouble if at all possible. But with the five murderers he could easily alter his code. They deserved a knife used slowly, methodically. He knew pain points in the human body that could be explored fully. Thinking of his revenge was all that kept him going as the agonizing miles and hours passed.

It was mid-afternoon when he was suddenly aware of a small band of Indians. They were on the lip of a mesa that jutted above the lush valley he had been crossing for an hour. At their backs a waterfall spilled down rock worn slick over the centuries. A rising mist produced miniature rainbows in the sunlight.

The Indians remained immobile as he pressed forward. When he drew near enough to be able to look up and see their faces clearly, they spun their ponies and dashed from sight. Some minutes later they appeared on a steep trail angling toward the valley floor. Puffs of dust rose from unshod hooves of ponies speeding toward him. Eight braves, each with a single feather in a headband.

He was within two dozen yards of them when they reined in and stared at him curiously. They wore leggings and breechclouts. Some were armed with war lance and bow and arrow. Two had rifles.

Cole made no move toward his own weapons. The palms of his hands were moist. He was thinking of the rumors of a band of renegade Indians on the prowl, a trading post burned. His parents murdered, this no rumor but fact. Both acts perpetrated by whites and blamed on the redman?

As he neared the Indians, he breathed easier because no war paint adorned their chests or their ponies. A hunting party, perhaps after buffalo. Although he had seen none.

A tall Indian rode forward. Cole halted and waited for the brave to reach him. The man had proud aquiline features, piercing black eyes. Cole's right hand was lifted, palm out, in the sign of peace. He sensed the brave was puzzled by the travois and the sight of a white man walking beside a horse instead of riding it.

The Indian reined in and pointed at the cavalry saddle and at Cole's dark blue hat. "Long knife soldier," he said coldly in English. "What do you seek among the lodges of the Crow?"

"It is welcome news that I am near their camp."

The brave had been sitting his pony stiffly, legging-clad legs clamped to the animal's barrel. But when he heard Cole respond in the Crow's language, his lips parted in surprise.

Cole gestured at the travois. For a moment the words seemed bottled up in him. Then he spoke. "My mother was White Elk. The Crow are her people. She should be with

70

them in death. I am also the son of the trapper, Badger Cantrell, who was an adopted Crow. Your people named me Two Trails."

The brave was no longer suspicious. He introduced himself as Tall Tree.

"How did your parents die, Two Trails?"

Tall Tree's dark eyes burned with rage as he listened to the story of a tragic homecoming.

When Cole finished the grisly tale, Tall Tree leaned from his pony and placed a hand on his arm in sympathy. Then he gestured to the other braves who rode up and listened grimly as Tall Tree spoke of the murders. When he had finished, war cries burst from their throats and they brandished weapons.

Cole shook his head and explained that as the son vengeance belonged to him alone. This they could understand, his determination to bring the white murderers to his own justice.

Cole had become more rational over the hours. "They'll face the law, if possible, and be hanged. If not, then I'll deal with them in my own way."

Tall Tree spun his pony, shouting, "You are welcome to our camp, Two Trails. *Kahay!*"

Soon Cole came within sight of lodges strung along a wide stream. Braves, herding a band of ponies to water, stared in surprise at the travois and the white man afoot. Smoke from many cook fires made a blue fog in the tall trees. Squaws tending the fires watched Cole's approach, then talked excitedly among themselves. Children bounded about with the enthusiasm of all youngsters. They were curious, as were the camp dogs who barked at the travois and the big black horse with the alien scent.

Word spread quickly concerning the reason for Cole's visit. Many of the Indians remembered him.

Cole selected a wide shelf of wooded land that overlooked the camp. They loaned him an ax which he used to fell saplings. Using the cottonwood poles, he erected two high platforms, firmly rooted into the shelf of ground he had chosen.

When this was done he used the hides of freshly killed buffalo as shrouds for the bodies.

Stepping back from the twin platforms that now held the bodies, he uttered a prayer in the Crow tongue, then in a monotone chanted a tribute to the dead.

Every Crow in camp had come to the high shelf of land to

partake silently in the "burial" of Cole's parents. Even the dogs seemed awed by the ancient ceremony and were quiet.

Cole knelt, placed his hat on the ground and faced the north star that was barely visible in the twilight sky. Head bowed, he prayed again: One prayer in English, taught him by his father, the other in Crow that he had learned from his mother.

Finally he put on his hat and stood up. It was finished. There was nothing more to be done here. His parents were already ascending to the land of shadows beyond the sky. He believed it. He recalled a passage in one of the books his father had insisted he read: "Without belief, man is lost."

He stood in silence, the evening breeze carrying a scent of freshly-cut wood, of wild waters and of the brush he had trampled. Onlookers below had drifted back to the camp. For the first time he felt exhaustion. Somehow in all the terrible hours he had been able to hold himself together. But now the lashings were coming undone and he was starting to unravel. Refusing to give way, he stiffened his knees and took one final look at the twin scaffolds. Above them the sky was brightening with stars, the last of daylight draining into reds and gold.

He started to leave. Then he had a sudden feeling that he was not alone there on the promontory. Tensing, he wheeled and snapped a hand to his gun.

12 He glimpsed a slim shadow some distance away. Then his hand dropped from the gun in embarrassment as he realized that the shadow was that of a woman.

"I thought I was alone," he said. "I didn't hear anyone come up here." In the stillness he leaned forward to try and get a better look. Something in the way she stood stirred a faint memory. But he couldn't be sure because of deepening shadows. When she did not move from her position near a towering slab of rock, he said, "Do you have something to say to me?" He felt her eyes on him although in the gloom he could not make out her features.

"It *is* you, Two Trails," she said.

"You know me?"

"Yes."

Again that tug of memory. "Why didn't you speak when I first came to camp?"

"I was not at camp."

"Somebody told you I had come?"

She shook her head. "I had a medicine dream that you would come, Two Trails."

"A medicine dream?" He squinted at the slender and shadowed figure, wondering.

"And in the dream I knew of your suffering. My heart is on the ground because of your sorrows."

She stepped from the deep shadows by the slab of rock and into the faint purplish twilight. Her skirt rustled softly about her ankles.

Cole's mouth fell open as he recalled her from other years. "A-Ho! Dark Star!"

"Yes, I am Dark Star."

Cole hurried to her and took her hands. They were warm, vibrant in his own. "You have grown beautiful since our childhood," Cole said softly, staring into the upturned face.

"I was not beautiful then?" she chided.

"You were. More so now."

His mind whirled back to his youth when he had vied with the best of the young braves in horsemanship, in footraces, tested his skill with bow and arrow, war lance and throwing ax. All to gain her nod of approval, her smile. How many years ago? Over a decade. So much had happened since those carefree days in the Crow camp when his father was running trap lines.

For the first time Cole was partially able to throw off the cold mantle of despair that had gripped him since his homecoming.

He studied her in the faint light, the high forehead, brows faintly arched, the eyes shining in this last of daylight. The nose perfectly shaped, the mouth generous. The tilt of the chin indicated strength and purpose.

"Your husband must be very proud of you," Cole said.

She shook her head. "I have no husband, Two Trails."

"Then the braves in this camp are blind."

"I am a medicine woman," she said gravely and he automatically released her hands. He recalled her mention of a medicine dream, but even so he was surprised at her confession. He had heard of certain women said to have supernatu-

73

ral powers but it was the first time he had ever stood in the presence of one.

He managed to speak. "It is a great honor that you remember me, Dark Star."

She smiled. Her teeth gleamed faintly through parted lips. She gestured at the glowing cook fires below, the dance of sparks in the trees. There was a faint buzz of voices from the camp.

"Come," she said, "you need food . . . and rest."

But he shook his head and turned to look significantly up at the twin scaffolds, somber in the growing darkness. "I have a long trail ahead of me. . . ."

"That can wait."

"Time is important."

"I will make you a great medicine for your journey." A touch of mystery was in her voice as she placed cool fingertips on the back of his hand. He felt a shock as one does when rubbing fur on a cloudy day and the sparks jump.

"I . . . I can't stay, Dark Star. I have business." His voice faded because the shock of her eyes on his seemed even greater than that produced by the touch of her fingers.

Her voice was musical, compelling. "You must stay. And do not worry about hunting the five white men."

"You heard the story of them in camp," he guessed.

"I saw them murder your parents."

He stared at her in wonderment. Then he shook his head. Nothing mysterious or mystical about her statement, he told himself. Some brave in retelling the story of the murders had in his excitement made it seem he had been a witness. She had picked up the story and changed it to suit her own needs. She seemed to read the cold logic spinning through his mind.

"I *saw* it happen," she repeated.

"You trying to say you were a *witness?*"

"Not a witness as you would call it. Not a witness in the flesh." An enigmatic smile clung to her lips.

He was weary and his brain was numbed and this was foolishness she spoke. "How do you mean you saw it happen?"

"You have forgotten much of the lore of your mother's people."

"Maybe, but even so . . ."

"Don't you remember what I told you? I am a medicine woman."

"I believe you." He conceded that much. "But it still doesn't make you a witness."

74

"Two suns have passed since I saw your parents killed in my dream. Killed by the men you seek. I knew then that you would come."

He shook his head in disbelief. "You claim you saw them in a . . . a *dream?*"

"Yes. And I can describe each man." And she did while he listened incredulously. "Of the five men, the one with flaming red hair is the most dangerous. He is the soft-spoken one, the deadly one.

Any number of renegades on the frontier would fit the descriptions she had given. And yet . . . His jaw hardened. "If you know so much, why were my parents killed?"

"That has not been revealed to me. All that need concern you for the present is the need to find those men. Not the reason behind their act."

"Tell me about the men who burned the trading post at Amber Creek," he demanded thinly. "Another medicine dream?"

She shook her head. "The trading post is in ruins, yes. But I do not know who did it. My dream was because of you, Two Trails."

He scowled. "I'd like to believe you, but . . ."

Dark Star spoke softly, her voice filled with compassion. "Even though I wept for your sorrow, my heart sang. Because I knew you were coming to me."

After all that had happened, it was almost too much. "I just don't . . . don't understand."

"There is no need to understand, only the need for an open mind. Just remember that many things in life are unexplained. You must have faith and believe that you are a part of the mind of the spirit that shines over us all. Not only on this earth but also on the land of shadows. It is what the white man calls God."

"If what you say is true, that you *saw* my parents killed . . ." His voice broke at the memory. "It is incredible."

"Do not think of your parents."

"Can I stop thinking of every fiber of my being that they gave to me?" he said sharply.

"It is a time to wash sorrow from your mind, Two Trails. That is what I mean. Tonight you must accept my counsel."

But still he held back. "I've got to take the trail of those killers."

"Listen to me and put all thoughts of vengeance aside," she urged.

"Easy enough to say," he muttered grudgingly.

"I will feed you and speak to you of the future. And then you must rest."

Again he was aware of the faint pressure of her fingers against his flesh. "Come, Two Trails," she said. "It is destined that we spend the night."

Her lodge sat apart from others in the camp, pole ends jutting from the smoke hole silhouetted against the starry sky. She drew aside the weather shield, then the inner flap and bade him enter.

"You are my guest," she whispered.

But he stood as if in a trance, faintly aware of odors drifing on the night air; the fresh grass trampled by horses, the scent of pine. A pleasant murmur of water over stones came from the nearby creek. The muted voices of braves and squaws drifted from deeper in the camp. Laughter of children, the barking of a dog.

"Don't be afraid of me," she said when he hesitated.

He managed a laugh that became partially wedged in his throat. "Afraid of such beauty? How could I be?"

Taking a deep breath, he ducked into the entrance and stood in the spacious lodge. A glow from a small fire in the center was reflected on the walls. What little smoke there was drifted out through the opening above. Dark Star gestured at a wide bed made of furs and buffalo robes.

He did not need to be coaxed. He flung himself down gratefully on the softness and stretched out his long legs. She knelt, smiling up at him, and gently worked off one boot, then the other. Soft fingers massaged his toes.

"I will feed you," she whispered, and got to her feet.

He ate ravenously, as grief finally gave way to hunger. Stewed antelope subtly flavored with wild herbs, greens and Indian bread. He finished off the sumptuous meal with wild berries, then settled back on the bed of furs. While he ate she knelt at his side, watching him, a smile of satisfaction curving her lips. When Dark Star moved there was a faint tinkling of her beads that reminded him of his mother's necklace. His jaws tightened and he stared up at the smoke outlet. A lone star shone through the scant opening.

Sensing his change of mood, she came to him quickly and peered into his face. "You must put such thoughts out of your mind," she ordered in a soft voice.

"How did you know what I was thinking?"

She explained modestly. "It is a gift." Then her eyes twinkled mischievously, reflecting the faint glow of the fire. "Or perhaps I only watched the expression on your handsome face. And from that interpret what goes on inside your head."

"Handsome," he scoffed. "You flatter me. I feel a hundred years old."

She slid her hands up under his shirt and made small circular motions on his bare chest. "I have a potion that will make you young again."

She backed away from the bed to give herself room. Reaching down, she caught the hem of her dress. It made a slithering sound against flesh as she drew the garment over her head. For a moment she stood, clad only in a shift that outlined the rich contours of her body. Then even the shift was cast aside. She knelt in front of him again and settled back on her heels, letting his eyes enjoy the sleek form she had unveiled for his pleasure. Never had he seen a woman more beautiful than this one, her coppery skin tinted by firelight. Breasts not large but ideally proportioned, the nipples small and erect, awaiting his pleasure. He did not need to be coaxed. When he leaned forward she gave a soft cry and pressed herself against his searching lips.

And as he brought pleasure to her and to himself, her fingers skillfully undid his buttons and his belt. Then she cast aside his clothing as she had her own.

"My warrior," she said almost in reverence as her own eyes feasted. "You want me and that is good," she whispered, both of her hands clasping him gently, warmly.

When she opened herself to him that residue of hatred and vengeance that still lingered in his tortured mind, slipped away.

Twice during the night he awakened and sought her again, each experience seeming to bring her even more delight than the others. In her arms he found a bliss lacking in the other women he had known. There was something mystical in the way she fused their bodies and their emotions. It was as if they alone drifted in a great, warm void somewhere beyond the most distant star.

Faint, dawn light touched the smoke hole. He saw that she was already at the cook fire. He yawned, stretched.

"You slept well, my warrior," she said. "Now you must rise and prepare for the war trail."

He was barely awake. Fully clothed now, she came to him and bent down to press her mouth against his.

The morning meal she prepared was fully as satisfying as

the supper. She laid out fresh buckskins to replace the worn clothing she had removed the evening before.

Attired in the new garments, he stepped outside with her. He put on his dark blue cavalry hat. But she was not through with gifts. Two hardy buffalo ponies were tethered to a stake. One bore his cavalry saddle, his Henry rifle and an Indian blanket.

Her look was grave as she said, "These ponies are strong and fast. They will carry you well."

He did not argue with her. But he had to know about Trooper.

"I will watch over your great black horse until you return. And return you will." Her eyes danced. "You must. My nights will be without pleasure until you do."

He glanced at the dimming stars. "You must have done all this in the dark."

"Perhaps I have the eyes of a cat and can see as well at midnight as at dawn." A tinkling laugh broke from her lips, then she grew serious and gripped his arms. "You must never forget me, Two Trails."

She removed a small leather bag from a pocket of her dress. Fastened to the neck was a loop of sturdy twine, dyed blue. He knew what it was and bent his head so she could slip it around his neck. Then she placed a hand over the small sack that now dangled beneath his buckskin shirt.

"My medicine," she whispered in that mystical voice she used when speaking of her gifts. "Carry it always."

"I will," he assured her gravely.

"May you find your enemies. And do with them what you will."

"They'll be found."

"And find them without injury to yourself."

It was time for him to go.

"*A-ho*, holy woman!"

She made no reply, only lifted a hand in farewell, as he rode off.

From a promontory he looked back at the camp, stirring now in the gray light. Last night he had been able to push from mind the tragedy of his parents, thanks to Dark Star. Her night of love had helped prepare him for the vengeance trail that he must ride until the blood debt was settled.

He fingered the medicine bag. Its magic would keep him alive until the last of the five men were dead.

He started riding hard, back the way he had come afoot

78

with the bodies on the travois. Every few miles he switched ponies so as to have a fresh mount always. Each mile narrowed the gap between pursuer and pursued. From time to time the descriptions she had given him of the five men flashed into his consciousness. They became locked in his mind, never to be lost.

He was crossing a land of rock, of towering mountains and fast-running streams. Sunlight flashed on swirling waters tumbling down a mountainside. A great yellowish animal the Mexicans called *El Tigre* leaped to a rock ledge ahead to look him over. Cole was not afraid, although the two ponies picked up the scent and snorted and twitched their ears. Cole did not worry that he would be challenged. No animal, unless wounded or starving would attack a human being. This one looked sleek and well fed.

Even as this crossed his mind, the great mountain lion bounded away.

"Happy hunting, fella," Cole said aloud, "and the same for me." He saw the animal later, a tawny streak through the trees far up a mountainside.

He reached a valley where he had set out trap lines as a boy with his father. His jaw hardened as he thought of Badger Cantrell, member of the fur brigade who had turned rancher. Murdered for what reason?

Dark Star hadn't been able to enlarge on her dream, if there really was one, and tell him *why* his parents had been killed. She said she'd know in time.

There would be time enough to credit her powers after he compared the descriptions she recounted from her vision with the killers in the flesh. He was on their trail now. Soon he would know for sure.

He came to a place where the killers had rested. It was the first time he realized they had exchanged moccasins for boots. Unfortunately there was nothing distinctive about any of the boot tracks.

But there was a difference in one of the hoof prints left by the five horses he had been following. Noting this again in the soft soil he smiled coldly.

Hours later he began to climb through sage and then into cedar. He switched ponies again on a spine of the highest point of land and turned to study the terrain below. He was too late for their dust to guide him, though from the signs he could tell they were taking their time.

The zigzag trail climbed higher, then dropped sharply into

a valley and climbed again. In his haste to take the trail he had not thought of food. But Dark Star had provided it; pemmican in his saddlebags. In a grove of aspens, some with trunks more than a foot around that shaded a spring, he made a meal of the sustaining food of the Indian. Dried buffalo and wild nuts, pounded into a mass, then dried in the sun. He also found venison jerky. As he rode, he ate sparingly, for he knew it was possible to go into battle at any time. At such a time the less food in the stomach the better. In the war those wounded after partaking of a heavy meal were more apt to succumb than those with empty bellies.

It had surprised him to find that the five men seemed unhurried. He had expected them to travel swiftly in order to reach Scalplock, still miles to the west, but the only settlement in the direction they were heading. They stopped often, perhaps to study their backtrail. Anticipation of a showdown quickened his pulse.

He watered the ponies at a creek that tumbled through rock walls and then spread out, a sheet of silver, across a valley floor. Later in the day he reached spruce that climbed into the sky and pine equally tall, the tracks of the five horses always before his eyes. His ponies, moving swiftly, made scarcely a sound on the matting, the result of decades of leaves and needles that had rotted into a carpet in the deep shade. He climbed again.

He rode now with the Henry rifle always loose in the boot. As darkness closed in he snatched a few hours of sleep.

There was never any doubt in his mind that he followed the right set of tracks because of the slight indentation in the shoe on the right forefoot of one of the horses.

He reached a camp site by late afternoon. He saw the remains of a cook fire. The ashes were cold. Last night's fire? He was closing in slowly but inevitably. Cole was about to mount his fresh pony when his heart twisted. His eyes fell on something that had belonged to his father. A prized possession, the Irish clay pipe, its stem snapped, the bowl crushed.

How he longed at that moment to have the murderers within gun range.

In his mad desire to catch up, he pushed on, recklessly now. But at full dark he had to stop before complete exhaustion claimed him as well as the ponies. Besides, only a lunatic would try and negotiate a mountain trail on a night when a thick mantle of clouds curtained off the unreliable glimmer of light from the stars.

80

Just before stretching out in his blanket, he realized he had miscalculated. He was not all that close to them. In his desire to catch up, he had ignored reality. Hell, they had two days on him. He had made up time, certainly, but not that much.

The showdown, when it came, would probably be in Scalplock. At least there he might have more of a chance against five men than on an uncertain trail strewn with boulders, or possibly while crossing some wild stream.

13

Sam Stark rode in the lead, eyes scanning the trail ahead. A few feet behind him Ed Lewt wore a bemused smile most of the time. Then came Dain and Cutter. Doak Lancer was several yards behind the others. His head, with its crown of red hair, turned every mile or so as he studied their backtrail. Apparently no one had picked up their sign. It might be days before anyone happened across the ruins of the Cantrell buildings in such a remote part of the country. By then, of course, predators would have finished off the bodies. Not that it mattered. There was enough Indian evidence to prove who had committed the crimes.

With no pursuit it meant they could take their time. It was unwise to push their horses, Lancer had said. An emergency could always arise. Foolish men on spent horses in such unpredictable terrain as this were soon dead.

For once, Stark agreed with Lancer.

Shortly before nightfall they were treated to a demonstration of Lancer's talents. A big buck deer appeared suddenly, veered at the sight of them and went bounding up a mountainside with dizzying speed. Lancer drew and fired his revolver before the others could hardly blink. The buck crashed to earth with a single shot through the skull. Stark and the other three exchanged glances. They were impressed.

"I never miss," Lancer said quietly.

Food for supper and breakfast was cut from the deer. They made camp in a grove of trees beside a small stream.

Lancer sat several feet away, eating alone. Stark wondered about him.

Creed had said, "Lancer will go along with you on this

Cantrell business." Then Creed jerked his thumb at a man they could see through the office window. He had a freckled and sunburned face.

"Who the hell is Doak Lancer?" Stark had demanded, not liking an outsider horning in and getting a share of the money.

"He's a good, tough man."

"Looks more like a peddler to me," Stark scoffed.

"What he peddles could make the undertakers rich."

That was Stark's introduction to Doak Lancer. . . .

It was the following day that they reached the old road to Scalplock. Up here in the high country a lot of it had been washed out. A newer road, miles away, angled in from the south.

Stark reined in, eyes intent on a fresh sign that a team and a heavily loaded wagon had recently passed.

"Not more'n an hour or so ago," Stark grunted in surprise. "What damn fool is tryin' to go through these mountains with a full load an' no road?"

"Mebby the road's all right ahead a ways," Cutter offered, shielding his eyes against the westering sun.

All five men were startled to hear a faint voice. "Fellas . . . fellas . . . help me!"

Their horses had been facing west toward a distant, narrow pass they intended to take. The voice snapped their eyes to an older man who was crawling on hands and knees around a bend in the road. He had thinning black hair and his eyes in a puffy face looked glassy. He was drooling.

Stark, wary of tricks, drew his gun. "Who the hell are you?"

"Peaceful I am, stranger. Put up your gun." There was a wild pitch to the voice that seemed on the verge of hysterical laughter. His lips twitched and formed a maniacal grin. He said his name was Buck Porter and that he was sickly. "Feel all swole up inside," he said. "Dizzy I am. But Flo's back yonder an' she'll put on her purtiest dress an' cook us all a fine meal. Cindy Lou, she's gone on up the mountain to see if there's any road left up there."

"Cindy Lou?" Stark murmured. Lewt, Cutter and Dain looked interested. Lancer's sunburned face was expressionless.

"I told Cindy Lou that it weren't no use to hike up there," Porter continued in that strange voice. "I said that some fine gentlemen like you would be along an' we'd have us a fine time. Then you'd show us how to get outa these mountains. . . ."

82

He ran out of breath. The once powerful frame sagged at the belly and chest. His silk shirt was ripped down the front. Crawling had worn through the knees of his wool pants. Stark put up his gun. "How far you crawled, anyhow?"

"Legs give out. Been havin' the sickness. Had it for two days. Flo got it bad, but Cindy Lou, she ain't got a trace."

Cutter's scarred face was suddenly taut with suspicion. "What kind of sickness?"

"Bad water, reckon." Porter looked up at them out of the glassy eyes. "Cindy Lou wouldn't drink none of it."

"Got any whiskey?" Lewt asked.

"Full jug. We'll have us a time while you fine gentlemen get our wagon back on the road, eh?" Porter tried to stand up, but his legs folded. "Weak as hell I am. Weak."

"Where was you headin' when you broke down?" Stark wanted to know. "Nothin' up ahead but Scalplock. That where?"

"Yeah. Aim to open up the finest house west of Missouri."

Cutter leaned over in the saddle and spoke to Stark. "Old bastard's crazy with fever. I seen others with it."

Porter started to ramble again. "Me an' Flo movin' nawth. Figure it's better up heah for business. Been down in Santa Fe, but can't get along with the damn *politicos*. Wanted me to slide as much gold across their palms as I give my gals."

"Gals," Lewt murmured excited.

"Yankee come to town an' opens up a new house," Porter cried, his voice cracking. "All the gals quit on me. All but Cindy Lou. I said to hell with the others. Me an' Flo we'll have us the best parlor house nawth of Santa Fe. An' Cindy Lou, she'll be our top gal."

"This Cindy Lou, she purty?" Lewt asked.

"Not as purty as Flo."

"Hell you say." Sam Stark looked pleased.

"Cindy Lou ain't been took with the sickness like me an' Flo has." Porter looked up out of vacant eyes. "Lemme tell you about Cindy Lou. She ain't like the others. Me an' Flo, we took her under our wing."

"Put her in your bed you mean," Stark snorted. He winked at the others. "How much she gonna cost us?"

"Flo's the one sets prices." Porter's head bobbed and he looked down as a wide wet stain appeared at the front of his dusty trousers.

Lewt let out a howl of laughter. "Peed his britches, by gad!"

Porter got both hands behind him, leaned back to look up

at the five men on horseback. "Somehow it ain't right, Cindy Lou doin' her favors for fellas out here in the mountains. Under a roof in a respectable house it's some difference."

"You old bastard, I wouldn't pay you a *centavo*," the pock-marked Dain said in disgust.

Cutter grinned. "Gotta be fair, Al." Then to Porter, who was trying to stand up in the road, only to fall: "How about a dollar for the bunch of us? Even give you two bits extra. Every pimp oughta have his share."

Four of the men laughed; Lancer remained silent.

"Flo sounds right for me," Lewt chuckled. "You fellas can fight over Cindy Lou."

"We better be moving along," Doak Lancer said.

Stark shook his head. "Hell, we been in the saddle since sunup. A meal, some whiskey an' . . . other things," this with a broad wink, "we can use."

Leaning down, he caught Porter by a wrist. With Lewt's help they got him astride the rump of Stark's horse.

They started up the mountain, the horses stepping gingerly over the washouts. They could see where the wagon had slid off the road two times, barely able to get back. The road worsened. At last they came to a sharp bend and saw the wagon tipped on its side. A cargo of boxes and trunks, cooking utensils had spilled out. The team had been unhitched and tied to a wagon wheel.

Someone was lying on the ground near the wagon, arms outflung. It was a woman about Buck Porter's age, in a worn blue dress with a dirty lace collar. A thick coating of lip rouge on a pale face made her look like a clown. Her eyes, with the same glassy look as Porter's, stared straight up into the sun, unblinking.

"Flo!" Porter wailed, sliding off the back of the horse. He staggered a few steps, fell. "Git up, Flo, an' put on a purty dress for the gentlemen. . . ."

Lewt pointed at the pitiful rag of woman. "That ol' hag is Flo?"

Stark dismounted and stalked over to peer down at the woman. "Dead," he announced. Reaching down, he plucked at one of the arms that was already stiff. "Hell, she's been dead for hours."

Porter sat on the ground. "Flo, you *hear* me? These gentlemen are gonna fix our wagon. . . ." Somehow the exertion of shouting at the dead woman snapped the tired threads that bound him to life. He eased over on his side, kicked a few times and was stilled.

A sudden screech of fear burst from Bill Cutter. "He's dead, sure as hell. An' you ask me, it's *cholera!*"

Lewt turned pale. "Let's get the hell away. . . ."

"If it's cholera, it'll travel fifty miles right on our heels," Cutter said, his voice shaking. "I *know!* My brother come west in forty-seven an' half that wagon train was dead afore they reached the Yellowstone." He flung himself from his horse. "Burn everything! Only way. Fire kills it! Only fire!"

They watched, slack-jawed, as he ran crazily to the wagon. He rummaged furiously through a trunk until he found what looked like account books. He ripped out page after page of columns of figures opposite female names. He struck a match. Lewt and Dain sprang to help him as flames flickered. They emptied the contents of two trunks into the growing fire. Dain cut loose the two horses that were kicking and whinnying in their great fear of fire. They wheeled in panic and went roaring down the washout, manes flying.

"Jeezus, why'd you let them hosses loose?" Cutter yelled at Dain. "Shoulda killed 'em, burned the carcasses."

But by then the two animals were pounding down the long slope through rocks and trees and out of sight around a shoulder of mountain.

Lewt braved the flames and salvaged a whiskey jug. He ignored Cutter's advice to throw it in the fire.

Clothing from the trunks helped feed flames that by then were eating into the bed of the upended wagon.

"Loco old bastard," Lewt snarled at the dead Porter. "Hell, there ain't no Cindy Lou no more'n there was a purty Flo."

"Burn every damn thing that's left!" Cutter shouted. "My brother said that fire cleans the air."

Cutter and Lewt threw the body of the woman on the fire. Just as they reached for the dead man, a girl began screaming at them. "What are you *doing!*"

She came running wildly down the hill, jumping over the great cuts water had gouged out of the road, her blue-striped dress billowing. Tears spilled down her cheeks when she saw that Porter was dead.

"Poor Buck!" she cried.

Cutter grabbed her by an arm. "They're both dead of cholera!" he yelled at the distraught young woman. "Likely you got it too!"

"No, no," she sobbed and tried to pull away. "It was bad water. Only bad water."

It was an incongruous sight as the limbs of the pair in the flames began to twitch. And the dead man actually sat up as he had on the road when alive. His hair flamed. The girl, still sobbing, retched at the odor.

Cutter shoved her over to a draw where a strong breeze kept away the stench. She sank to a rock, face buried in her hands. She was still gasping for breath from the hard run down the mountain.

"Not cholera at all," she said in a more normal tone. Flames crackled and spit. "Flo died just after sunup and when the wagon tipped over her body spilled out. I . . . I just couldn't move her. Buck was too far gone to help." She brushed away tears with the back of a small hand. She had a gamin face, moist from exertion and tears.

"Where you been, anyhow?" Stark demanded, his eyes darting over her trim figure.

"I . . . I thought maybe I could find a cabin," she said, gesturing wearily over her shoulder at the higher elevations. "Or maybe find another road. But there was nothing. I was about halfway back when I saw the smoke and started running." She shuddered. "Poor Buck, dead along with Flo."

"Yeah, but you're alive," Lewt said with a grin.

She seemed not to hear. She exhaled a deep breath, puffing out her cheeks. She rubbed at her brown eyes, then said, "No need to have burned the bodies. I know they do that when there's a cholera epidemic, but this was not cholera. "You'll help me dig graves . . . ?" She looked anxiously into each of their faces like a small child asking grown-ups for help. She met stones' faces, swallowed and looked away.

Lewt's eyes were bright. "Reckon you're Cindy Lou."

She flinched. "That isn't really my name. It's . . ." Her mouth began to shake from sudden fear.

"With her face washed she'd be kinda purty," Al Dain said eagerly.

Stark turned to Lancer who sat some distance away on a deadfall, away from the fire that still burned. "Might's well have some fun, eh Doak?"

"Let's move on," Lancer said, the pale blue eyes flicking a contemptous glance at the frightened girl.

"For once, *I* say what we do." Stark took a long and defiant pull at the jug Lewt had rescued from the fire.

"Buck had fever and must have talked wild," the girl said

in a trembling voice, not quite matching the false smile she tried to keep on her pretty mouth. "You can't believe anything a person says when they're burning up with fever as poor Buck was."

Lewt, grinning, caught her by an arm and dragged her struggling up a cut bank and into a thick stand of trees. She screamed and tried to hit him in the eyes. But Lewt ducked and laughed. He hauled her across his hip, held her firmly with one hand then worked off her boots with the other. She kicked and sobbed, but finally her feet were bare. Lewt turned her loose then. He took careful aim, then tossed her boots from the cut bank down into the fire, scattering cinders.

"Purty good aim, huh?" he said, winking at the others.

"We do all right around fires!" Sam Stark laughed as he scrambled up the bank. "Ain't the first one we had this week!"

Doak Lancer shouted a warning. "No more talking, you damn fool!"

"Who wants to talk? We got somethin' better to do!"

"Keep a holt of her, Sam," Ed Lewt said, "till I can git my britches off."

But the girl twisted free and was running barefoot up through the trees like a panicked fawn, hair and skirts flying.

"You let her get away," Bill Cutter complained as he came slipping and sliding up the cut bank.

"She won't go far on them tender feet," Lewt assured him. "Why the hell you think I burned her boots?"

Lewt's long-legged stride caught up with her. He dragged her back.

"Please, I know what you think of us," the girl cried, "but they were good people, Flo and Buck. They treated me well. Better than I'd ever been treated before. At home I was a slave. . . ."

Lewt, still holding her by an arm, turned to Stark. "Sam, you an' the others draw straws to see who's next after me."

"No need to draw straws." Stark's smile was icy through the black beard. "I'm first. You hombres can fight over her afterwards."

"Sam, that ain't fair," Lewt complained. "I'm the one went after her. . . ."

Stark seized her by the other arm. For a few moments it was a tug of war. Finally Lewt released her.

87

"The rest of you take a walk," Stark ordered. "I'll yell when it's time for the next one."

"It isn't right," the girl sobbed in her anger, as she fought unsuccessfully to free herself of the thick fingers.

"For money you'll do it?" Stark's grin was vicious. "That what you want . . . *pay?*"

"No, it is *not* what I mean!" she protested as Stark threw her to the shadowed ground under the swaying trees. She tried to sit up and claw his face, but one hand caught both of her slender wrists. His weight pinned her to ground.

"Flo and Buck are dead," she said shakily, "and they deserve a decent burial. Please . . . please, don't treat me like this. . . ."

Stark laughed. He drew his gun, cocked it and pushed the muzzle against her cheek. "Which you want, me or this?"

She had learned to endure a stepfather when she was twelve. These men who had upon her here in lonely mountains she also endured. All that night and the next morning.

"Take her with us or leave her behind?" Bill Cutter wondered aloud when dawn was cracking the eastern sky.

"We leave her, one way or the other," Stark said thickly. He'd consumed most of the whiskey and was still half-drunk. "She can't get far with them bare feet." He grinned at her. "Redskins will find her, likely. They'll know what to do with the likes of her."

"I'd rather be with Indians than renegades like you!" she said, clenching her fists.

The back of Stark's hand popped against her cheek, knocking her down.

He stood over her, glaring. "Redskins get hold of you you'll wish I'd blowed out your brains. We know all about injuns, eh boys? Like them settlers we killed back in Beaver Valley."

Lewt gave a broad wink that the distraught girl, dazed from the backhand, failed to see. "Shoulda brung along my war bow." Lewt gave a howl of laughter and slapped his knee.

"Wonder how she'd look scalped, like we done to that squawman," Stark chuckled.

"Let's clear out." Doak Lancer was already mounted. His pale blue eyes flicked to each of the bleary faces.

They started to ride away, Lancer lagging behind as usual.

"I guess you know what I've got to do," he said as cooly as if he might be asking for a beer. "I listened to Stark spill his guts to her. He did everything but draw her a map of Beaver Valley."

88

Stark reddened. "Hell, a little whiskey talk . . ."

Lancer twisted in the saddle and looked back at the girl on the ground, looking pitiful and frightened, her cheek beginning to swell. She just sat there unmoving on the gentle slope under the thick trees. Lancer's gun hand made a blur. He shot her in the head. Reverberations of the gunshot racketed against the slope. She fell back. One side of her face, turned now to a cloudy sky, was dark with blood.

Lancer gave the four men a meaningful look that lingered on the bearded Stark. "You talked too much about the Cantrells. It doesn't matter this time because she's out of it. But from now on, keep your mouth shut. That goes for all of you."

Stark's throat muscles worked, but he made no reply.

"Everybody satisfied that I had to kill her?" Lancer asked softly, looking around.

Lewt nodded. "Better'n leavin' her alive." He tongued his gold tooth, Lancer's cold gaze making him nervous.

"How about you, Dain?" Lancer asked.

"Yeah." Dain's small eyes blinked in the pockmarked face.

Lancer looked directly at Cutter. "You agree?"

"Better her dead than us shakin' hands with the hangman." Cutter tried to laugh.

"Haven't heard from you, Stark." Lancer drawled.

"You done what you had to do," Stark said, not looking at Lancer.

Only then did Lancer jack the spent shell from his gun. He reloaded his weapon and holstered it. He was the last man through the narrow passage in the mountain that eventually would take them to Scalplock. Lancer knew that as soon as the human scent faded, the predators would come. All that would be left of Cindy Lou would be bones. Probably not enough of them to half fill a gunnysack.

14

Cole switched ponies on a spine of mountain, then at a gallop cut down into a valley darkened by great stands of spruce and pine. The hoofprints reached a road that had been ravaged by storms. A team and wagon, from the looks of the sign, had tried to negotiate the bad road. A fool driver, Cole thought grimly.

He followed the tracks of the horses and the wagon for a ways. After half a mile the road was completely gone. To his left, down in a hollow, was a heap of ashes. Metal brackets indicated the remains of a wagon. There were bits of charred cloth and the partially burned lid of an old trunk.

Drawing his Henry rifle, he rode closer and saw bones gleaming in the ashes. Two skulls with eye sockets upturned seemed to question his right to stare.

All around were the tracks of horses. And boot prints. It was another set of tracks that caused a cold prickling at the nape of his neck.

These were fresh, made by bare feet.

He bounded from his pony, tied both animals because the lingering stench from the ashes made them nervous. He looked carefully around. Nothing moved. The only sounds that of a rising wind humming through trees above a cut bank. The barefoot tracks led up into the trees and down again. Several sets of them, all fresh.

Leaving the edgy ponies, he studied the footprints and realized they had been made either by a boy or a female.

"Step out so I can see you!" he shouted. He switched from English to Crow and a smattering of other Indian languages he had picked up over the years. But there was no response.

"Damn it, show yourself!" he shouted in English. "I won't hurt you!"

At last there seemed to be a faint movement where the shadows in the trees were deepest. But he couldn't be sure because clouds that had been piling up for over an hour had thickened and covered the sun.

He saw a figure above, moving slowly in the shadows. It halted. "Easy now," he called. "No tricks. I won't kill you. But try anything and you'll have a bullet in the leg."

He had about made up his mind that the footprints had made by a boy. Then he saw a bedraggled-looking girl step out in the dimming daylight from the sanctuary of pines.

Her hair, brown and tangled, hung loosely. The dress was white, or had been, with blue stripes. It was smudged with dirt, torn at a shoulder. There was a long rip down one side that she modestly tried to hold together so as not to expose a leg.

She took another step. She seemed in pain, unsteady on her feet. Then in a brighter streak of sunlight he saw the ugly wound at her left temple, saw the caked blood on the side of the small face.

She started to speak, but her mouth collapsed. As did her legs, folding abruptly so that she fell headlong across the thick carpeting of pine needles.

He booted his rifle, then ran to her, swung her up in his arms. Almost weightless, a child. He carried her around a bend in the ruined road, back down the way he had come. Here the air currents were strong enough to keep away the lingering odors from the fire.

He set her down on a flat rock. Her brown eyes were red and swollen, possibly from weeping. One cheek was purplish.

"What happened to you, child?"

She just stared up at him, dazed and fearful. He took a closer look and saw her breasts, the mature curve of thigh, and knew she was older than he had thought. The soles of her feet were bruised, stained from dirt. She watched him warily from slitted eyes.

After making sure the tracks of the five horses headed west toward a slot in the mountains, he returned to her. Without protest she allowed him to carry her to a small stream that angled in from some boulders below the road. He bathed her head gently and washed away the caked blood. She winced and made small sounds of pain.

"Looks like a gunshot wound," he said.

"Yes . . ."

"Who shot you?"

But she shuddered and for a minute seemed unable to speak. Then she started talking about people named Flo and Buck. The bones in the remains of the fire, he supposed.

"They were deathly ill because of bad water I refused to touch," he said. "It tasted terrible, they said. Maybe arsenic."

"It killed them?"

"Eventually. Some men came along. . . ."

"Five men," Cole offered and felt his jaws ache from clenched teeth when she nodded her head. "They thought Flo and Buck had died of cholera. They burned everything. All my clothes, the bodies . . . everything."

"And your shoes, I guess."

"One of the men pulled them off and threw them into the fire."

"It's something they'd do," Cole said with such vehemence that she gave him a startled look.

"You *know* them?"

91

"I'll know 'em better," he said in that cold voice that made her shoulders twitch.

"You sound as if you hate them."

"I do."

"So do I!" She screamed it and began to weep. After a few moments she straightened up and wiped her eyes on her fingertips. She brushed back loose strands of brown hair. Then she stood up and took a few wobbly steps. He steadied her.

"I'm dizzy is all," she explained, sinking to a slab of rock, knees together primly, one hand holding closed the long rip in her dress. "I've lost all tracks of time. I think it's two days since I've had anything to eat. Oh, a few berries, all I could find."

"They've been gone that long?"

"I . . . I think so. I hid in the trees, afraid to move except at night. I thought they might come back and . . . and make sure of me this time."

"So they left you for dead. Killing's their business." Hatred flashed in his eyes like summer lightning. He asked the girl her name.

"Cindy Lou . . . Well, not really. My name is Helen, but Flo, who was from the South, thought Cindy Lou was better."

He gave her jerky and pemmican from his saddlebags. She was famished. He had to warn her to eat slowly.

As she ate, she talked of Flo and Buck. "They were good to me. I ran away from home and my horse died on me. I was wandering, about dead from thirst when some freighters found me." She gave a despondent shrug. "By the time we reached Santa Fe I didn't care much what happened to me. Flo and Buck took me in. I may not be much of anything else, mister, but I'm loyal."

"Not much of that these days."

"I might as well tell you the rest of it," she said, wiping a shred of jerky from a lower lip, "although I expect you've guessed it already."

"No need to talk," he said, staring at the horse tracks heading westward.

"When they closed up the place in Santa Fe and decided to come up here I came with them. The other girls quit!" She looked him in the eye. "You do know what I'm talking about?"

"Yeah. But I don't give much of a damn, Cindy Lou . . . or Helen. . . ."

"Helen." She tried to smile, but there was evidently too much pain. The wound, even though superficial, needed attention. The nearest place for that was Scalplock. "By the way, I'm Cole Cantrell."

"Cantrell." A tiny frown puckered the forehead that he had washed clean of blood and dirt. "Those men spoke of Cantrells."

"Bragging?"

"What did they do to you, Mr. Cantrell?"

"They killed two people mighty precious to me . . . my parents."

"How awful." She shuddered.

"We'd better get moving." He glanced at the darkening sky.

"If I'd have had a gun, I think I would have killed myself, after those men left. . . ."

"Not you." He patted her on the shoulder. "Not if you could survive everything you've been through. Only weaklings kill themselves, Helen. You're too strong for that."

"I don't know just how strong I am." She stood up awkwardly, her bare feet on the gravelly ground.

"How's your head feel?" he asked.

"Not pounding and painful as it was."

"Good. We've got some riding to do."

She tried another smile; it was shaky. "Thanks for taking me with you. I was worried you might not."

Much as she would slow him down, he could not abandon her.

He gave her his slicker for warmth, then helped her aboard the spare pony, her skirts hiked up her slim legs. They started along the path made by the horse tracks so familiar to him. As they rode he decided to see if she had recovered sufficiently from shock to describe the five men. She did, even though some of the horror had been blocked out of her mind.

Cole was amazed at how closely the descriptions matched those given to him by Dark Star.

He looked around at the small figure, bared legs clamped to the barrel of the sturdy Indian pony, her hair blowing now in the strong wind.

"What names did they use?" he wanted to know.

She frowned, trying to think. Rock walls towered on either side of the pass. She said that one of the men was called Bill. Another Newt or Lewt, she wasn't sure which. "And the black-bearded one was Sam."

"What about the redhead?" Cole asked, keeping his eyes

now on the rough country ahead. He didn't think there was a chance for an ambush, but he couldn't take chances. The five men might take it into their loco heads to come back and see if the girl was dead.

Helen spoke of the redhead. He seemed aloof, she said, and was the only one who hadn't raped her. "I guess he thought that me being what I am was beneath him to touch." She spoke bitterly.

"Any name for the redhead?"

"I . . . I honestly can't remember. There seemed to be bad feeling between him and the others."

"You speak well, Helen. You've had schooling."

"I went to school on money my father left us. Then my mother fell in love with that . . . that Riley, my stepfather. He beat me and . . . I stopped my schooling."

"Life hasn't handed you very much."

"But I'm alive and that's important." She was watching a covey of mountain quail caught in a strong down draft and fighting their way to calmer air. "There were times when I thought my stepfather might kill me. And those five men . . . I can endure almost anything."

A mountain storm that had been building all afternoon suddenly lashed the high country they were crossing. Cole found a cave for shelter, large enough to hold the two ponies. Because of a strong odor of bear, he cocked his Henry and tiptoed deeper into the cave. If he should find cubs, he and the girl would clear out. He wanted no confrontation with a returning she-bear who might have gone to prowl for food. Even though it was late in the season for cubs, he had to be sure. Far back in the cave the wild odor was even stronger. He would kill a bear only in defense of his own life. Never would he kill a cub. But when finally he reached the end of the cave, he found it empty. It had been used the past winter, he guessed, by bears hibernating. Their strong odor had lingered.

"No worries," he told Helen when he had returned to where she waited apprehensively near the cave mouth. The welcome news seemed to take the last of her strength. She slumped to the cave floor, leaned back against a wall, the oversize slicker billowing out like a yellow tent.

He stared sourly at the sheets of rain. "Lucky it's not winter," he said over his shoulder, "or we'd have deep snow out of a storm like this."

Lightning flickered above higher peaks. Closer in, a great

jagged fork of it cut through the gloomy day with the brilliance of a July noon. Thunder jarred the ground, reminding him of the last great cannonade of the war.

"The storm will wash out their tracks," Helen said, speaking of the men he sought.

"Won't matter. I'll get 'em eventually."

"Will you turn them over to a sheriff?"

He could barely make out her slight figure in the gloom beyond the ponies. "Way I feel now, I'll be my own sheriff."

"Kill them and you could be the one on the gallows," she said, getting up and coming close to where he leaned against the stone wall of the cave. "Or do you have proof that they murdered your parents?"

"Proof enough in my own mind." Thunder crashed, making the ponies jump.

"You've been kind to me and I don't want to see you hurt." She looked down at the damp floor. "If I were an ordinary woman, I could speak up and tell the law what those men did to me. Reason enough to do away with the lot of them on that score alone. But nobody would listen to me . . . because of what I've been." She swallowed and stared out at the deluge.

"Remember this," he said, touching her arm. "Nobody knows about your connection with Buck and and his woman Flo. And what business you were in down in Santa Fe."

"Those five men know about it."

"They won't be alive to talk for long."

She peered up into his face. "*You* know all about me," she reminded.

"Believe me, I'd never let on to anybody."

He had hoped the storm might be dying but it roared with renewed fury. Daylight faded. He made a decision; they'd have to spend the night in the cave. She was resigned to it. Weak as she was, she insisted on helping him gather dry wood scattered along the cave floor and pile it under a smoke-blackened fissure in the ceiling, far back from where he had tethered the ponies to a rock slab that had been dislodged from the cave wall.

Despite a drizzle of water from the break in the cave roof, he managed to get a small fire going that threw enough heat to dry them out. They sat with their backs to the wall, enjoying the warmth.

He asked for more details concerning the five men, but she could add nothing to what she had told him earlier. After they had eaten more pemmican and jerky, Helen could hardly

95

keep her eyes open. Although she protested, Cole made her take his blanket.

She looked at him as if expecting him to say something more that would define her obligation to her rescuer. But he put the blanket around her, made her lie down. He managed to keep the fire burning despite gusts of wind that occasionally swept into the cave mouth.

By the time he turned and looked at her again, she was sound asleep.

They left the cave early. The storm had ended while they slept and the skies were clear. In the warming day Helen no longer needed the slicker he had loaned her.

The tracks of the five horses had been wiped clean by the deluge, but no matter. He would never forget that distinguishing track left by one of their horses. All else failing, he would find that hoof print if he had to search clear to the Pacific.

The meager supply of food that he had nursed before meeting Helen, was gone. He kept one eye on the grassy slopes, looking for antelope or deer. But the matter was solved when he saw a faint haze of smoke through the trees. Drawing his rifle, he warned the girl to stay back. He rode on ahead where he could look down on a collection of buildings. The source of the smoke was a chimney on the roof of a fair-sized ranch house. There was a barn, some corrals and two sheds. Not more than a few miles to the west he saw more smoke from cook fires. A small town. It had to be Scalplock, an easy distance from the ranch he could see in the valley below.

Just as he was turning away he glimpsed a plump woman step from the house. She carried a basket of laundry to clothes lines that laced a corner of the yard. Two girls, the eldest about eleven or so, followed her, each carrying smaller baskets.

Cole made a decision. He rode back to where Helen waited for him anxiously.

"What does the smoke mean?" she asked.

He told her about the woman and the two girls. "If you go into Scalplock with me, those men may see you. And spread gossip about you."

And probably finish the job they botched, he thought, but he didn't say it.

"I've endured before," she said with a shrug. "I can again."

"You don't have to endure anything," he snapped. "Stop using that word."

96

"I've upset you and I'm sorry. I've been a terrible burden."

"I couldn't ride off and leave you in the mountains."

"Most people would have."

"You're a human being and you needed help and it was sheer luck that I came along when I did."

"You've done so much for me. And asked nothing."

He didn't reply to that. He told her what he hoped would work out. "I'm going to see if I can't convince that woman to let you stay at the ranch for a spell. Out of sight. Until I can take care of those scum."

"You can't face up to five men by yourself."

"Don't worry, I don't figure to rush blindly into trouble. I'm not that big a fool. I'll put my ear to the ground and take one step at a time."

"How do you know the woman would let me stay?" Helen asked. "What about her husband? He'd have something to say."

"General Sheridan used to say that I was a good convincer. I'm going to do my damnedest to convince those people to let you stay under their roof. But you've got to do your part."

"In what way?"

"By keeping your mouth shut about Santa Fe and Flo and Buck and all the rest of it."

She frowned and absently plucked strands of hair from the gash just above the left temple. Some hairs had stuck to the raw flesh. She winced. The wound needed to be dressed. A ranch house would be stocked with bandage and arnica.

"I can't just stay there and not pay anything," she protested.

"Help with the chores when you feel stronger. There's always plenty to do around a ranch."

"If you think it will work. . . ."

"I'll make it work." He forced two double eagles on her, which she was reluctant to accept. "You'll need clothing. I'll get word when it's safe for you to go to town."

The plump woman was still in the yard, hanging up wash, when they rode down the long slant. The woman heard them approach. She looked around, dropped her laundry and hurried to the house, the two little girls scrambling after her. The woman reappeared a few moments later with a rifle.

Cole reined in twenty feet away and gave the frontier sign of peace, right hand lifted, palm out. Her plump figure was rigid as she studied them warily. Perhaps the Indian ponies worried her, Cole thought. Or more likely it was just the sudden appearance of an armed stranger in buckskins.

Cole raised his voice. "Ma'am, this young woman needs rest and food. And she's willing to work." Cole spun a tale, some of it true, of how Helen had come north with an older couple, how their wagon had been wrecked on the washed-out road. "She survived, they didn't. But she got a bad cut on her head out of it."

Cole rode closer and dismounted. The woman eyed the holstered gun at his hip, then looked up into his face. Some of the hard suspicion in her eyes was replaced by compassion whenever she glanced at Helen in the torn and mud-splattered dress.

"She lost her clothes, everything," Cole went on. "Not even shoes." He held out two double eagles, the gold coins catching the sunlight, money intended for his parents. "It'll help pay her keep for a spell," Cole finished.

The woman spoke for the first time. "Mercy, all that money . . . for me?" She lowered the rifle. "I'd let her stay without money. But it's welcome all the same. We don't see much of it up here."

The woman beckoned to Helen, who had dismounted a few yards away, her bare feet on damp ground, holding her pony's lead rope.

"You go in the house an' dry out by the stove. My man's gone to town today to see about settin' up a church in Scalplock. Though them devils there don't seem of a mind to worry about the Lord."

"You'll take good care of her?"

"My word on it." The woman tucked the rifle under her arm and thrust out a hand still damp from handling the wash. "An' the money you give me will sure help."

Cole shook her hand. He gave Helen a pat on the shoulder. "Might be our paths will cross again one of these days."

"I hope so," she said in a small voice.

"Mercy, that place on your head looks bad, honey," the woman said now that she had a close look at the scalp wound." Her eyes swung to Cole. "How'd you say she got it?"

"She doesn't remember. But she probably hit her head on a wheel rim when the wagon tipped over. Plain luck that she didn't fall into the canyon with her friends and the team."

"Wasn't it luck, though." The woman made clucking sounds.

Cole had done all he could. Helen was on her own now, which was nothing new, he supposed.

He gave them a final wave of the hand, then rode out, leading the spare pony. When he reached the main road leading to town, he looked back. His throat tightened, for the place reminded him of his father's place in Beaver Valley, the last time he had seen it whole, before going off to war.

He faced westward again. Scalplock lay ahead. He checked revolver and rifle, then with a hard smile quickened the pace of the two ponies.

15

Cole was surprised at the changes a few years had made in Scalplock. On his last visit before the war there had been only one building, a combination store, saloon and boardinghouse for the handful of miners who worked the settlement's only asset, a lead mine.

Now the town was on a new north-south freight road. The old road that Flo and Buck had taken by mistake had been abandoned. Experts claimed it was easier to build a new road over a better route than try to repair the old.

Off the main street in open country was an oversize livery barn where he left his ponies. Down the slant was a narrow building with a lettered sign on a small window: T. TAGGART. TOWN MARSHAL.

Cole kept his gun loose and had himself a drink at the Pines, the first of the two saloons that had sprouted in Scalplock. He nursed his whiskey and listened to the talk.

It was mostly talk of a railroad that would turn Scalplock into more of a boom town than it was at present.

Cole spoke to a fat bartender, bald and missing a front tooth. "Is it possible, a railroad through this rough country?"

"Railroad men rode every foot of these mountains," the barkeep confided with faint bitterness.

Cole tensed as he began to wonder. A railroad that spawned killers? He looked around. A dozen or so men were at the bar, four more at a deal table. The place smelled of new lumber, sweat, whiskey and coal oil from an unlighted overhead lamp that had been overfilled.

Cole scanned the faces. Even though the day was still bright, shuttered windows kept out most of the sunlight. He saw no redhead, but there were several heavy black beards. These beards, however, were on short men. And he saw no stocky man with a pockmarked face. Nor one with heavy shoulders and a scar on nose and cheek. The only lanky man in the place had no gold tooth in front.

"What's the name of the railroad?" Cole asked the barkeep.

"Centurion Pacific."

"Strange name for a railroad," Cole commented.

"Strange fella at the head of it, so I hear."

"Strange? In what way?"

"They say he's fat as a waterlogged buffalo, but he's got a purty young wife."

Although the barkeep was reluctant to talk, Cole did learn that a company called Python owned Centurion Pacific.

Cole fought to make himself sound amiable. "Anybody in here work for the railroad?"

"Naw. These are miners, drifters. A few ranchers in for supplies. They come in most every Saturday."

Cole had lost all track of days. He swallowed. "But no railroad men."

"They got favorites in town, so it seems," the barkeep said, bitterness creeping back in his voice again. "The Pines ain't one of 'em." The barkeep leaned plump forearms on the bar. "You a lawman?"

"Just out of the army and looking around. Why you ask?"

"The way you sized me up put a chill down my back. You been lookin' at everybody else the same way."

"I just got through fighting a war. Gets to be a habit, I guess. Thinking you might meet the enemy any time you draw a deep breath."

"Sure you ain't got a badge pinned to your undershirt?"

"Tell me more about this railroad."

"Go up to the Shamrock," the bartender said in a sour voice, "if you want to hear about railroads. I'm sick of the bastards. Free whiskey they'll pour up there. But not here at the Pines. That ain't fair."

That was all Cole could get out of him. He paid for his whiskey, then went out to the busy walk. There was no use trying to make anything out of the maze of hoof prints in the rutted street. All the tracks were fresh, older ones having been wiped out in the same deluge that had lashed him to the east.

The Shamrock was a squat rambling structure at the far western edge of Scalplock. It stood alone, but it wouldn't be so for long. A building was under construction on adjoining vacant land. Near it, a stocky man with a hammer was drinking water from a dipper. Cole recalled the ranch woman

100

remarking that her husband was in town. In his haste to continue his trackdown, he hadn't even gotten the woman's name.

"This going to be the new church by any chance?" Cole asked the man, hoping to start a conversation.

The workman laughed. "This'll be Annie's new place. She's got two gals now, but she's bringin' in a new batch all the way from Saint Louie. Where'd you hear about a church, anyhow?"

Cole mentioned stopping by a ranch on his way into town. "Woman there said her husband was interested in starting one."

"That'll be Lockwood. If he's in town, he'll be down at the store tryin' to get donations. Ask me, he's wasting time. After four years of war, nobody's got time for a Bible shouter."

"More time for a place like Annie's, eh?"

"Hell yes."

"Railroad coming through will boom her business."

"That's how come we're buildin' her a new place here."

Cole tried to speak casually, but it was one of the hardest things he had ever done. "Beaver Valley," he managed without choking on it. "The railroad coming through there by any chance?"

"Right through, is the way I hear it. All of a sudden you looked kinda pale, mister."

"Need food. Had a long ride...."

"Chong can fix you up in the Shamrock."

"By the way, what happened to the settlers in Beaver Valley?"

"Railroad bought 'em out."

"You sure?"

"I ain't sure about nothin' except my own name."

"Any railroad men in town?"

"You want word about the railroad, go to Basin City. That's their headquarters. But surveyors'll be through here soon, so I hear."

Cole thanked him, then took another tour around the saloon building to try and quiet his nerves. Beaver Valley settlers bought out by the railroad, the workman had said. Not quite all of them. Taking a deep breath, Cole entered the Shamrock. It had a dance floor, not in use this time of day. To the left of a long bar was a small kitchen, a counter and four tables. A Chinese cook, pigtail draped over a narrow shoulder, was busily chopping meat with a long-bladed knife.

Because he'd need strength and endurance for the job ahead, Cole seated himself at one of the tables. It wasn't easy to down a meal of steak, eggs and fried potatoes because Beaver Valley kept intruding. Somehow he got through the meal, while looking over the saloon patrons across the big room. So far, the place wasn't doing the business of its competitor, the Pines.

After paying his bill, Cole walked over to the bar. The bartender had a narrow face and furtive eyes. He seemed unfriendly. No wonder they weren't doing much business, Cole thought. Drink at his elbow, Cole kept one eye on the patrons. Still no sign of a redhead among them. There were two men with heavy black beards. One was dressed as a miner and asleep at a deal table. The other was a spindly little man with a sample case. His loud voice proclaimed that he was a drummer who peddled items that not only appealed to housewives but also a special line for girls such as the pair at Annie's down the block. There was much laughter as he regaled the grinning customers with stories of the various establishments he visited.

Cole wondered if the next time he came through Scalplock he'd find that Helen was one of Annie's girls. He hoped not. But the choice was hers.

Cole felt let down. The five killers must have pushed on. They were the kind of men who'd frequent a saloon. And what else was there to do in a place like Scalplock? There was Annie's place, of course, but sometime a man had to come up for air.

While this was running through his head, a man with a black beard shoved through the doors. This one was tall, heavyset, wearing a brown suit. The bartender, who had been surly to most of his customers, beamed at this new arrival.

"Hiya, Sam," the bartender said, and Cole tensed at the name. Helen said the bearded rapist had been called Sam by the others.

Sam came up to the bar, grinning. His teeth were oversize. "I'll take the special bottle, Fred."

A tag attached to the bottle Fred set out made Cole's nerves hum. Printed in large block letters: COURTESY OF E.J. CREED. CENTURION PACIFIC R.R.

Sam poured for himself. "Any important people in town, buy 'em a drink, Fred. Don't bother with drifters." He turned and looked Cole over. "Won't do you no good to stare at the bottle, mister."

Cole forced a smile. "Was thinking that I knew a man named Creed in the army."

"This Creed," Sam said, slapping at the tag on the bottle, "never did no fightin' in the war that I ever heard of."

"Must be another Creed."

Sam's black eyes were cold. "This Creed sets at Basin City with his feet on a desk. While me an' a few others do all the work."

"Creed must be a big man with the railroad if he can let somebody else do the dirty work."

Sam stiffened. Cole matched him in height but the other man was heavier through the upper body. Cole could see the heel plates of a revolver worn under the brown coat.

"Why'd you say dirty work?" Sam demanded.

"Slip of the tongue, I guess." Cole's smile was lazy. He spread his hands, his right only inches from the butt of his holstered .44. Some men at a nearby table looked up. Two customers drinking at the bar moved quickly to the far end as if sensing trouble. Sam evidently had a reputation for it. Cole knew he'd have to watch his speech from here on out. "Dirty work" had made Sam suspicious. "Meant nothing by it, stranger," Cole said to Sam. "Been a long time in the saddle. Too long, I guess. Muddled my head."

Sam thought about it then seemed to accept the apology. Cole forced his smile to remain in place while he thought of what Dark Star had said about the bearded man. *Your height, Cole, but heavier. And with a black scowl.*

Sam's voice snapped his musing. "Have a drink of railroad whiskey, Mr. . . . Mr. . . . ." Sam was pushing the bottle toward him. "Didn't get your name."

"Call myself Latigo," Cole said.

"First or last name?" Sam kept his hand on the bottle while the black eyes bored into Cole's face.

"Just Latigo." Cole matched the hard gaze.

"You on the dodge?" Sam asked abruptly.

Cole lifted a shoulder as if considering the question. Then he said carefully, "Was in the army. Had a fight with a sergeant. Been ridin' ever since."

"Kill him?"

Cole gave Sam a direct look. The shoulder lifted again. He let it speak for him.

Sam mentioned the dark blue hat. "Officers wear a hat like that."

103

"This one belonged to a captain." Cole let him read whatever he wanted into it.

"A sergeant an' a captain. Army remembers you, I bet."

"Yeah."

Sam looked him over again. A corner of the bearded lips curved. Then he spoke softly about the railroad possibly needing tough hands to protect surveyors and later the tracklayers. He poured whiskey into Cole's glass. "You interested, Latigo?"

"Some." Cole tried not to appear anxious. But what luck if things worked out and he could corral the five of them all at one time.

"You don't talk much, Latigo."

"If need be this talks for me." He casually stroked the butt of the .44.

"Gun hand," Sam said quietly. "Figured as much." He drained his glass and shoved the bottle at the bartender. "Lock 'er up, Fred."

Fred grinned and locked the bottle in a cabinet in the back bar.

"Got business to take care of, Latigo," Sam said heartily, slapping Cole on the arm. "Meet me here later if you're interested in what I said. Or tomorrow. I'll be here for a few days."

"Thanks, Sam." Cole took a sip of the drink as Sam stomped toward the doors, lifting a hand to some men in a poker game. They called out a greeting.

"Folks around here cotton to the railroad," Fred the bartender said. "You work for Sam an' you'll earn good money."

Cole nodded. But was he really sure that Sam was his man? It crossed his mind to bring Helen to town for positive identification. But it would expose her to danger. No telling what might happen if Sam was one of them and saw her alive.

"Railroad whiskey's good, Fred." And it was. Cole made a show of smacking his lips.

"Got two cases of it out back."

"Sounds like a great outfit to tie in with," Cole remarked. He wet his lips with the whiskey. Of all times he didn't want his brain even slightly off center from alcohol. Yet he couldn't refuse to drink what Sam had poured. Not without arousing Fred's suspicion. Cole cleared his throat and said casually, "Sam got a redhead workin' for him?"

Fred was busy rinsing glasses in a tank and perhaps hadn't heard the question.

Cole tried another. "How about a fella with a pockmarked face? He one of Sam's friends?"

Fred straightened up from the tank, eyes in the narrow face bright with suspicion. "Next you'll be askin' me to count pimples. A redhead an' now pockmarks?" So he had heard the question after all.

Cole managed an easy laugh. "Hell, only havin' a little joke. It's about a redhead an' a pockmarked gent who had this dancehall gal, see . . ."

"Lemme give you a little advice, Latigo. Sam's pockmarked friend is damn touchy about it. Don't never make a joke about pockmarks. Not where he can hear you."

Cole whistled softly. "Glad you told me. What's his name, so I'll remember to step light when he's around."

"Al."

Cole waited for the rest of the name, but Fred hurried away to wait on new customers. Had Helen mentioned an Al? Dark Star had described one of the killers as having a pockmarked face. And one of the rapists was similarly scarred, according to Helen. But pockmarks were no rarity. Even so, he couldn't quell his elation over the possibility that the jaws of his trap might be ready to close on the guilty.

A man well over six feet tall but thin as a lodge pole stalked in. Fred greeted him. "Hiya, Toby."

Toby Taggart wore a badge. At his thin waist hung a holstered .45 with ivory grips. He grunted a greeting at the bartender, then shifted a sawed-off shotgun a little tighter under his arm as he turned to look Cole over.

He introduced himself. "Town marshal."

"Howdy."

Taggart assessed Cole out of light gray eyes while fingering a thick mustache. "Down at the Pines they claim a fella fits your description was askin' a lot of questions."

"I'm new in town. Just wanted to get the lay of the land to see if there's any work."

"Don't recollect anybody sayin' you mentioned work. Mind tellin' me your name?"

"Latigo."

"How many sheriffs lookin' for you, Latigo? With a name like that, your picture must be on some sheriff walls." Taggart spoke loudly, playing to an audience of bar patrons who laughed dutifully. Before the laughter died and trouble possibly developed, the bartender, Fred Byson, leaned close.

"Toby, I got a hunch Sam wants Latigo to work for him."

"You mean Sam Stark?"

"He was just in here."

"So Sam's back in town." Taggart didn't seem too pleased about it. "Where'd he go?"

"Try Annie's."

"Was just there. Line half a block long. Couldn't wait. Annie needs more gals." More laughter swept the saloon.

Cole wasn't listening. His heart thumped. For the first time he'd heard a full name. Stark. Sam Stark.

Fred set out the special bottle. "Drink here instead of at the Pines an' Sam will see you get free whiskey. Compliments of Centurion Pacific Railroad."

"They hate Stark's guts at the Pines," Taggart muttered, without explaining why. He put the sawed-off shotgun on the bar and helped himself to a drink. He looked at Cole. "Mr. Latigo, you look kinda peaked. If you figure to work with Stark you better have some of his railroad whiskey. It'll put color back in your cheeks."

Cole shook his head and gestured at the whiskey he hadn't finished. "When I drink this, it'll be enough, marshal."

"You work for Sam Stark, you'll need one good leg for standin' on," Taggart said in his loud voice, "and the other for fillin' with railroad whiskey." This followed by more laughter and some knee-slapping. Taggart drained his glass, gave Cole a look, then picked up his shotgun and sauntered out on his long legs.

Cole felt obligated to finish off his own whiskey. He did. It burned all the way down, setting a name afire in his head. *Sam Stark.*

Cole suddenly needed fresh air. When he got outside, the palms of his hands were moist, his heart pounding. Over higher peaks to the west the sky was roseate, laced with gold. Hours had slipped away. Although he was reasonably certain that Stark was his man, he needed proof. Out of habit he again studied horse tracks around the saloon hitch rail. This time he found what he had been seeking. A hoof print made by a big roan horse now tied to the rail.

He bared his teeth in a grin of triumph but quickly had to caution himself. It didn't prove that Sam Stark had been riding this roan. And just because Sam Stark worked for the railroad and had a pockmarked friend didn't necessarily connect him with murder. Whiskey tasted sour in his stomach as he considered the possibility that the railroad might not be behind it after all. Perhaps the crimes were committed by five murderers on their own. But in the next second he refused to accept it. And he couldn't toss away his strong suspicion that the same railroad money that furnished good whiskey for employees and well-wishers had also paid for murder.

Cole walked to the stable to check on his horses.

16

Upon leaving the saloon, Sam Stark went down to the Scalplock Mountain Store for tobacco.

At the back of the store some men and a few women were bunched near the bolts of muslin and calico. A stocky blond man of about forty, with a windburned face, was addressing them about the need for a church.

"This'll be a growing community once the railroad gets built," Jed Lockwood told his visitors. "And a church must be part of it."

A gaunt man with sideburns asked, "Jed, how much you figure it'll take to put up a church?"

"I'll see if we can't get Python to donate a building site. It's the way it could get started. They own all the vacant land along Center Street. . . ."

At mention of Python, Sam Stark turned his head. Out of curiosity he strolled to the edge of the gathering. Those fools had about as much chance of getting anything free out of tight-fisted Python, Stark thought, as they had of building their church out of bear grease.

Stark was about to turn away when a boy of about fourteen dashed into the store. Jed Lockwood at the time was speaking about the males of the town cutting timber for the new church. "A few Sundays and we'd have the job done. The ladies can keep us fed from picnic baskets. . . ."

"My Jane can saw a board good as me," spoke up one of the men. Others joined in. Their wives could drive nails, help carry rock for the corner stones. They were pioneers, most of them, used to working alongside their men. Sure they'd furnish the food, but also help with the labor.

107

"Else how we gonna feel that we helped put up the church?" a woman in a sunbonnet declared shrilly.

Jed Lockwood opened his mouth to speak. From his height, looking over the heads of the others, he noticed the boy at the front counter for the first time.

"Ralph, what you doin' in town?" he bellowed.

"Didn't want to bother you, Pa, you speakin' an' all. . . ."

"Go ahead and bother me. I asked what you're doin' in town? When you're s'posed to be out at the place bein' the man to your ma an' your sisters."

"Ma sent me in for arnica an' laudanum. We're runnin' low."

Lockwood pushed through the crowd and caught his tall son by a shoulder. "Somebody hurt? Your ma? One of the girls?"

The boy, realizing he was the center of attention, positively beamed with his new importance. "Young lady was brung to the place." He paused for dramatic effect. "Ma says she'd been shot."

"Shot?" Lockwood's mouth fell open. A ripple of surprise swept the gathering. "Who shot her?"

"Fella that brung her didn't say, so Ma claimed. He said she hit her head, but Ma got to doctorin' her wound an' said it sure looked to her like it'd been made by a bullet. The gal finally admitted it. I was movin' some cows when I seen the fella ride off."

"What'd he look like?"

"Wore a dark blue hat an' buckskins. Ridin' one injun pony an' leadin' another."

"We better get to lookin' for this fella," Lockwood exclaimed and there were nods of agreement.

Ralph Lockwood said, "Wasn't him shot her."

Lockwood frowned at the boy. "Then who did shoot her?"

"She was travelin' with a man an' a woman. They drunk bad water. She tried to tell 'em, but they wouldn't listen. They died."

"Ralph, will you tell us who shot the young lady?" Lockwood's patience was thinning.

"She claims five bandits come along. They shot her. But the bullet only put a gash on her head. She was unconscious an' said that likely them seein' all the blood, they figured she was dead. This fella with the injun ponies come along an' found her an' brung her to our place."

"What's his name, she say?" Lockwood asked, peering down at the excited face of his son.

"She said his name was Cole."

Andy Lushard, the owner of the store, was wrapping arnica and laudanum in a sheet of newspaper after adding the purchases to the Lockwood bill.

"I'll be goin' home with you, Ralph," Lockwood said. "Tie your hoss to the back of the wagon. I sure hope the young lady ain't too bad hurt." They were walking toward the door.

"Weak an' lost blood, Ma says."

"We better get a description of the men who shot her. . . ."

That was the last thing Sam Stark heard as Lockwood and his lanky son left the store.

Stark wheeled for the door, but Lushard called him back. He had forgotten to pay for his tobacco. Scowling, Stark dug coins out of his pocket and flung them across the counter. He hurried out.

Of all the stupid luck, he thought as he strode rapidly in the direction of the Shamrock. He saw Lockwood and the boy heading east out of town in a wagon, a saddle horse trailing on a lead rope. Supplies in the wagon bed bounced and shifted whenever the wheels struck deep ruts.

It was that damn Doak Lancer's fault. "Never miss," Lancer had bragged. Main thing now was to make sure this time that Cindy Lou stayed dead. Tomorrow by daylight he'd take a rifle and watch for her to come outside. Even if it took a week, she was as good as dead.

Head down to keep his bearded face out of a rising wind, he plodded toward the west end of town. Where had he heard the name Cole? Cole what? Or was Cole the last name? Ed Cole. Ben Cole. Hadn't Creed, when he was giving instructions about Beaver Valley, mentioned Cole somebody or other?

It came to Stark suddenly, like a jolting fist in the mouth. "Cantrells have a son," Creed had said. "Captain in the Union Army. Name of Cole . . ."

"Jesus Christ!" cried Stark with such vehemence that miners slogging along with their lunch pails turned to stare at him in surprise.

He was remembering that the hat worn by the man called Latigo was dark blue. The kind worn by cavalry officers. And he was wearing buckskins like the Lockwood kid had described.

As he hurried, he checked the loads in the gun worn under his coat. Then he slipped it back into a shoulder holster. . . .

* * *

109

Cole was still standing on the far side of the Shamrock. He wanted to see if Stark would claim the roan. As far as Cole could tell, the roan's hoof had left the track he had followed for so many miles. He was almost certain that Stark was his man. If the roan belonged to Stark, it would be proof enough of murder.

To see fear in Stark's dark eyes would be gratifying; to witness the collapse of features in the bearded face in that split second when Stark realized he was doomed.

"So there you are, Latigo," Stark said heartily. "Come inside. Got things to talk about. Important things."

Cole looked around, and was startled to see Stark's bulk by the saloon doors. Cole had been watching the horse and had failed to see the man arrive quietly from the other side of the saloon. Stark gave a friendly grin, then elbowed his way inside. The doors flapped shut behind him.

Cole followed him in. The saloon crowd had thinned. Miners who had stopped in for a drink were now at home or the boardinghouse for the evening meal. Stark was leaning at the bar. A swamper was on a stepladder, lighting one of the overhead hanging lamps. Its soft glow spread over Stark's broad back in the brown coat. The Chinese man was wiping off one of his tables. The deal tables were empty. Two men stood at the cafe end of the bar, heads together. They didn't look up.

Fred Byson was behind the bar. He was bent over, reading something on the bartop. Possibly a letter. His lips moved as he read silently. He was directly behind Stark who lounged at ease. A railroad bottle and two clean glasses were by his elbow. Stark looked around, grinning. Black eyes in the bearded face reflected lamplight. He gestured at the bottle.

"Have a drink . . . Cole," Stark said softly.

Cole managed to look blank and glanced over his shoulder as if looking for someone named Cole. He faced around, a puzzled look in his eyes. "Who's Cole?" he asked, walking to the bar.

"Mebby you?"

Cole squinted into the broad face. "Latigo's the name, remember?"

"Sometimes Cole?" Across the room the swamper was climbing his ladder to light another lamp.

"You mean sometimes Smith or Jones or whatever name I pick up in my rambling?" Cole gave a short laugh. "Latigo's good enough for me. Coal's something you dig out of the ground with a pick."

"This one's Cole." Stark spelled it.

"All of a sudden you sound suspicious as hell."

"Pays to be suspicious in my business." Stark watched him closely.

Cole said, "What business you in, Stark? You haven't told me much, for sure. All I know is that if I work with you I get free whiskey out of the railroad bottle."

"Speakin' of whiskey." Stark gestured to the bottle. "Help yourself, Latigo."

"So now you remember my name all of a sudden," Cole said with a tight smile. He sensed that Stark wanted him to reach for the glass and bottle, to have both hands busy and away from a gun.

Cole shrugged. "You first, Stark."

"Sure." Stark tilted the bottle, splashed in an inch of whiskey. When Cole just stood there, Stark hesitated, then poured a like amount in Cole's glass. No one was looking their way, Cole noticed. The two men at the far end of the bar were arguing about the price of lead.

"Been down since the war ended," said one of the men loudly. He was older, with a graying mustache.

"I predict the price'll go up," the other one countered. He was red-faced and wearing a bowler hat. "Government will need lead for bullets to handle the Indians. In order to open up this country, they'll have to be cleared out. The ones left alive can be pushed into Canada."

Stark laughed. "That fella speaks good sense. How you feel about cleaning out the redskins, Latigo?"

"They were here first."

"I'll tell you somethin' . . . Latigo."

Cole did not miss the stress put on the name. He felt a cold rippling sensation in his gut, as he used to get in the war just prior to battle. "What'll you tell me, Stark?" Cole asked easily.

"Was just up to the store. Rancher's kid come in with a wild tale."

"Kids are full of wild tales." Cole reached for the whiskey glass with the left hand.

"You was drinkin' right-handed before."

"I change around." Cole's smile was spare.

"This kid's pa was up at the store, tryin' to get money for a damn church," Stark went on. His eyes drilled Cole, who

111

drilled back. Mention of a church and Stark being suddenly suspicious meant Helen was going to get mixed up in it. This Cole hated, but it couldn't be helped.

Stark said, "Can you figure a man wantin' to build a church?"

"Maybe the town could use one." Cole stood with knees loose, glass of untasted whiskey in the left hand. His right hovered near the butt of his holstered gun. Down the bar the two men still argued lead prices. The Chinese cook was not in sight and the swamper had disappeared with his ladder.

Stark spoke of a wounded girl being left at a nearby ranch. "Kid claims she was left by a gent in buckskins an' cavalry hat. Like yours."

"Maybe the kid needs eyeglasses."

"Kid claimed this fella's name is Cole."

"So that's where you heard it." Cole chuckled. His eyes never left Stark's face. "You say the gal was wounded. Probably got a fever. People ramble when they've got a fever. Don't know half of what they're saying."

Cole measured the dark eyes where the contents of his whiskey glass would be hurled if necessary. He would then spin and cover Fred Byson who was still reading the letter. Or pretending to. The argument between the two men still continued at the far end of the bar. Cole hadn't wanted a showdown before witnesses. But Stark was forcing it. There had to be some way to get Stark outside.

Cole lowered his voice to a confidential tone. "Stark, let's you and me get some air. If there's anything you want to know about me, I'll be glad to tell. But not in here. Too many ears." He nodded toward the pair down the bar. It was what a man on the dodge would say.

Stark seemed to think it over. "Mebby you're right, Latigo. You talk straight to me an' you'll have a job. Good pay."

"Let's go, then. . . ." Cole took a step away from the bar. Stark did not move. Fred Byson had put away his letter.

There was a stomp of booted feet down the boardwalk.

"Let's go before we have more company," Cole urged.

The men on the walk outside passed the saloon, coming from the direction of the mine, and went thumping off down the block toward the center of the town.

"Soon's I have a drink we'll go," Stark said. He lifted the whiskey glass with his right hand, but did not drink. Cole watched him dig his left hand into a coat pocket. He removed something from the pocket that was hidden in his hand. It

112

wasn't large enough to be a derringer. Still watching Cole, Stark placed the left hand on the bar, palm down. He opened the hand.

"You got a kind of injun look about you, Latigo. Take a look at this . . . tell me what you figure it's worth."

He withdrew his hand, leaving exposed on the grainy wood the object it had covered. Blue beads and intricate silver work caught the dim light from overhead lamps.

In that shattered second Cole's heart bumped coldly. Poison in his bloodstream burned like acid. But his voice was toneless. He couldn't help himself: "That necklace belonged to my mother, you son of a bitch!"

"So you *are* the one!"

Stark spun away from the bar, hurling his whiskey glass. Liquor made an amber-colored fan in the air. Cole ducked, felt some of the whiskey splatter his forehead, dangerously close to an eye.

Stark shouted at Byson behind the bar. *"Fred, get him!"*

Byson was bent down, reaching toward a shelf under the bar. He didn't make it because the barrel of Cole's .44 caught the back of the bent head. Byson disappeared behind his bar.

Stark was dancing aside, a .45 with bone grips spitting in his hand. The first shot ricocheted off the bartop and slammed into a far wall.

Desperate to keep Stark alive, Cole gambled. He tried to club him as he had the barkeep. But Stark, firing again, arched his big body out of range. Cole's gun barrel missed the chin by an inch. But the jerking movement tilted Stark's gun so that the shot instead of drilling Cole, put a hole in the ceiling. Down the bar the two men were scrambling for safety. A bowler hat rolled across the floor.

Cole was raging at Stark. "You killed my parents for their land! Who else was in on it . . . !"

But Stark was giving no answers. A faint desperation touched the eyes. He'd wasted two shots on the dodging, weaving figure in buckskins who was trying to use the .44 in his hand as a club. Stark reached out a long arm and seized a chair from an empty deal table. He hurled the chair at Cole's head and fired at the same moment. Chair and bullet crashed into the bar just as Cole tried for a leg shot.

But a piece of the shattered chair struck him on a cheekbone. It jarred him so that instead of his bullet striking a leg, it ripped into the soft underpart of Stark's bearded chin and upward into the brain. The impact drove Stark back on his

113

heels. He teetered for a moment. Then it seemed as if every inch of supporting bone was suddenly withdrawn from the big body. He went limp and crashed, raising dust from the plank floor.

17
Down the street somebody was yelling for the marshal. "Get Toby Taggart. Trouble down here. A *shootin'!*"

Answering voices came from a distance. There were sounds of men running toward the saloon.

Cole was down on one knee, dazed. He tasted blood. Everything he saw was doubled. Stark appeared as two mountains of inert flesh lumped on the floor. Cole shook his head to clear it. He climbed to his feet.

Men poured into the saloon, saw Cole with the .44 in hand. Stark lay dead on the floor, the back of his skull blown out. Those in the doorway froze, then began backing into those trying to get inside. The two men who had been arguing lead prices at the end of the bar had stampeded in panic to the small dining room.

"I saw it all!" one of the men shouted to those in the doorway. "The big one dead on the floor drew his gun first. Fella in buckskins nearly got killed, I tell you . . ."

"*I'll* ask the questions!" roared Toby Taggart. Men stood aside to give the marshal room. Taggart strode in, sawed-off shotgun under an arm. "What happened here, Fred?" he demanded of the bartender.

Cole saw that Byson, bleeding from a gash on the back of the head, had regained his feet. He clung to the edge of the bar and stared, white-faced, at Stark crumpled in a widening pool of blood. Then he shifted his gaze to Cole. Terror streaked his eyes. It took him a minute to find his voice.

By then the marshal had reached the bar and was leaning over, the shotgun loose under an arm. "Fred, you hurt bad?"

Byson managed to level a trembling finger at Cole. "He . . . he tried to rob me. Stark seen what was happening an' butted in. Looks like he got killed. . . ."

Taggart had had eyes only for Fred Byson. Now he wheeled, but Cole moved faster. He jerked the shotgun from under a long arm before Taggart could tighten his grip.

Cole leveled his .44. Blood ran down his face from the gashed cheek. "Listen to me, marshal."

"Latigo," Taggart snarled. "I figured right off you'd be trouble for this town."

"Let me talk, damn it. Everybody keep clear. I mean it. You too, Fred." The bartender had started to back up, but froze in his tracks behind the bar.

"Latigo, put up that gun," the marshal ordered.

"Not till you hear me out. Fred, tell the truth. You know damn well what the row was about. Stark had an Indian necklace. . . ."

"No necklace at all!" Byson cried.

Cole's quick glance flicked to the spot on the bartop where Stark had placed the necklace. It was gone.

The gray-mustached man who had been at the end of the bar, spoke again. "Stark drew first. I saw it!"

Taggart ignored him, his gaze riveted on Cole's bloodied face. "Lockwood wants to build a church. I figure we better build us a gallows first." There was an ugly murmur from men bunched at the doors. "Latigo, you're under arrest for the murder of Sam Stark!" Taggart said in a loud voice. "Now gimme that gun. . . ."

Cole knew that any second a bullet could scream from a window or from the bunch hovering by the front doors. Some hothead deciding on his personal brand of mountain justice. And Cole knew that unless he could convince the marshal otherwise and get Byson to confess, he just might be standing on the new gallows.

In one movement Cole holstered the .44 and cocked the sawed-off shotgun. He caught Taggart by the belt, spun him around so that his back was turned.

"Taggart, we walk out of here . . . together. Tell the crowd to watch it. I don't want you dead. I want you alive, to listen to what I've got to say."

"You got so much to say, say it here." Taggart looked over his shoulder. His face was slick with sweat that glistened through the hairs of his mustache.

"Outside!" Cole shoved him toward the door. "Remember what I said . . . no trouble."

Taggart, realizing his position, added his own voice, shaky at first then stronger. "Better do like he says, boys. If he does get away, he won't get far."

"What if he makes you go with him?" asked a bearded man in miner's garb.

115

"If you find me dead, you boys know what to do with a rope when you catch up to him."

"That we do, Toby!" a dozen or more of them chorused.

Outside was full dark with only a hint of moon low in the sky. Men tried to crowd in close but Cole shouted them back.

"March toward those trees, Taggart," Cole ordered.

"Then what?"

"We talk."

The threat of the shotgun seemed to hold the crowd. But even so the odds for success weren't promising. Cole hoped he could get away with it before someone else died. He gave Taggart some low-voiced orders. Taggart accepted them grudgingly.

"Boys, stay out of this!" he yelled, not breaking stride as he and his captor headed for a dark row of tall trees fifty yards beyond the saloon where the ponies had been left.

At each step Cole talked. He spoke of the war, of his parents on their place in Beaver Valley. Of his homecoming. Finding them dead, everything burned out.

They were halfway to the trees by the time Cole finished.

"It's a lie about the railroad, Latigo, or whatever the hell your name is," Taggart snapped. "A lie to try an' save your own skin. You tried to rob the Shamrock. Stark took Byson's part and got killed for it."

"Byson's the one lied!"

"*You're* the liar!"

Cole tried again with the same result. In the faint wash of moon and starlight Cole read cold hatred in the marshal's eyes each time the man glanced back over his shoulder. At first Cole had taken the man for a blowhard. But now he was forced to a grudging respect. Cole had no intention of killing him, but Taggart did not know it. Even so, he would not unbend.

Upon reaching the trees, Cole backed Taggart into the shadows and released his hold on the belt. Quickly he unloaded the shotgun, threw the shells away and tucked the weapon under his arm.

"Just so you won't try and grab it," Cole said, "and the damn thing goes off and kills us both."

"Latigo, you got no chance."

Again Cole tried to convince him of the truth, knowing that the sands in his hourglass were getting dangerously low. Any second the crowd that he could see bunched in the light from the saloon windows might be spurred into a reckless attempt to rescue their marshal. All it took was someone to strike the first spark.

Taggart sneered his reply. "You're dead, Latigo. The railroad won't let you forget that it's their man you murdered."

"I'll deal with those bastards later."

"You're mad, loco in the *cabeza*."

"I'll find a newspaper that'll print the story. Or a magazine."

Taggart laughed. "You'll never find anybody to believe your lies. Biggest people in the country are the railroads. What they want they get."

"Murder for it, you mean."

"They've got money to pay for what they want. They don't have to kill for it."

"You ride back to Beaver Valley with me and I'll show you different. . . ."

"Not on your life. An' speakin' of life, you ain't got enough of your own left to pack into a thimble."

"I'm trying to reason with you, Taggart!"

A shout came from the men bunched in front of the saloon. "You all right, Toby?"

"Hell yes, I'm all right. . . ." And as Cole reached out to untie the ponies, the marshal spun quickly and started sprinting out of the shelter of trees. In half a dozen strides he reached open country. It was then that the truncated shotgun, spinning like an Indian war club Cole had learned to throw as a boy, caught him at the back of the knees. Taggart sprawled headlong, the unloaded weapon skating across damp ground.

"I'm comin', boys!" Taggart yelled, jumping up and running headlong toward the crowd. "Cover me!"

Cole couldn't shoot him in the back. And by now Taggart, at a lumbering, long-legged gait, was too far away to risk trying to wing.

Something slammed into one of the trees to Cole's right, showering him with dwarf pine cones. A wink of muzzle flash from the direction of the crowd, then another. Cole wasted no time because he could hear them coming at a hard run. Sounds of thudding boots reminded him of stampeding buffalo.

Cole untied the ponies, leaped aboard the saddled animal, seized the lead rope of the other and pounded at full gallop deeper into the trees and away from town.

It didn't take long for him to tell that horsemen had joined the chase. He heard someone shout, "Bring a rope!" "Got one!" another voice responded loudly.

117

As he rode, head down, the second pony thundering in his wake, Cole touched the bag that Dark Star had hung around his neck. If ever he needed the magic of her medicine, it was now. No doubt but what he was in for the ride of his life.

He prayed for a little luck. A rainstorm had washed out the tracks of Stark and company. Maybe he'd be as fortunate. As he pounded deeper into the mountains the moon climbed, brightened, the great curve of sky filled with glittering stars. Not a cloud in sight that might herald a downpour. Wind from the fast pace made his eyes burn. He swore at himself for letting everything get out of hand.

At the crest of a long grade, Cole pulled up, watered his ponies at a spring and switched saddles. In the distance he could hear the sound made by two dozen or more horsemen coming up the grade. Experience in the cavalry had taught him to gauge the number of riders just from the sounds of their pounding horses.

Then he was riding again. Hours later he halted to switch saddles. Reaching into his shirt, he gripped the medicine bag suspended from the thong around his neck. Without knowing it, perhaps, Dark Star had saved his life by insisting he take two strong buffalo ponies. Trooper, gallant as he might be, wouldn't have been able to put such a distance between pursued and pursuer without tiring.

Or had Dark Star known what was ahead for him? Had she gazed into her secret fires and seen the future revealed? Or seen it written in the stars?

He pushed on, the brief respite diminished now by the necessity for survival. Toward morning he snatched an hour of sleep. For the first time in his life he knew what it meant to be hunted. Hunted like an animal. Cole felt he was bucking not only the outraged citizens of Scalplock, but Python.

Cole bared his teeth at the morning wind as he galloped on. Python was Centurion Pacific Railroad. Railroad meant tracks, shining rails through Beaver Valley.

A python squeezed the life out of its victim. As Python would do to the frontier. Anyone who stood in their way, white man or red, would be destroyed. Cole set his jaw. "Not while I'm alive!" he shouted and shook his fist at the sky.

Although it was hours since the gunfight at the Shamrock his nerves were still strung tight. His ponies were weary. Pursuit still pounded in his wake. Somewhere they had picked up fresh horses. He was riding for his life.

18

Fred Byson didn't ride with the posse. What he wanted was a stake for himself alone. Through his association with Sam Stark, Byson believed he had been well on the way to acquiring a stake. Although Stark hadn't said too much, Byson knew that Python had great wealth, which meant power. And now Stark was dead and he was on his own.

Four years of Civil War had made him realize that a short life could best be lived if one had money. He had done no fighting during the war, but had been shot at more times than he had fingers and toes during his four years hauling artillery shells to various battle fronts.

Byson doctored his gashed scalp at his hotel room. Even though each step sent a rocket of pain through his skull, he got ready for a quick trip out of town.

Bernie Halloran, who owned the Shamrock, had come at a run from his boardinghouse when he heard about the trouble. He was a big man with a bald spot the size of a dollar, and half his right ear missing. He surveyed the damage. Only a broken chair, a few bullet holes in walls and ceiling and a rather large stain on the plank floor.

He didn't think much of Sam Stark, but decided to give him a wake. Good for business, it was. When Byson entered the saloon he showed no sympathy for his bartender's gashed skull.

"I heard what happened, lad," Halloran said, scowling. "Next time keep out of trouble. You're paid to tend bar an' nothin' else."

"I want two weeks off."

Halloran snarled at him. Things were bad enough already. There'd been a killing and the town marshal marched out of the place at gun point and a big posse riding hell-bent after the killer.

"And just because this Latigo hombre gives you a bump on the head, you want a vacation." Halloran was disgusted.

"Not a vacation." It hurt to talk and Byson kept it to a minimum. "Got business in Basin City."

"A new whorehouse opened up there I s'pose," Halloran said caustically.

"Business . . . with Python."

Halloran studied the thin face of his bartender. "What kind of business?"

Halloran knew that Byson and the late Sam Stark had had long talks. That the cases of Python whiskey had been left by Stark in care of Fred Byson, instead of with the owner of the saloon.

Byson decided to be mysterious. "Can't say what kind of business, Bernie."

"Private business, huh?"

Byson shrugged.

"You got a bad bump on the head, Fred. It's a long ride to Basin City. You feel up to it?"

"Important that I go."

"You'll be back in two weeks?"

"Might be a little longer, Bernie."

"If you figure to make that long trip just to tell Python about Latigo killin' Stark, I'd save my strength was I you. By now the boys've hung Latigo to a tree and are on their way home with his body."

"Mebby not." But Byson fervently hoped Halloran was right. "There's fifty or more of them. One of him. He's got no chance."

"He rides like an Indian. He's got two Indian ponies. I've seen the redskins outride anybody by switching ponies. Like he'll do."

"You talk like you kind of admire the bastard that knocked you in the head."

"I hate his guts. But I got to admit if he hadn't knocked me down, I'd likely be dead along with Sam Stark. He was just too goddamn fast for me. And sure as hell he was for Stark. If I hadn't run out the back door . . . thinkin' he was inches away . . ." Byson broke off because the pain had moved to his jaws. He fingered the Indian necklace he had instinctively snatched up from the floor before making his break for the rear door. It might prove useful in some way.

Halloran said, "You and Stark were friends, huh?"

"Sort of."

Halloran rubbed his bad ear. "I'm in business in this town, Fred, so I oughta know what kind of future we can expect. Are them rails Python is gonna lay a spur line for the lead mine? Or do they figure to push on west?"

Despite the pain, Byson couldn't resist bragging a little about things Stark had let slip. "They'll push west."

"Nothin' out there but redskins an' jackrabbits."

"Might be they figure to go clear to the Pacific Ocean."

Halloran grew confidential. "Fred, I missed my chance to buy up half of Scalplock for a handful of dollars. Now if you hear anything good in Basin City, don't spread the word. Save it till you get back. There just might be a new town planned for out there somewhere. A Python town." He gestured to the west. "Fella who gets in first makes the money. You bring back good news from Python an' you'll be my partner."

Byson smiled to himself as he left Scalplock. If there was any good news of wealth, he'd keep it to himself. He owed Bernie Halloran not one damn thing. . . .

Later in the week Fred Byson introduced himself in Basin City to a thin-faced clerk wearing eyeglasses. A sign on the door of the modest office adjoining a saddle shop announced that E. J. Creed was the western representative of Python Corporation.

"I want to see Mr. Creed."

The clerk looked at the narrow face, the dusty clothing. There was a bad cut on the scalp. A drunk, the clerk thought disdainfully, looking for a job. "Mr. Creed is very busy. . . ."

"It's important news. About Sam Stark."

Byson noticed a man in a chair tipped back against the wall, cleaning his nails with a penknife. He had bright red hair and cold blue eyes which put a little shiver down Byson's spine.

"I'll see if Mr. Creed is interested," the clerk said stiffly and entered an inner office. He closed the door.

Doak Lancer got to his feet, dropping the knife in a pocket of black pants. "What's this about Sam Stark?"

"I prefer to talk to Mr. Creed."

"I asked a question, friend." The voice was soft but carried the unmistakable crack of a three-ply whip. Byson swallowed. He'd tended bar in enough frontier towns to recognize a killer.

"Sam Stark's dead."

At that moment the clerk opened the office door and beckoned for Byson to enter. He stood aside until Byson was in the office, then stepped out and closed the door.

Creed wore a gray suit, white shirt and string tie. He smiled. His teeth were crooked. Byson thought he could have been a town banker or a faro dealer.

Creed waved him to a chair. "I recall Stark mentioning you, yes. I consigned some whiskey at his suggestion in your

121

name. Now, did Stark send you here or did you come on your own?"

Although Creed still smiled, his eyes had the same chilling quality as those of the redhead in the front office.

Byson told Creed the whole story about Stark's run-in with Latigo. Creed pursed his lips.

"Obviously this Latigo was too quick on his feet for either one of you," Creed said softly.

Byson squirmed in his chair. "A tough son of a bitch," he admitted.

Creed asked, "Just why was Stark so intent on doing away with this Latigo?"

"He never said."

A personal grudge, thought Creed with a twist of lips. Stark, the fool. He stood up.

Byson was dismayed and tried desperately to think of something that would delay his obvious dismissal. Creed looked at him with distaste. Byson wasn't surprised; people were always doing that.

Creed said, "If I were you, I'd have a doctor look at that head wound. The doc here in town shouldn't charge you more than four bits."

Byson was desperate. He climbed to his feet and stood awkwardly, hat clutched in both hands. "I thought maybe I earned myself some money because I tried to help your man Stark."

Creed laughed. "That's more like it. Come to the point. Don't beat around the bush. I have the feeling you didn't give one damn about Sam Stark personally. I certainly didn't."

Creed removed three twenty dollar gold pieces from a big safe in the corner and dropped them into Byson's outstretched hand. "That'll repay you for your pain. Keep your eyes and ears open in Scalplock. Anything that would interest Python, you can pass on to the man I'll send to replace Stark."

Byson bit back his disappointment. "I was hoping I might be that man."

"Python does not tolerate failure. Sam Stark was a braggart and he drank too much. And he failed. And so did you . . . to a point."

"I failed . . . how?"

"From what you told me of that setup in the saloon, it was clumsy. Stark should have shot Latigo in the back, not tried to drag you into it."

Byson flinched at the cold-blooded way Creed spoke of

shooting a man in the back, showing about as much emotion as he would in bringing a boot heel down on an anthill.

"Anything more about this Latigo?" Creed asked after a pause.

Byson leaped at the opening. He spoke of the girl who had been left at the Lockwood ranch. "Sam tried to trick Latigo into admitting he was the one who dropped her off there."

Creed seemed interested. "Why did Stark think this was so important?"

"All I know is that Sam said she'd been wounded, left for dead. Name of Cindy Lou."

"Sam knew this girl Cindy Lou?"

"Well, he was sure upset because she was alive."

"Sam's the one shot her?"

"Sam didn't get to tell me too much." Byson was perspiring under his dusty clothing. He was about to reach for the necklace wrapped in tissue that he'd placed in his pocket. Something stayed his hand. He said, "Everything went to hell when Sam put an Indian necklace on the bartop. Latigo went to pieces right then and there. He shouted that the necklace had belonged to his mother."

Creed rubbed a fingertip over one of his crooked teeth. "Then what happened?"

"It was right then that Sam yelled at me to get him. But Latigo spun so quick I didn't even see him move. I got whacked over the head and I was out of it."

"What happened to the necklace?"

Byson swallowed, looked out the window where a man in a vacant lot was cutting wood. Creed was obviously upset. Byson felt he had done one of the really smart things in his life by keeping his mouth shut about having the necklace with him.

"I found the necklace later where it had fallen behind the bar," he said blandly. "I hid it."

"Just keep your mouth shut about the necklace . . . and that Cindy Lou." Creed was emphatic.

"I could ride out to the ranch and have a talk with the girl and see what she knows," Byson said innocently.

"I'll send someone else to do that, Byson. And also pick up the necklace." Creed smiled; if an icicle could smile, Byson thought.

"When you see the doctor about your head wound, tell him I said to put his fee on the Python bills." Creed gave him three more double eagles. "That's over a hundred dollars for

123

being loyal to Python. Not the last of the money, of course."

Byson was delighted. He enjoyed the jingle of all that gold in his pocket. "I'm loyal, all right."

Creed let no doubt about loyalty reflect on his face. They parted at the door. "Thank you for coming, Mr. Byson. Remember, eyes and ears open, mouth shut. Just keep pouring Python whiskey at Scalplock. To those who deserve it. The new man I send along will tell you who."

Creed gave Byson a little shove toward the outer door, then beckoned to the redhead who still lounged in a chair near the front door. "Doak, would you mind stepping in here, please?"

Creed seated himself behind his desk, fingers laced across a flat stomach. Creed repeated what Byson had told him.

"Two things worry me, Doak. A wounded girl left at a ranch by this Latigo. And an Indian necklace that would cause a gun hand, like Latigo evidently is, to fly to pieces."

Lancer came to the point. "I warned Stark not to take the necklace. He wouldn't listen."

"You should have gunned him down."

Lancer shrugged. "He was your man. I was new."

"You're not new now. You replace Stark."

"I figured." Lancer laughed.

"Now tell me about the girl."

"A pimp and madam and their girl. Bad water got the man and the woman. The girl was smart enough not to drink it. Stark was the first to rape her."

"Raped her because of the kind of woman she was?"

"She could've been a nun. Wouldn't have made any difference to Stark."

"You said Stark raped her first. How about the rest of you?"

"Stark tied her up. I don't blame Lewt or Cutter or Dain. A good-looking female, whore or not."

"How about you, Doak?"

"I left her alone."

"Conscience?" Creed asked with a hard smile.

"Born without one. A woman I don't know anything about, I leave alone. Whether preacher's wife or whore."

"Who shot her?"

"Stark did." It was the only lie. Lancer would speak to the other three who had been along that day. They'd back him up, now that his position with Python had been established.

Creed steepled his fingers above a thick gold watch chain draped across his stomach. "I've got more important things

124

for you to do, Doak, so I'll send Lewt to Scalplock. I'll tell him to watch his chance. Kill the girl. Leave the usual sign to make it look like an Indian did it. We'll be pushing across more of their lands soon and we'll need every possible excuse to get them out of the way. So, two birds with one stone."

"Lewt will get the job done."

Creed nodded in agreement, then said, "I didn't expect a slipup in the Beaver Valley business. The Cantrells are supposed to have had a son in the army. A captain. Could Latigo and the son be one and the same?"

"Bet on it."

Creed sighed. "Now comes the hard part of my job, Doak. I'll have to put everything that's happened into a report to Claudius Max. I don't dare leave out one detail."

Ed Lewt arrived in Scalplock on a Wednesday. The first thing he did was go to the Shamrock and ask a balding man with a weak chin where he could find Fred Byson.

"I'm Byson."

Lewt almost laughed. No wonder Stark, with his big mouth, got himself killed. Tying in with the likes of this. Lewt managed a straight face and put his hand across the bar. Byson's handshake was moist and lacked firmness, which was no surprise.

Lewt grinned, showing his gold tooth, and told Byson that he had been sent by Python to replace Sam Stark and to keep an eye on things. "With you helpin' me."

"Be glad to do anything I can." Byson bubbled in his enthusiasm, already anticipating the weight of gold in his pockets.

Lewt waited until Byson got off work, then had him point out the important people of the town. By another day he knew these people by sight. He also met Toby Taggart who assessed him with eyes tight at the corners.

"Just don't step on my toes, Lewt," Taggart said, "and I won't step on yours." The marshal smiled with his teeth. "I sometimes come down hard."

Ed Lewt shrugged that off with a grin. "Hell, we'll have no trouble. I hear half the town's off chasin' somebody named Latigo."

"Yeah. The one killed your friend Stark."

"They must be chasin' him all the way to Chihuahua."

"He's good as dead no matter where they chase him."

Lewt hung around the bench in front of the Scalplock Store

and swapped lies with some of the men who paused for a rest and to stretch out the legs. Lewt didn't mention a girl named Cindy Lou; he waited for someone else to do it. No one did.

But he acted interested in news of the proposed church, learned that it was being promoted by a rancher named Lockwood. "That's him now an' his boy Ralph," said a supplier of information, straw bobbing in a corner of the mouth.

When Lockwood entered the store, leaving the boy with the team, Lewt sauntered over. He could be pleasant enough when his viper blood was reasonably cooled. "Nice lookin' team you got there, kid."

Ralph Lockwood turned a freckled face to the pair of heavy-footed work horses as if wondering what the stranger found so interesting. "Just plain ol' hosses," the boy said, turning back and leaning against the wagon.

"How's Cindy Lou gettin' along these days?" Lewt asked innocently.

The boy looked puzzled. "Don't know any Cindy Lou."

Lewt had to resist an impulse to flatten the kid's nose. He turned the name over in his mind. Cindy Lou was the name Creed had supplied, he was sure of it. He had even written it down.

"I mean the gal I heard was stayin' out at your place," Lewt said with a warm smile.

"Oh . . . her." Ralph Lockwood studied a distant peak. "You'll have to ask my pa."

"Reckon she's probably able to get around by now. Take a walk . . . get outa the house for some fresh air, huh?"

Ralph Lockwood climbed into the wagon and sat with arms folded.

Lewt itched to pull him off the seat. "Heard she got shot in the head," he called up to the boy. "Was just interested is all."

By the time he reached the hotel where he'd taken over Stark's room, he had calmed down. After all, he had the information he needed.

He got his high-powered rifle from a shelf where it had been hidden under a pile of spare blankets. Sitting on the bed, he dismantled the weapon, gave it a thorough cleaning, then reassembled it. He sighted the rifle through the hotel window at the back of a woman's head over a block away. His aim did not waver.

Satisfied, he got his horse at the livery barn, booted the rifle and said he was going out to look for a deer. He listened to the hostler tell him through gapped teeth where he was most likely to find a buck. Lewt thanked him, waved and rode in that direction. But once out of town, he doubled back. Byson had talked enough about the Lockwood ranch so that Lewt felt he could find it easily.

Thirty minutes after locating the ranch, he found what he was looking for. A shelf of rock that overlooked the house. Fortunately it was downwind from two big dogs asleep in yard dust warmed by the sun. He waited patiently one hour, two. There seemed to be no one around, which was disappointing. Then he suddenly spotted movement. Someone had come out of the house by a different door than the one he was watching. It was a young female in a gingham dress. He picked up his rifle. On the way back to town he would try his damnedest to find a deer. It would look better if he came back with a haunch of venison that he would present to the hotel cook.

The girl stepped behind a spring wagon with a missing wheel and leaned down to pick up something from the ground.

Lewt found the skull in his sights, centered on a neat part in the light hair. Drawing a deep breath, he held it. At the last second he realized with a shock that the target was only a girl of ten or so. She came skipping out from behind the wagon to disappear around the far side of the house. The close call chilled him.

You could murder your way across the West and with luck escape the gallows. But murder a kid, especially a female, and you were dead. All the territories west of the big river, and half of Mexico wouldn't be big enough to hide in.

Lewt was still shaky when he got back to town by a circuitous route. Next time he wouldn't trust the uncertain light of late afternoon. He'd pick a clear morning.

But after today there had to be a change of plans. He'd forget the ledge screened by brush and try and catch her away from the house while she was taking a walk. It was better, he reasoned, if her body was never found, that she simply disappear.

Cindy Lou was as good as dead.

19 Twice the posse nearly had Cole boxed in what appeared to them to be a blind canyon. But each time the agile Indian ponies scampered up an almost impossible trail. Rifle shots slammed dangerously close into rock walls. One of them knocked granite chips against the back of a hand, drawing blood. He fired over their heads, trying to scatter them. They took cover. Voices reached him faintly as they cursed in their anger and frustration. One of his shots hit a horse by accident when its rider spurred recklessly to higher ground. At first it seemed that rider as well as horse had been hit. The man struck the ground, rolled loosely, arms flapping. This brought on another wave of epithets Cole could barely hear as he reached the canyon rim. Looking back, he saw that the downed rider had regained his feet. The man weaved for a moment, then scrambled up behind one of the other riders. Cole knew he had only been momentarily stunned by the fall. For some days they had done their damnedest to run him to ground, but so far he had not even winged one of them.

They were tenacious, he had to give them credit for that. By now pursuit might have faded had they not been lucky enough to swap for fresh horses at mountain ranches. But by this the fourth day their mounts were wearing thin. So were his, for the pace had been furious.

That night Cole had to sleep with a bandanna over his face to keep off mosquitos. But by morning a sudden change in the weather put a light frost on the ground. He got up, his muscles stiff from the cold. Alert for the first sign of danger, he washed his face in the icy waters of a creek, then finished off the last of his cold biscuits and beef he'd gotten from a freight outfit.

He needed fresh meat, but hated to risk a rifle shot that might give away his position, because he had seen no sign of pursuit most of the previous afternoon.

At last upon reaching a promontory, he looked back and was gratified that he could no longer see posse dust filming the pale sky. Because of relentless pursuit, he had been forced to circle miles south and to the east in his attempts to throw them off his trail. He had come at last within sight of a natural hole in a red stone escarpment, a V-shaped opening barely large enough to admit a single horse at a time. He knew it as a hideout used by outlaws and Indians engaged in intertribal warfare. His father had visited it many times when coming this far south to the fur trapper's rendezvous. Cole recalled his father telling him how he had met Kit Carson at the rendezvous one year. His father liked Carson at the time but Cole wondered if his feelings had changed drastically because of Carson's part in the Navajo massacre at Canyon de Chelly. Cole had learned of it during the war.

As this went through his mind, Cole continued the climb toward the V in the rock wall. A dangerous trail, the footing poor over loose rubble. A lesser horseman might have dismounted and walked, but Cole pressed on, the ponies stumbling but surefooted. They reached the gap, spent, spraddled-legged, streaked with sweat.

Cole swung down tiredly to stare across flats far below that stretched endlessly toward a horizon boiling with cotton clouds. From this high point there was no sign of pursuit. He breathed easier. At times they had been close, for some of the posse men obviously knew this stretch of country better than he did. But he had finally worn down those few who stubbornly remained in the chase.

For once, no one else seemed to be using the hideout. He needed rest. So did his ponies. He prowled on foot, shot an antelope and had a filling meal. Then he settled down near the V in the red rock wall where any sound of men or horses in the rubble would bring him instantly awake. Here one man could stand off many. . . .

Heading back, he made a wide circle, intending to stop off at the Crow camp. But at an isolated trading post he happened across an old copy of a Basin City newspaper. A few lines told of the Cantrell place in Beaver Valley being burned out by renegade Indians. Although there were signs of massacre, no bodies had been found.

Cole's jaws tightened. He was about to crumple the paper when another story caught his eye, this one even shorter. In a few lines it told of Marshal Toby Taggart of Scalplock offering a reward for the apprehension of the man known as Latigo. Wanted for the murder of one Samuel Stark. . . .

What a grim coincidence, he thought, a story of dead parents and of a son wanted for murder appearing in the same edition of a frontier newspaper.

Cole knew what he had to do, take one of the longest gambles of his life. There was no other way. . . .

On a Monday at twilight, Fred Byson paid a visit to the privy out back of the Shamrock. It had been a slow day and he had two more hours to put in before Bernie Halloran arrived to take over. There were only two customers.

When he stepped from the privy he saw a shadowed figure and at the same moment felt a revolver muzzle shoved against the soft pouch under the narrow chin. He stood, eyes round with fear when he realized who was searching him for a weapon.

"Wh . . . wh . . . what do you . . . w . . . w . . . want?"

Cole's smile was icy. "Keep your mouth shut."

"You've come back to m . . . m . . . murder me," Byson gasped.

"You'll stay alive if you do as I say."

"You better get out while you can. All I have to do is open my . . . my mouth and yell."

"Do that and you'll have no chin. Probably no head. Remember how Sam Stark looked?"

"Jesus."

"Start walking, Byson."

"W . . . w . . . walk where?"

"Marshal's office."

"Likely he won't be in. . . ."

"Then we'll bust in and wait for him."

"Oh gawd," Byson groaned.

As they started across open country, the mine whistle blasted up on the mountainside.

"They'll be comin' down the hill for whiskey," Byson said shakily as he looked at the implacable dark face of his captor. "There'll be all hell bustin' loose when they find nobody to wait on them. . . ."

"They won't miss you. Chances are they'll wait on themselves."

"Bernie'll kill me," Byson groaned.

"Or I will, if you try anything."

Byson shuddered. Cole linked arms with him as some men came out of the livery barn and headed downslope, talking together, toward the main street. Byson knew better than to cry out. He didn't want to risk a rib cage blown apart by that gun rammed against his side.

Perhaps if the light had been strong the group of men might have noticed Byson's pallor. But they didn't even

130

glance their way. Cole breathed easier. He had passed one test and not been recognized. Some of them might even have been members of the posse.

A lamp competed with the twilight in the marshal's cubbyhole of an office. Through a narrow window Cole could see Toby Taggart, slouched in a chair, feet on a rolltop desk, reading a newspaper.

As they approached the small building, Cole gave Byson instructions. Byson started to protest. Cole punched hard with the gun. Byson winced, bent over as the weapon dug into his ribs.

"And don't forget what I told you," Cole warned the terrified barkeep. "You stay alive only if you follow orders."

"I . . . I . . . I understand."

Taggart removed his feet from the desk and leaned over to turn up the lamp, to give him more light for his paper. His head jerked around as Cole flung open the door and shoved Byson inside. Taggart's lips whitened below his mustache. Hunched awkwardly in the chair, he recovered from his surprise and started a hand toward the gun grips of a holstered revolver.

"Don't," Cole hissed. He kicked the door shut behind him, groped behind him for the bolt, slid it into place. Rage began to darken the marshal's face as Cole, keeping both men covered, jerked curtains across the single window.

Mules in the livery barn up the hill began to bray. A few horses became agitated and neighed and snorted. An irritated voice came faintly, "Shut up back there!"

Taggart's right hand dangled at his side, the eyes rolled up coldly to stare at a trembling Byson and at the cocked .44 in Cole's hand.

Taggart found his voice. "You're a nervy bastard, Latigo. I'll say that for you."

"Byson's got a little speech to give. *Tell* him, Fred!"

Byson licked his lips, made a couple of false starts, then blurted, "Toby, I . . . I . . . lied."

"Lied about what?" Taggart demanded, straightening up in the chair.

"Latigo didn't try to rob me like I claimed." When Byson hesitated, Cole nudged him with the gun. "Stark figured to murder Latigo . . . but he wanted me to help, just in case." Byson's narrow face was wet. He licked his lips.

"Go on, Fred," Taggart said when the bartender hesitated.

"I pretended to be reading a letter. I had a gun on a shelf. Stark wanted me to . . . to . . . shoot him. . . ."

131

"In the back, he means," Cole said.

"That right, Fred?" Taggart demanded.

"Y . . . y . . . yes."

Marshal Toby Taggart got slowly to his feet, long legs spread, hunched slightly as he stared at Byson. A vein pulsed at his forehead. "Is what you're saying the truth? Or has Latigo scared the starch outa you."

"Don't let him kill me, Toby. . . ."

"He won't. Answer my question, damn it."

Byson swallowed. "The truth, I swear it, Toby, but I was only trying to keep Stark from turnin' on me. . . ."

"So you agreed to shoot a man in the back." Taggart's lips curled. Then he swung his cold gaze to Cole. "Latigo, you made me look like a fool that night. Marched me outa the saloon in front of half the town."

"Better I stay and maybe hang?"

"You wore out some good hosses when the boys tried to catch up with you."

"They pushed me to the limit."

Taggart had to agree. "I'm also remembering you could've shot me in the back when I made my break."

"You haven't heard it all." Cole briefly sketched the bloody business at Beaver Valley and Sam Stark's part in it. "The only proof I've got is my mother's necklace." He turned on Byson. "Stark put it on the bar. You saw him."

Byson swallowed. "Jeez, I don't remember any necklace."

"Liar!"

"Wait a minute, Latigo," Taggart snapped. "I believe you about the shoot out in the Shamrock. Byson sure admits his part in it. But I don't figure to tangle with Python about that Beaver Valley business just on your say so. Hell no. I'm not that big a fool."

"Byson's lying about the necklace. . . ."

Taggart held up a hand. "I'll spread the word that you didn't gun down Sam Stark in cold blood. That I got proof of . . . Byson standin' there like a whipped cur admittin' he lied. But I only got your word about Beaver Valley. . . ."

Cole turned on Byson. "There were four other men in on the Beaver Valley killing with Stark. Who were they . . . ?"

"Hold on there, Latigo. I let you come bustin' in here an' shove a gun in my face. I listen to you when I really felt like bustin' your head. I figure to kick Byson outa town. . . ."

"That ain't fair, Toby," Byson protested.

"You open your mouth about Latigo or Cantrell or what-

132

ever the hell his name is and you'll be damned old before you get out of our jail!" Taggart exploded.

"Toby, Toby . . ." Byson wailed.

"Don't use my first name," the marshal snapped. "It's reserved for my friends. Not a liar!"

Cole knew he had pushed his luck to the limit already, but he tried again to get Taggart to listen to him about Beaver Valley. But Taggart refused to hear anything that might involve Python.

"Stark worked for Python and you're willing to believe the worst about him. . . ." Cole began.

"Python's got no love for Sam Stark, that I know."

"What do you mean by that?" Cole demanded suspiciously.

"I'll see that the real story about the shooting at the Shamrock gets in the paper. But that's all I'll do. . . ."

There was a sudden sound of boots outside the office, voices. Someone rattled the doorknob.

"Toby, we're goin' down to the Pines for a drink. Come along."

Taggart stiffened, stabbed Cole with a tight glance. Cole felt a prickling sensation at the back of his neck as he awaited Taggart's next move. If it wasn't the right one, somebody could be dead.

Taggart cleared his throat. "Boys, I'm busy. See you at the Pines in a few minutes."

"Hell with bein' busy," said another voice, slurring the words. The doorknob rattled again.

In that moment Fred Byson spun away from Cole, his mouth flying open. But Cole's left fist was already slamming the point of the narrow chin. Whatever cry Byson was about to utter died in his throat. He slumped. Cole made a desperate attempt to catch him, but too late. Byson crashed against the wall, then the floor.

"What the hell was that?" cried two or three men outside.

"Fell over my chair," Taggart said loudly.

Cole expelled a tightly-held breath. For an instant he had thought Taggart might make Byson's stupid diversion a cover for pulling his gun. But he didn't. His lips under the mustache showed strain. There was more doorknob jiggling.

"Who you got in there, Toby?" the one with the thick voice persisted, slurring his words again.

Taggart added scornfully, "For Chrissakes, will you boys go on down to the Pines? I got private business to take care of first."

One of the men tittered. "A lady in there, by gad."

"No wonder he's got the window covered. That right, Toby?"

"I won't admit one damn thing," Taggart said.

"See you at the Pines." Laughing, they trooped off down the hill, stumbling a little in the rubble.

Cole drew a long breath. "Thanks, Taggart."

"You get outa town till I can clear your name of that Stark business. Otherwise, the boys spot you here I might have to shoot somebody to keep you from gettin' hung to a tree."

"I'll take Byson with me."

"He's leavin' town . . . for good! But not with you!"

"I need some answers from him . . ."

"Don't push your luck, Latigo. You lose your temper and kill Byson . . ."

"I won't kill him, damn it."

"Won't chance it. Get out. Latigo. You treated me decent that night when you could've blowed my head off. So I'm givin' you this chance. Next fella rattles that doorknob will get straight answers."

Cole gave him a nod, looked at Byson just beginning to stir on the floor. Cole unlocked the door, peered carefully both ways on the shadowed hill, but saw no one. Quickly he closed the door and hurried away before Taggart could change his mind.

Only when he was in thick trees where he had left the ponies, did he draw a reasonably normal breath. His gamble had paid off to a point. Taggart believed him about the business at the Shamrock but refused to discuss Beaver Valley. He supposed he couldn't blame the man. Accusing Python of murder, without proof, could cause a man to lose more than a badge.

Emma Lockwood was just setting a platter of biscuits on the table when the dogs started barking. The two girls hopped up and ran to the front window. "Papa, there's a man in the yard!"

Young Lockwood pushed back his chair, but his father shook his head. "Lemme see who it is first, Ralph."

"Mr. and Mrs. Lockwood!" somebody called from outside. "I'm the one who dropped Helen off here. Can I speak to her, please?"

"Poor Helen," Mrs. Lockwood said with a sad shake of her head.

Lockwood picked up his rifle. "I'll go see what he wants."

"What'll you tell him about Helen?"

But Lockwood had stepped outside. He quieted the dogs. His jaws were working and Cole knew he had called the man away from the supper table.

134

"I just stopped by to see if Helen's safe and well. . . ."

"She's gone."

"Gone where?"

Lockwood said when she was feeling stronger he let her ride one of the horses to town. Helen never returned. But she had left the horse in the livery barn for him.

"Maybe something happened to her," Cole said, concerned.

"There was a freight outfit in town that day. Might be she hitched a ride." Lockwood lowered his voice. "I never told the missus about the freight outfit 'cause she'd worry. A nice girl like Helen traipsin' off like that. I said that Helen run into some friends who took her away."

Lockwood's son appeared at the doorway. "You all right, Pa?"

"Yeah. You finish your supper. You got schoolwork to do." The boy ducked back into the house. Lockwood said, "No school here yet, but I buy books for all my kids."

"My father did that for me," Cole said, his throat tight.

The dogs sniffed the ponies suspiciously.

"We was growin' right fond of Helen. An' she was goin' to help the missus with the church. Oh, well, she come with nothin' an' she left the same way. . . ."

"How's your church coming along?" Cole felt he should ask.

"Python donated land right behind the store, which surprised me," Lockwood said. "Reckon we can get the church up in a month or so."

Cole wondered about Python generosity. To blind the citizens to murder committed in the name of a railroad?

"Good luck with your church, Lockwood."

"I heard in town that a fella named Latigo rides two ponies like you an' wears buckskins. But Helen always called you Cole."

"I didn't murder Sam Stark." Cole related Byson's confession made in the presence of the town marshal.

"Latigo was about the only talk I heard for a few days," the rancher admitted. "I tell you one thing, though. A lot of us didn't think you could be as bad as some folks painted you. You could've killed our marshal. You didn't."

"Taggart realizes that now."

"Don't know why you killed Sam Stark, but I never liked the man. Python didn't either, so I hear."

"I thought he was their man."

"They was set to fire him, is the story I heard."

No wonder Taggart hadn't minded believing the worst about the Stark shooting.

135

"Do you happen to know the men Stark worked with?"

Lockwood shook his head. "Python was kind enough to give us land. I don't know their private business, an' I don't *want* to know."

"Yes, I can understand." Cole picked up the reins.

"Come in an' eat. I'll have the missus set out an extra plate." Lockwood gestured behind him at the lamplighted window.

The offer was tempting, but Cole shook his head.

"Thanks, but I've got a lot of miles to cover," he said.

Cole rode away, feeling depressed. Helen running off with a freight outfit had come as a surprise. What else to believe? It was how she had gotten to Santa Fe and then ended up as one of Flo's girls. The same pattern repeated, he supposed.

He thought perhaps he had convinced her otherwise.

Apparently not and it was too bad.

He couldn't deny that Helen had disappointed him.

Fred Byson knew his job at the Shamrock was done, even if Taggart hadn't ordered him out of town. As he approached the place, he could hear the shouting and laughter. Miners and other patrons, finding no bartender, were no doubt helping themselves.

Chong wouldn't venture from his kitchen to try and restore order, that was for sure. Bernie Halloran would be furious.

Byson kept to the main street, not wishing to risk another encounter with that cold-eyed Latigo. Midway up the block he sank to a bench so he could try and think his way out of the trap he had made for himself. All because he had listened to Sam Stark. His only hope now, he felt, lay with Ed Lewt. It was unfortunate that Lewt was out of town on Python business. If Lewt were only here now he'd whisper in his ear that Python should get rid of the town marshal. Then he reconsidered, having learned enough about Python to renew the surging fear. If there was anyone to be gotten rid of, the more likely victim would be one Fred Byson.

Although Byson had tried to pretend otherwise, he sensed that everyone at Python, from E.J. Creed on down, regarded him with contempt. A nuisance bug underfoot. Which he had been most of his life, except for the interlude with Sam Stark. He had listened to Stark's stories, laughed at his jokes, even though he'd heard them before. Stark had treated him like a human being. Now Stark was dead and he had no one.

He had to admit, now that he thought it over, that trying to

136

get close to Ed Lewt would be about as sensible as carrying a live rattlesnake under his shirt.

As he sat on the bench watching the Basin City stage being readied for its morning run, Byson's desperate and crafty mind searched for ways that would earn him enough money to quit the country. And at the same time even the score with Cole Cantrell, alias Latigo.

20

Once before Cole had found solace in a pair of warm arms. He hoped to again. It was a time for rest, for regeneration, to think carefully of the violent future that awaited him. He approached the Crow camp from high ground, seeing the great sprawl of lodges, the bands of horses. Smoke from low fires drifted into the trees. Squaws tending racks where meat was being dried had turned to stare at a band of warriors who chanted and milled about, some brandishing war lances and bows. A few had rifles. Cole reined in, wondering why the camp was aroused. Excited voices from below drifted to the brushy promontory where he sat his pony. As he watched, he saw chiefs appear, carrying war shields that were symbolic, hardly protection against modern rifles. Voices were stilled now as the chiefs led a solemn procession of braves away from the camp. Clouds drifted in, dimming the sun.

His two ponies negotiated the steep trail. When he reached level ground there was no sign of the departing Indians; only their dust lingered.

Dark Star's lodge was where he remembered it. The flap was open. About all he could see of her in the shadowy interior of the lodge were her shining eyes.

She came out as he dismounted, giving him her hands. "I knew you would come, Two Trails."

"Another medicine dream?"

She placed a hand over her left breast. "In my heart I knew."

At first the Crow tongue seemed awkward to him, then it came easily as before when they spoke a little stiffly of weather and ponies. She clapped her hands. Two Indian boys appeared, eager to do her bidding. She instructed them to care for the ponies.

Cole unsheathed his rifle, then ducked to enter the lodge.

At once he felt the sense of peace that had been a balm to his tortured mind at a time of tragedy.

"You have had much trouble, much danger," Dark Star said as she dropped the two flaps and secured them.

Placing his rifle and belted revolver on the floor of the lodge, he stretched out on the bed, thankful that for the moment at least he was no longer running for his life. The departure of the band of braves, led by chiefs, troubled him. He asked what it meant.

"There is to be a council of chiefs." She gestured northward with a slender hand. "They will decide how to prevent the shining rails from crossing Indian lands."

How successful would they be? he wondered. But he was too weary to give it more than passing thought. At least it had not been a war party.

As Dark Star moved lightly about the lodge, beads making a rhythmic sound while preparing a meal, she wanted details of his life since their last meeting. He told her the story.

Later under the robes of the soft bed, he felt the silken fire of her soft bare flesh against his. As before, his power caused her to cry out in pleasure. And she brought to him a joyous respite from the steel-edged world beyond the deerskin walls of the lodge. It helped release for the moment those hatreds that had been bottled up inside.

In the morning she spoke of the council of chiefs and wondered if he thought it would be wise for him to catch up with them. "Ride with them to the powwow," she finished, watching him intently. "You were once a part of the white man's army and could suggest ways of solving the problems without bloodshed."

"They wouldn't listen to me."

"I shouldn't have suggested it," she sighed. She seemed suddenly grave. Reaching for his medicine bag, she transferred the loop to her own neck. The small buckskin pouch dangled between her breasts.

"When you are hunting down those men," she said softly, "place your hand on this bag and think of me."

"I have done so many times," he told her.

"Vow that you must stay alive to return to me." Then she added soberly, "Also, it will remind you of my powerful medicine."

They made a ceremony of restoring the bag to his own neck. Under his shirt the pouch was warm from her body.

Before leaving, he went to see Trooper and found the big horse sleek and well cared for. Trooper snorted a greeting and trotted over to nuzzle his arm. "I still need ponies for fast riding," Cole said, stroking his muzzle. "But one day soon I'll be back, old friend."

Dark Star walked with him back to her lodge. "Be careful," she said in parting, "because your life is also mine."

He mounted up. "*A-ho!* Holy woman." Lifting a hand, he wheeled the ponies and trotted through the camp. Squaws at racks where chunks of venison and buffalo were being dried, paused in their labors to look at him. Camp dogs were curious as usual. A few of them barked. Children stared solemnly as he rode out.

On the bright early morning something compelled him to swing from the narrow mountain pass he had intended to take, and instead retrace the route of the travois on that day of the dead.

He rode at ease under a clear sky, the ponies eating miles. Dark eyes always alert, scanned the backtrail, the high peaks to the right, lower forested areas on the left. And beyond, the endless miles of open country. Had it not been for the hat of midnight blue, he could have passed for an Indian, with his black hair, hawklike nose, lean build.

Finally within sight of the scene of murder and arson, cold sweat dampened his palms. Ruins of the house and barn had been hauled to this side of Beaver Creek and dumped under cottonwoods. Blackened timbers and a pile of metal, bolts, square-head nails, ranch tools that had resisted the conflagration.

On the far side of the creek were tents and two wagons, the teams staked on the grass where Badger Cantrell used to turn his stock out to pasture. Cole's hand, coldly moist, clamped the butt of his .44. As if through a red haze he saw eight men huddled where the house had stood. They were studying what appeared to be a large map spread out on the tailgate of a wagon.

One of them, lank with a pale beard, a rifle under his arm, was the first to see Cole. His shout brought the other seven men swinging around. They stared in surprise at a white man astride an Indian pony, leading a second.

Cole saw the stakes outlining a narrow area, the width of a railroad track. Surveyors at work. Most of these appeared to be in their twenties, with city faces reddened from wind and sun. They wore wide-brimmed hats and wool shirts. Their pants were tucked into high-top lace boots.

"I suppose you know you're trespassing," Cole said to the staring men.

139

The spokesman for the group introduced himself as Ben Sampsel. "Trespassing?" he said incredulously. "You're mistaken, Mr. . . ."

"Latigo."

"Mr. Latigo, the railroad owns this land now."

"Badger Cantrell was the legal owner," Cole said through his teeth.

"I've seen the transfer of title, Mr. Latigo," Sampsel said.

"Seen it where?"

"In Basin City. In Mr. Creed's office. This man Cantrell you mentioned signed it over. Perfectly legal." Sampsel, a little older than the others, with chin whiskers, seemed sincere. Only the man with the rifle looked apprehensive at the moment.

"Creed, eh?" Cole said, remembering the name.

"Creed appears to be a reasonable man," Sampsel went on when Cole continued to stare coldly. "Certainly he would do nothing underhanded, if that's what you're implying." Then Sampsel mentioned that they were about to partake of their noon meal. "Join us, Mr. Latigo, and we can discuss this further."

Cole shook his head and drew a deep breath. If he tried to push the eight men off the land, somebody would be dead. Even me, he conceded. Luck could only stretch so far.

Cole's silence caused Sampsel to perspire and scrub a shirt sleeve across his moist forehead. "One thing I don't want is trouble," he said, swallowing. "We were assured there'd be none. All we were hired to do is run a survey. . . ."

Cole knew it had probably been foolish to come here, but the compulsion had been strong. And he had learned a name. Creed, with an office in Basin City.

In contrast to the mountain boom town of Scalplock, Basin City was well named. It was truly a city, with hotels, saloons, two livery barns, one with a wagon yard that took up half of a square block, saddle shops and several stores. And the usual establishments found in a frontier settlement that catered to the pleasures of lonely and womanless men.

Cole was a little surprised at the modest building that housed the western headquarters of Python.

A thin and harrassed clerk demanded to know his reason for wanting to see Mr. Creed. The harrassment turned to apprehension when Cole gave his name.

"Cantrell?" the clerk blurted, eyes widening behind half-moon spectacles. His worried glance involuntarily fell to the holstered gun at Cole's belt. Then he turned and rapped

140

nervously on an inner door and let himself in. Cole put his back to the wall, so he could watch not only the street door but also the one to the inner office.

Cole had his second surprise of the day when a man wearing a gray vest, a watch chain, matching trousers and boots with a high polish, opened the inner door himself.

"Mr. Cantrell, do come in, sir. I'm Creed." He stood aside so Cole could enter. But Cole waited until the clerk was out of the doorway and again seated at the reception desk. Even a slightly-built, inoffensive-looking clerk could put a gun to a man's back.

This Creed noticed and smiled as he closed the door. "Don't blame you for being suspicious, Mr. Cantrell. These are trying times. Most trying." He gestured to a straight-backed chair, then seated himself before a large flat-topped desk littered with papers. Several large topographical maps on the wall reminded Cole of a field headquarters. A squat iron safe filled one corner.

Cole turned his chair so as to keep one eye on the door, the other on a single window that overlooked an alley. This move also was not lost on Creed as he held out a humidor. Cole shook his head. Creed took one of the cigars, bit off one end which he dropped into a polished spittoon beside the desk.

"I heard about your parents and I'm terribly sorry," Creed, said lighting his cigar.

Cole studied this man he had been prepared to dislike intensely. While Creed might not have participated in the murders, he most certainly had been instrumental in furnishing money to those who had.

Creed stared through cigar smoke. "Did you hear me? I am very, very sorry about what happened. My sincere condolences."

"I heard you."

Creed blew a cloud of good tobacco smoke at the ceiling. "You're upset, Mr. Cantrell, and I certainly can't blame you."

"I saw surveyors on my father's land. I told them they're trespassing. Now I'm telling you."

"Our land, Mr. Cantrell," Creed said in surprise. "How could you think otherwise?" Without waiting for a reply, he opened the safe and rifled through some papers. Cole touched the butt of his .44, prepared for anything. Even a hideout weapon in a safe.

But Creed produced no gun, only a printed form which he passed over. "A quitclaim deed signed by your father and witnesses."

Cole studied the document while Creed resumed his seat. Cole met Creed's direct gaze. "A forgery," Cole said flatly.

In the silence that stretched thin, came a creaking of wagon wheels from the street, a braying mule. A young boy laughed.

"You're making a serious charge," Creed said at last.

"I am," Cole snapped.

"I happen to know where these witnesses are today," Creed informed him smoothly. "They can be produced to swear they witnessed your father's signature."

"Neighbors you bought out or scared out . . ."

"As for your father, unfortunately he cannot be produced." Creed shook his head sadly. "But I assure you, Mr. Cantrell, everything is in order, perfectly legal. Python does business in no other way."

Cole's smile was icy. "What happened at Beaver Valley wasn't exactly legal. . . ."

"A despicable act on the part of those renegade Indians," Creed interrupted.

"Renegade Indians? Not quite."

"Hear me out, Cantrell." Creed leaned forward, all serious business. "We paid your father five thousand in gold for that land. Oh, I admit he was stubborn, wanting to hold out. But we finally convinced him that there was even better land to the north that he could take up. He finally agreed. I imagine those Indians got wind of the gold and tortured your parents to learn where they had hidden the money."

"A fine story you tell."

Creed stiffened. "I've never been called a liar before."

Cole spoke softly as he told of Sam Stark's attempt on his life in Scalplock. He spoke of an Indian necklace that had triggered the final violence. "My mother's necklace, Creed," and voicing that part of it was the hardest part.

Creed acted surprised. "A necklace? That can't be. . . ."

"I saw it, Creed. Stark knew damn well that sight of it would throw me off balance. It did. He counted on it giving him an edge. It didn't."

"My God, I had never heard any of this. I had word that Stark was dead, of course." Creed seemed genuinely concerned, but the pupils of his eyes reminded Cole of sunlight reflected off cold steel. "Killed by a man named Latigo," Creed went on. Then he looked at Cole with faint surprise. "I gather you and Latigo are one and the same."

Cole didn't answer. He shoved the quitclaim deed onto the desk. "My father never signed that."

"As I said, you make a serious charge. . . ."

142

"Murder is about as serious as you can get," Cole said bluntly.

The brief glint of steel vanished from Creed's eyes and he again became the affable, concerned representative of a powerful company.

"Let me say this, Mr. Cantrell. We have done business in the East, but out here we travel unknown trails. And perhaps some unscrupulous individuals may attatch themselves to our coattails, so to speak. Now I'm not saying that Stark murdered your parents just because you say he had in his possession a necklace that belonged to your mother. He could have found the necklace. Or perhaps traded for it. We thought we had a good man in Stark, but I confess we were wrong. He was to have been discharged for drunkenness and refusing to obey orders. So, you see we had already realized our mistake in taking him on." Creed placed his cigar in a small metate on the desk. He rubbed the cigar out, leaving a smudge on the stone.

Cole stood up. "Four men traveled with Stark. I want their names."

"Stark traveled alone, so far as I know." Creed looked blank. "I have no idea who his friends might have been."

"You think I'm fool enough to believe that?"

"I'm asking you to believe it, Mr. Cantrell. *Asking* you."

Creed reached across the desk to pick up the quitclaim deed. Cole reached it first. He folded it carefully, put it in a pocket.

Creed said, "That's Python property."

"Somewhere around here is a forger," Cole said softly. "I figure to find him."

"You are making a grave mistake, Mr. Cantrell." Creed sounded hurt. "And I was prepared to offer you a position with us at a most generous salary. . . ."

Cole's laughter had the quality of glass breaking.

"Mr. Cantrell, I am quite serious. I know of your Indian blood. We need someone who can help us quell the rage of the tribes. They seem to be in an uproar over our plans for a railroad."

"Because those plans will destroy their way of life!"

"No, no, you are quite wrong. . . ."

Cole jerked a thumb at the cigar in the metate on the desk. "A squaw once used that to grind maize. Food for her family. You use it for cigar ashes. See what I mean? It's a small thing, but it proves you don't give one damn about the Indian."

Creed frowned at the metate. "Believe me when I say I didn't realize it's true purpose. A man here in town made me a present of it. I had no idea it had something to do with food for the Indian."

"In the war I met great liars. Some wore gray and some blue. But if they handed out medals for pure mule shit, you'd be a winner."

Creed did not seem offended. "Please sit down, Mr. Cantrell. I am sincere when I say that hiring you would be an advantage to . . ." Creed's gaze slipped to the closed door, then to Cole's taut face. "Let us discuss our differences."

"Stall, that's your game. Keep me talking until you can get some help."

Creed's mouth worked ever so slightly, then curved into a warm smile. "You are altogether too suspicious."

"Probably." Cole backed to the door.

"You can be a great help to us in dealing with the Indian." Creed reached for a desk drawer but Cole shook his head.

"Touch it and you've go no fingers," Cole warned.

Creed settled back in his chair, hands in sight. "I only wanted to show you notes that I've taken in our dealings with the Indian. We are sincerely trying to negotiate. . . ."

"How sincere you are in everything," Cole snapped.

"If we fail in our negotiations," Creed continued, unperturbed, "then we may have to call on our own men for protection. . . ."

"Such as the late Sam Stark. Listen, Creed, I came here for the names of the four men with Stark that day. Do you give 'em to me, or do I go through that safe?"

"As I've said, Stark worked on his own. But I did hire the man, which I admit. And he probably brought in . . ."

A sudden thump of boots; a man running from the street and into the outer office caused Creed's affability to vanish as ice before a morning sun. He grinned, shouted, *"Doak, get in here!"*

The door crashed open. Cole was already moving, gun drawn. But the man who stormed in from the outer office surprised them both. Creed's jaw dropped and he looked ill.

Instead of the redheaded Doak Lancer, it was Fred Byson, bartender, late of Scalplock. Byson gripped a .45 that in his thin hand loomed like a fieldpiece. Cole thrust out a leg as Byson, at a hard run, tried to pivot and bring his weapon to bear on Cole. But he tripped over the outthrust leg. Momentum carried him headlong, the gun discharging as he and the gun crashed to the floor.

Creed was yelling frantically, "Doak, Doak!"

He made a desperate grab for the desk drawer. He got the drawer part-way open as Cole pivoted. Creed was coming up with a pearl-handled revolver, really a lady's gun. A shot

144

from its barrel whistled, crashed into the wall at Cole's back. The hammer of the .44 snapped downward. For the third time a roaring filled the small office. Creed was flung back into his chair, the gun spinning away. In his eyes was reflected the awesome certainty of a man about to die.

"Don't . . . don't kill me, Cantrell . . . please . . ."

Creed gripped his right arm just above the wrist. Blood bubbled through the shirt sleeve. He tried to stand up but his legs suddenly gave way. The whole episode since Byson had come crashing into the office had not taken more than five seconds.

From the street came shouts, sounds of men running toward the office. Cole kicked Byson's gun out of reach. He ran to the window, doubled his tall frame to slip through. He dropped to the alley. At a hard run he dodged around a building, glimpsed men streaming toward the Python office. He veered, found an alley and finally reached a street where he had left the ponies. Just before mounting up, he slapped a hand to his hip pocket where he had stuffed the folded quitclaim deed. It was gone. He'd lost it either while scraping through the tight fit of the window or in the hard run to his ponies. He swore. A wasted day and he hadn't even learned what he had come for: the names of four men. He had a first name, possibly. Doak!

At the moment, with all the shouting and commotion a block away, he knew he had to put miles between himself and Basin City. But he'd make a return visit. Next time E.J. Creed wouldn't be so lucky. . . .

Creed's thoughts were a jumble. Slowly he picked himself up, lips tight from pain. Dazed, he stared down at Byson, out cold on the floor. Creed heard the turmoil out front and knew he had to act. Byson could regain consciousness at any moment and start to babble. Answering questions from a crowd was something Creed didn't need at such a time. For one thing, he was too upset, too much in a state of shock to give straight answers.

On wobbly legs, trailing blood, he made it to the outer office, closing the door at his back. Several men were just bursting in from the street.

"We heard shootin'!" a bearded man panted excitedly.

"Just an accident," Creed managed to say. "If one of you will kindly fetch the doctor . . ."

Creed's calmness, despite his dripping wound, settled them

145

down. If Python wasn't upset about a bullet hole in a man's arm, why should they care? Men began to file out, one of them running for the doctor. Creed had to repeat his story before lurching to the inner office. Byson was sitting up on the floor, a hand pressed to his right cheek that was open to the bone. A corner of the desk had caught him when he plunged to the floor.

Creed stared, white-faced. "If you *had* to butt in, why in hell couldn't you have done it right?" he snarled through his pain.

"I . . . I didn't know anybody was behind the door."

Creed flopped to his chair. While wrapping a silk scarf around the upper arm as a tourniquet, he glared at Byson.

"That goddamn Latigo," Byson moaned.

This only deepened Creed's wrath. "Any man with an ounce of brains would have found a shotgun someplace and blasted through the door."

"My head hurts somethin' awful. . . ."

"So does my arm. One thing I cannot abide is incompetence. Byson, you're a worm. Born to be trampled under somebody's boot heels."

That stung. Byson got shakily to his feet. Blood ran down his narrow jaw.

"I come to Basin City 'cause I figured you'd let me work for you here. Or in some other town . . ."

"Get out of my sight. Jesus Christ, where is that doctor!"

Creed looked relieved when there were hurrying footsteps out front. It was not the doctor, however, but the thin and panting clerk who opened the office door. "I heard there was a shooting. . . ." He looked surprised and a little sick at the sight of blood.

"I sent you to get Doak Lancer!" Creed shouted, and he had. "Why the hell didn't you?"

"I hunted all over, Mr. Creed," the harrassed clerk replied, wringing his hands. "Then I remembered you sent him north. But I went to the Ajax Livery Barn to make sure and the hostler said Mr. Lancer had left town just before dawn."

Creed sagged in his chair. Shock and anger deepened his pallor. "Yes, I did send him," Creed was forced to admit in a more reasonable tone. "It completely slipped my mind. Adams, go see if you can't hurry the doctor."

The clerk, glad to be out of Creed's sight, sped away. Creed noticed that Fred Byson had not moved but still stood on the far side of the desk, dripping blood on the floor. "I told you to get out," Creed said angrily.

146

"Mebby you better listen to what I got to say."

Despite his pain, Creed caught a note in Byson's voice that alerted him. "Go on . . . speak your piece, Byson."

"That young lady out at the Lockwood ranch near Scalplock."

Creed was suddenly wary. "I don't know what you're talking about. Explain."

"I told you about her last time I was here. Well, she's gone, Mr. Creed. Cindy Lou's disappeared."

"For God's sake, how does that concern me?"

"Ed Lewt was askin' questions about her. One day I followed him. Just outa curiosity, you might say."

Creed swallowed. "Pays to be curious sometimes. Continue, Fred."

"I spotted Lewt on a shelf of rock near the ranch house. Right above a path where this gal took a walk every day, so I overheard Lockwood say once in town. Reckon Lewt heard it too. Well, this day Lewt had his rifle with him. He had showed it to me one time when he first hit town. It's high powered an' can knock off a fly's ass at a hundred yards, as he put it."

"Well, that means nothing. . . ."

"She's *disappeared,* Mr. Creed. Gone. Vanished!"

Creed loosened the tourniquet, his lips twitching at the painful though superficial wound. He waited until sure that he had his voice under control before saying, "I don't really know what you're talking about, Fred. But as one of us, of course I expect you to keep your lips sealed about such things. No use in people speculating over what never happened. I'm sorry I lost my temper a minute ago, but that Latigo, that Cantrell . . ." He looked up at the ceiling. First, Sam Stark, the blundering braggart. Now Ed Lewt. Everything so goddamn funny to Lewt. So proud of his damn gold tooth. And so empty-headed he not only talked too much to another empty-head like Byson, but didn't even look around to see who might be prowling his backtrail. If Byson could be believed, that is.

Before he could dwell further on his miseries, the doctor came bustling in. A fat little man with a black medical bag, he peered at Creed and said, "Ah, it seems we've had a bit of an accident."

"Doctor, take care of my friend first, if you will. Fred seems to be in considerable pain."

Byson looked surprised, then turned his head so Creed couldn't see his sly smile. Never in his life had he felt so tall, so powerful. As the doctor swabbed the ugly cut on his cheek, Byson endured the pain by remembering how he had put fear

147

in E.J. Creed, the pompous bastard, just by mentioning Ed Lewt's connection with the missing girl.

He knew that if he kept his head and did nothing foolish, he could be on the Python payroll for some years.

And the matter was settled formally the moment the doctor, after caring for Creed, had departed. The office door was closed to give them privacy. Creed handed over four double eagles which he termed a bonus, then mentioned other financial considerations.

Creed suggested he stay in Basin City until needed elsewhere, which suited Byson just fine. His salary would be forty dollars a week, with twenty dollars extra when he traveled for the company. And in addition there would be a generous bonus from time to time.

Byson considered it loafing money. Basin City offered many attractions where he could spend it. He headed for his favorite saloon.

What was most galling to Creed about this whole slipshod business was having to report in detail to Claudius Max in New York. He dared not try to cover up any of the facts. If Max ever caught him in a lie . . .

He thought of Doak Lancer again. The arm wound throbbed, making him edgy. That goddamn Latigo. It had taken sheer guts for the man to walk into the Python office, Creed had to admit.

"Damn Doak. The son of a bitch took a convenient time to be out of town," Creed muttered aloud, forgetting for the moment it was he who had sent him away.

The day, however, ended with one bright note. Someone had found the Python document in the alley and returned it; the Cantrell quitclaim deed. Creed decided to have it done over again, by another forger. Cantrell hadn't been fooled into thinking it was his father's signature.

When Al Dain and Bill Cutter returned to town at the end of the week, Creed lost his temper again. "Why didn't you kill Cole Cantrell along with his parents!"

"He wasn't there." The scar-faced Cutter was affronted.

"Mr. Max will not tolerate loose ends." Then Creed got hold of himself. "This next job I give you must have no loose ends. None at all."

"What kind of job?" the pockmarked Dain wanted to know.

Creed told them. . . .

A week later Toby Taggart was reading the latest edition of the *Basin City News* that had just arrived in Scalplock by freighter. An obituary caught his eye. It seemed that Fred Byson, formerly of Scalplock, had been killed in the crash of a spring wagon when his team of horses ran away on a mountain road.

"And I figured he was the kind of a weasel to die of a gunshot wound or a knife," Taggart mused, and turned the page to more interesting news.

This concerned a gold strike in a remote mountain area somebody had dubbed El Dorado Gulch.

A tough town like Scalplock was bad enough, but a gold camp was hell's front gate, where human life had about half the value of a rusty horseshoe nail.

Taggart had seen one gold camp, had worn a badge there for a month. He still had nightmares.

21

Theodora couldn't forget last night when Claudius had padded about their bedroom in his bare feet, his obese figure stiff with rage as he used the foulest language in connection with someone named Cole Cantrell.

"That fool Sheridan made him a captain!" Claudius had raged and flung his plump fingers toward the cupids in bas relief on the pale pink ceiling. "Gad, no wonder the war dragged on."

"But the war lasting so long was to your benefit," Theodora pointed out.

"There is a point in any undertaking when one stops making money. Even in war."

He had been unusually violent in their bed. Even in the moment of shuddering completion he uttered the name of the man out West: "Cantrell. . . !"

So in effect she felt almost as if this unknown Cantrell had been fused with her instead of the tyrant she had married. She would have to ask Lorne about the man, when Claudius made his next trip out of town. It happened later in the week.

Theodora Max knew the game she played with Lorne Payne was exceedingly dangerous. But excitement made it worth the risk.

As usual, whenever Claudius left town . . . this time for Philadelphia . . . she patronized her favorite bookstore. Sometimes a connection was made, sometimes not. It depended on circumstances. Lorne was no fool; he took few risks.

149

Claudius had married Theodora four years ago when she was seventeen. Claudius said he loved her. Theodora's father said they needed money. Being married to an obese husband with stumpy legs wasn't as horrible as she had imagined. One newspaper cartoonist had portrayed him in caricature as a tarantula crouched behind a desk and ready to suck the life blood from every living thing within reach.

As she waited in the bookstore, she thought of how Claudius had met her father when making a contribution to the college where the old man was a professor of Roman History. At the time, Max also contributed generously to numerous orphanages. It was done, Theodora was to learn later, to counteract a vile rumor that he was selling munitions not only to Federals but to the Confederates as well.

Throughout the wedding ceremony, one of the most fashionable that could be managed during the dark war period, she kept giving the ponderous bridegroom apprehensive sidelong glances. At the Academy Theodora had learned how the thing between man and woman was accomplished. One of her classmates had even produced forbidden sketches filched from an uncle's library of erotica. So Theodora wondered how she could ever survive such a smother of monstrous weight in the marriage bed. But Claudius Max made adjustments and she was satisfied.

Satisfied until Lorne Payne of the Viking hair and arctic blue eyes, the splendid shoulders, the easy laughter, had joined Python.

At the house one evening Lorne had commented on a statue of Caesar. "Your husband is quite taken with the subject of Rome."

"That's what he and my late father had in common."

"And you live in the splendor of Rome in this grand house."

"When I am alone with my husband I sometimes wear the sheer robes in the style of Roman ladies." She knew Lorne was impressed that she could so casually mention an intimate part of her life with Claudius. "At times my husband pretends I am the Empress Theodora."

"You are certainly beautiful enough."

"He had a crown fashioned for me. I imagine it's quite valuable. Should I ever decide to run away to the Sandwich Islands or far China, I shall be able to live quite well." She laughed to show it was said in jest, and covered her attractive mouth with a fan.

"He's given you jewels by the ton, I expect," Payne said, also laughing.

"Only by the pound," she said lightly.

At that point Claudius waddled over, almost grotesque in evening clothes, brusquely elbowing past a butler and nearly causing the poor man to drop a tray of drinks. Should that have happened, it would have cost the man his job. Claudius never tolerated mistakes except with Theodora.

"Mr. Payne is proving to be my good right hand," Claudius said, the small eyes swinging from her own flushed face to that of the smiling Viking addition to Python.

A week later Claudius was using a bootjack in their bedroom when he suddenly flung it aside. "You remove my boots, Theodora."

As she knelt and started working off one of the polished boots, he spoke to her bowed head. "If I ever suspect you of infidelity, I will make it my business to see that you are unhappy. Extremely so."

It worried her, his roundabout way of making threats when he was not enraged. It was somehow more ominous than if he had come right out and said, "I'd kill you!"

Theodora couldn't help her indiscretions, even though, as Lorne Payne once put it, they were the same as walking barefoot on a greased rope stretched across a canyon filled with upright Roman spears.

Today he came in off the street, jauntily as usual, climbed the short flight of stairs to the loft with its shelves bulging with books. As usual he looked surprised to see her sitting at a small table by the window.

"Good afternoon, Mrs. Max," he said formally with a slight bow. "What a coincidence you being in my favorite bookstore."

Only two other readers were nearby, both older men. Neither looked up from their books.

"Good afternoon, Mr. Payne," Theodora murmured, barely glancing at him. She was scanning a rare volume devoted to Pliny when Lorne surreptitiously slid a key under her gloved hand. Long ago they had decided it would never do for her to have his key permanently. She suspected that Claudius searched her room. Of course Lorne could have left the door to his lodgings unlocked. But he was never quite sure of the timing and an unlocked door invited unwanted visitors. And there was no safe place to hide the key at his hotel.

He selected from a shelf a small volume of Sir Francis Bacon. He held it up for her to see.

She shrugged. "I find him rather dull."

"I've been searching for this volume. My lucky day. Good afternoon, Mrs. Max."

151

She nodded as he trotted off downstairs to pay a clerk for the book. She saw him later on the sidewalk below. He did not look around. It would have been unwise. Her excited eyes followed him until he was lost in the crowd.

She read for another ten minutes. Then she casually returned the volume to a shelf. She told the clerk that perhaps another day the book would be reconsidered. It was quite expensive. The price was six dollars.

She window-shopped on the autumn afternoon, then walked through one of the stores to an alley exit. A block away she entered a brick building by a side door, avoiding a main entrance with its awning and potted plants. A boy in blue livery kept the short and narrow street immaculate with a wide broom. By the time she reached the third floor by a rear stairway her heart was pounding not only from exertion from the steep stairs but also from anticipation. She let herself into the small, tastefully furnished apartment. Removing her hat, she lay down on the bed to wait. A tilted mirror gave her a good view of her fine dark features, glossy hair, lively eyes and a nose her father once said was designed for sniffing disapproval at maids and butlers. When she was growing up they had neither. A professor might be intellectually superior to a blacksmith, her mother would say, but seldom matched his income.

It was over two hours before she heard Lorne Payne's light step on the main staircase. Despite the long wait she was wildly excited; usually he arrived within the half hour.

He let himself into the apartment, looking grim. He said that Lackman had flagged him down on the street. Claudius had not taken the early train to Philadelphia. Lorne was wanted at the office.

"He'll take a later train, thank God," Lorne said, slipping out of his coat. "Has already gone, as a matter of fact," glancing at his watch. "What a day this had been with Claudius steaming about Cole Cantrell, alias Latigo."

"So he has an alias." For some reason it pleased her.

"Cantrell leads a charmed life," he said sourly as he undressed.

"Tell me about him." She was unfastening small pearl buttons at the side of her dress.

"Cantrell is a cold-blooded killer. He shot a man to death in a saloon and kidnaped the town marshal. Fortunately, the marshal got away from him. A large posse couldn't even run Cantrell to ground."

She should have been shocked. Instead she was fascinated.

"Cole Cantrell," she murmured, dropping her last petticoat. "An easy name to say."

"Saying his name sticks in my throat."

"I wonder what he looks like."

"Personable enough, so they say. Half Indian." Lorne Payne swore. "His latest depredation was to walk boldly into our Basin City office and shoot our man Creed in the arm."

"He must have buccaneer blood in his veins."

When Lorne came to her, he seemed pleased by the reaction. "I say one thing, the long wait has made you even more exciting."

Smiling to herself, she settled down to enjoy. But for some reason the physique that usually intrigued her, now touched by strips of sunlight through a slight gap in the drapes, seemed overshadowed by that man of mystery halfway across the continent.

Usually their meetings in the large Victorian bed were tumultuous. But today she noticed a certain reserve in Lorne. Finally she collapsed prettily in his arms and idly ran a forefinger through the tawny forest on his chest.

"You're worried about that Latigo, Lorne."

He rolled to an elbow, his eyes brooding. "When things don't go right for your husband, when someone thwarts him in even a minor way, he can be a tyrant."

"Oh, yes," she agreed with a strained little laugh.

She urged him to give her details and he did, speaking of the times her husband had erupted in fury because of the delay caused originally by Cantrell's father. "An old trapper who stirred up a handful of neighbors. And when Claudius learned that the son was proving as great a threat as the late father, he flew into one of his towering rages."

"Cantrell's late father? What happened to the man?"

Lorne hesitated, then said, "Massacred by Indians. Both he and the wife, Cantrell's mother."

"How awful. But why isn't Cantrell going after those Indians," she asked thoughtfully, "instead of making trouble for Claudius?"

"He thinks we had a hand in the dirty business. . . . We didn't, of course," he added quickly.

"Tell me the truth, Lorne. Did Claudius hire someone to kill Cantrell's parents?"

His eyes suddenly hardened. "Dangerous enough to even think such a thing. To speak of it is sheer madness."

"I admire anyone who has the nerve to defy something as formidable as Python," she murmured and punctuated it by finding his lips with hers. What had first excited her about

153

Lorne was the fact that he had the cold nerve to make a cuckold out of Claudius.

Lorne broke away from her lips. "Don't admire an idiot like Cole Cantrell. And only an idiot would defy Python."

She got him to tell her about the right-of-way through Beaver Valley and its importance to the railroad, and about Cole Cantrell, the war hero whose desire for revenge was now interfering with Python's great plans.

"What will happen to Cole Cantrell now?" she asked

"Let's not think about it."

He swung long bare legs over the edge of the bed and reached for his clothes. "Let's forget we even had this discussion."

"Discussion you call it now, our meetings in your bedroom?" She was teasing him, but with it a faint anger.

He buttoned his shirt. "Forget the names I mentioned," he said harshly. "I mean it, Theodora. I shouldn't have talked so much." He touched her chin. "You are a delightful adjunct to Python, but must have no share of its problems." He smiled.

"Don't have Cole Cantrell killed."

Her tone surprised him. His face darkened. "Damn it, Theodora, this is not woman's business!"

"Remember I would never have known these details about Cole Cantrell if you hadn't told me."

Although she spoke innocently he studied her eyes for a long searching moment. "Don't build fantasies around a man you haven't even met. Who will no doubt end up on the gallows . . ."

"You'll see to that, I suppose."

"Careful, Theodora," he warned.

Something in his eyes startled her, but she was determined to show no fear. Calmly she climbed out of bed, strolled across the room to the chair where she had carelessly flung her clothing. She felt his eyes on her back. She stood there, taking her time to pick up a camisole and smooth it carefully.

He said in a taut voice, "I find a sudden renewal of interest in things other than Python." He gave his schoolboy laugh. "Our bed awaits."

She faced him, holding the camisole over her breasts. "But we've wasted so much time, Lorne. And there are things I have to do." It pleased her almost as much to refuse him as it had earlier to accept his attentions.

He looked petulant. "You're angry."

"Slightly, that you consider me a fool."

When he reached out from the bed to try and pull her into his arms, she danced aside. "Damn it, will you stand still?"

154

"Python murdered those Cantrells, that man and his wife. And you plan to do the same to the son."

For a moment he made no reply, but sat on the edge of the bed like stone. She almost wished she hadn't spoken so rashly, but it was too late now. Her chin lifted defiantly.

"Claudius and I get along because we're alike," he said in the coldest voice he had ever used with her. "He saw in me a man equally as ruthless, equally willing to take risks. Don't press me, Theodora. Any more than you'd dare press Claudius."

"You threaten me?"

"Theodora, you've spoiled the day."

She dressed quickly and hurried down the rear stairs and out into the alleyway. As she walked away she felt his eyes on her from the third floor window. It would be unwise to call attention to herself by waving to him. Even if it weren't, she would not give him that satisfaction.

He would have to make the first move if they were ever to resume their relationship. On that point she was adamant.

22 Cole Cantrell's second visit to Basin City was under cover of darkness. He knew the risk, but he needed information. And it was long overdue. This time he looked the place over more carefully than on the previous visit. That time he had been interested only in Python's office and had paid little attention to anything else. But now in the wan glow of an early moon he saw the framework of numerous buildings under construction, the loads of freshly milled lumber dumped on vacant lots. The sight of surveying stakes reminded him of the ones on the charred soil of the Cantrell homestead. It was a minute before he could regain control.

Keeping to back streets and alleyways he headed toward a saloon he had seen on the edge of town. With luck it might be a source of information. He needed some names.

Beyond the saloon he saw a large cook fire on graded land. The nearest building was a block away and so new its sign was not even hung, but rested on end against the building. Firelight was reflected on three high-wheeled freight wagons and bull teams tethered nearby.

He sniffed a strong aroma of boiled pork and cabbage. Cole

dismounted, trailed the reins of both ponies. He looked carefully around but saw no one but the eight or nine men who lounged around the fire. One of them with a great slope of belly got up to sample the contents of a pot hanging from a tripod over the cook fire.

In the distance someone was banging on a piano. A horse neighed and the feeding bull teams snorted and snuffled.

"Howdy," Cole said, walking toward the fire. Men lounging on the ground, some with their backs to wagon wheels, were passing around a jug. They looked up, grew silent.

"Hiya," a couple of them responded in a reserved way.

"If you fellas come through here often maybe you could help me," Cole said.

The fat man at the kettle said, "Help you how?"

"Lookin' for a redheaded hombre used to run with Sam Stark."

"Stark got kilt up at Scalplock," one of them said, jerking a thumb in that direction.

"Yeah, I did hear about him bein' done in," Cole said. He tried to remember the name Creed had shouted that day in his office. "I had this redhead's name written down, but lost it. Figured to find out from Stark. It was Loke or Doak, something like that."

"Why you want this . . . this redhead anyhow?" The fat man holding a long-handled spoon was cautious.

"Got a message . . . from a lady. Things happened mighty fast and I had to leave town in a hurry. The lady scribbled his name, but like I said, I lost it. . . ."

The fat man finally laughed, which seemed to relieve tension in the others. "Stark worked for Python. They can tell you. Office about four blocks from here."

A thin, bearded man resting the back of his head against a wheel hub, spoke to the fat man. "Oh, hell, Herbie, go ahead an' tell him."

Herbie wasn't to be swayed; there was a matter of frontier ethics involved. A man did not give out information unless there was a good reason. "Who's lookin' for this redhead besides you?" he asked Cole.

"The lady in question . . . well, she wanted me to warn him about somebody."

"Her husband?"

"You could say that." Cole's grin was faint in the firelight.

The bearded one resting against the wheel hub hooted with laughter. "Her husband's the one better do the worryin', not that cold-eyed son of a bitch Doak Lancer."

Doak Lancer. The name was written in fire across Cole's brain. Two down, three to go.

"Any idea where I can find this Lancer?"

"He ain't in town." He pointed at a thin man by the fire. "Slim there with the jug owes him money from a game last time we was through here. We made sure Lancer wasn't around. But if he was, Slim figured to stay hid under a tarp till we pulled out tomorrow."

Herbie's belly jiggled from his laughter; the others joined in.

Cole laughed with them. He needed more names, but how to get them without arousing suspicion?

He innocently mentioned the contents of the cook pot. "Smells good, Herbie." Cole made a great show of sniffing the aroma.

Being the kind of men they were, he was invited to share. Before he had finished a tin plate of greasy cabbage and shreds of pork, he learned what he wanted: the names of three men who had ridden with the late Sam Stark—Ed Lewt, Bill Cutter and Al Dain. It was remarkable when they drunkenly supplied descriptions of the trio how they matched up with those Dark Star had given him.

"Lancer's only been ridin' with 'em a short spell," Slim offered. "Bastard slicked me with a pair of Spanish dice last time I came through. Dice that'd only roll *his* way, I swear. Then he had the guts to say he'd cut his initials on my belly if I didn't pay up next time I come through. By gad I almost told Herbie that I wouldn't make the trip up here this time even if I did have a full load an' it'd mean losin' money."

Cole offered to pay for his meal. But it was only a gesture because his offer was refused as he knew it would be.

He got up, brushed off the seat of his pants, then casually mentioned Helen, although he called her Cindy Lou, which name he supposed she'd be using by now. "Heard she might've hitched a ride with a freight outfit outa Scalplock." He described her.

"We'd never have that much luck," Slim said with a screech of laughter. "Only kind ever wants to hitch with us an' we bed down under the wagon is snaggle-toothed an' so skinny it'd take two tries afore she could even throw a shadow."

Cole left them to their peals of laughter that competed with the banging piano on another street. The freighters and their swampers were already rolling up in blankets. Part of their cargo they had unloaded in Basin City. Tomorrow they would head into the mountains with the remainder, to a boom town called El Dorado Gulch where a prospector with a lucky toe had kicked at a stone which turned out to be a gold nugget.

When Cole bedded down that night under clouds that partially obscured moon and stars, he spoke the names aloud so they would never be forgotten. Ed Lewt, Bill Cutter, Al Dain and Doak Lancer.

Meanwhile, Creed complained by telegraph that he needed more men. "Do with what you have for the present," Claudius Max shot back.

There was trouble for Python. *Amison's Weekly* had published a story questioning the rights of the railroads crossing the Indian's hunting grounds.

Creed was called to Omaha for a conference. A name kept coming up, Cole Latigo Cantrell. . . .

23 Roger Amison, nephew of the owner of the popular weekly, was in his early twenties, quite thin and suffering from respiratory problems. He was a fine journalist and an excellent artist whose subject was life in the postwar West. Young Amison's talents had helped boost the weekly's circulation. His uncle, who had agreed to let him travel about the West with a horse and pack mule, was surprised and delighted. Eastern readers seemed fascinated by the artist-reporter's stories of Indian life, his sketches of chiefs, of battles, Equally popular were those he did on the outlaws encountered during his travels across the frontier.

Cole tracked him to a camp site north of the Yellowstone. He and young Amison hit it off immediately. Over a camp fire Cole related the story of the Beaver Valley massacre. Roger Amison listened grimly and made notes and sketches.

The story that appeared in *Amison's Weekly* proved to be a sensation, although Python denied any connection with the tragedy. According to Python, Badger Cantrell had been paid for his land in gold. Renegade Indians had learned of it and had committed the vicious crimes for which others were blamed. The Python spokesman, Lorne Payne, was indignant at the charge.

Even before the story appeared, the vengeance trail had come to a sudden dead end. Creed had dropped from sight, replaced in Basin City by a man named Cummings, who dealt not in guns but columns of figures. The four survivors of Sam Stark's band of killers disappeared. One rumor claimed they had been sent to Mexico to get them out of the public eye.

The white roofs of another high country winter had given way to melting snows under a spring sun. Cole was forced to take a job, riding shotgun for Intermountain Stage Lines, but he kept his eyes and ears open. Still there was no trace of the four killers.

During one of his visits to the Crow camp, Dark Star gazed into her medicine fire.

"The men you seek will be back before another winter," she said solemnly in Crow. Cole smiled grimly. Dark Star had always been right so far.

That was when he exchanged his two Indian ponies for the stalwart Trooper.

Cole had a date to meet Roger Amison at a mountain trading post when spring thaws finally cleared the roads.

Roger Amison was talented with a sketch pad and the written word, but foolish in some ways. He was, after all, a tenderfoot. He risked traveling a mountain pass in deep snows where avalanches were frequent. Although warned by mountain men, he refused to listen.

Some freighters saw the tumbling mass of snow crash down on Roger Amison, burying horse and pack mule. They tried to dig him out, but were too late.

During those months as shotgun guard, Cole kept his ear to the ground. But he heard nothing of the four men. Three times on his job he thwarted would-be holdup men. The fourth time his stage coach was attacked he had been forced to kill a man. It sickened him. Cole had had enough of the job.

Mounted on his black war horse, he rode south. At a trading post he had news of Python. The trail that had turned cold over so many months was now hot again. . . .

Jeremy Van Horn had come out from Ohio to get rich. In Basin City he had acquired two mules, one for riding, which he named Stonewall, and the other to be used as a pack animal. This one he had not bothered to name because of its unpredictable temper. Noting his narrow-brimmed hat and black suit, a mule trader in Basin City had remarked, "The dude's dressed like an undertaker, but bet he ain't even half as smart as one."

The remark made within Van Horn's hearing had not upset him. He was used to jibes.

159

On this early afternoon he decided to make camp. A good chance to rest up before reaching his destination, El Dorado Gulch. A boom town drawing the sum total of greed and depravity in man, where human life had less value than the useless rubble found in the bottom of a gold pan.

So he had been told by a hotel clerk in Basin City who was subtly urging him, in so many words, not to try his luck in such a raw frontier settlement.

Van Horn wasn't easily swayed. He outfitted himself and started out. Aside from a small band of Indians who looked him over curiously, he met few people. The fact that the Indians made no attempt to do him harm bolstered his philosophy that if a man offered friendship he need have no fear.

On this afternoon he erected his ridgepole tent, pleased that he was proficient at last in assembling the confusing pack of canvas, poles and guy ropes.

In his larder was enough meat and dried vegetables to make a stew. He got a fire going, then breathed in the clear mountain air, enjoying magnificent vistas of craggy peaks, forested slopes and in the far distance a dot of blue he knew to be a lake.

With the stew bubbling away, he walked to where his mules had been staked out beside a creek flowing down between tall trees. Stonewall nuzzled his arm. The other mule, cropping short grass, did not look up. The creek made a pleasant sound. He spoke aloud to Stonewall.

"A beautiful country but your saddle has put a shine on the seat of my pants. At a place where they are quite thin, by the way." Van Horn laughed delightedly when Stonewall bobbed his head as if in complete agreement. Van Horn rambled on, explaining to the mule his hopes for a bright future.

It was the voice that alerted Cole. He was some distance above Van Horn's camp on a trail that angled down from higher country. He reined in, frowning because the conversation he overheard seemed one-sided.

Out of curiosity Cole stood up in the stirrups to peer down through the trees. He saw the slender figure in the town hat and black suit. No wonder he had heard only one voice.

"Eat hearty, Stonewall," the young man was saying. "By this time tomorrow we'll be in El Dorado Gulch and on our way to a fortune in gold." Van Horn laughed, slapping his leg. "Not impressed, eh? Well, I suppose great wealth does mean more to men than to a mule."

Cole shook his head, thinking, the poor damn fool. He thought of younger Roger Amison who had refused to accept a warning about a possible avalanche. Roger was dead. In Roger's memory Cole decided to make an attempt to advise this young man. He started to rein Trooper from the trail so he could descend through the thick pines to the camp below.

A sound of horses and voices caused him to pull up.

Two men rode from behind a large outcropping covered with lichen. Van Horn greeted the pair pleasantly, eyeglasses catching sunlight.

They dismounted. One of them wore a slouch hat. He was big, with a beard that covered the lower half of a long bony face.

"My camp is yours, as the Spanish say," Van Horn said, after introducing himself.

The bearded man said, "You travelin' alone?"

"Y . . . yes . . ."

"Take a look, Monk, an' make sure."

Monk did and reported the tent was empty. Monk, who had stringy yellow hair, laughed and pointed at the fire. "What you got cookin' in the pot?"

"Stew," Van Horn reported nervously.

"Ain't only a cook but a gold miner," said the black-bearded man, jerking a thumb at gear piled beside the tent. "Mebby we oughta sell him that salted mine. . . ."

"Easier way than that Petey." Monk smiled and drew a large revolver. "What you got under that shirt, dude?"

"Why . . . why nothing at all."

"Either you're fat around the middle," Petey Grimm said, "or you got a money belt." He gestured with a long-barreled .45.

"Take a look, Monk."

Monk Allenby holstered his gun and hurried to reach under Van Horn's shirt. "A money belt," Monk said happily.

"Please, that's every dollar I have in the world. . . ."

Petey Grimm stepped close and touched Van Horn on the chin with the snout of his .45. "Do you give us the belt? Or do we take it?"

Cole couldn't hear the rest of it because the two mules started braying energetically. As he eased his Henry rifle from its saddle scabbard, he wondered if it was possible to take a hand in the business below without endangering Van Horn's life.

Monk untied the money belt from a trembling Van Horn, who made feeble protests. Monk peered into the belt. "Must be a coupla thousand in gold coins," Monk said to his partner.

"My life savings," Van Horn cried.

"Life savings you won't need." Monk's voice hardened. "You done about all the livin' you're gonna do."

161

Grimm grinned through his beard. "Hate to kill a man while he's standin' up. Get on your knees, tenderfoot!"

"This is . . . is inhuman!" Van Horn protested.

Monk shoved him to his knees. "We need your money. And you've seen our faces."

One moment the bearded Grimm was cocking his gun, aiming it at the terrified Van Horn. In the next instant the gun was ripped from his fingers. A rifle crashed from above. Grimm screamed.

Monk spun around, facing into the thick trees above the camp. Flinging aside the money belt, he made a desperate grab for his gun.

Cole's voice cracked like a bullwhip. "Hold it!"

Monk froze as Cole rode into view on a big black horse.

"Seems I interrupted cold-blooded murder," Cole snapped.

"We wasn't gonna kill him," Monk protested, eyeing the rifle. "Only funnin'. Ain't that right, Petey?"

Grimm was massaging the tips of his bruised fingers. "Yeah," he managed to get out. His gun lay in the dirt a few feet away. Van Horn was rigid, still in a kneeling position.

"We . . . we was next gonna make him dance," Monk said, showing large teeth in a strained smile, "then we'd be on our way."

"With his money belt," Cole broke in. "Ease out your gun and let it fall." Monk did as he was told.

Then both men were ordered to turn their backs. Cole told Van Horn to get behind them. "You feel a gun under a shirt, you take it. If either one of 'em tries to grab you, he's dead."

Spoken so calmly it was more of a threat than if Cole had shouted it.

There were no hideout weapons, Van Horn reported in a trembling voice. Cole told him to get the rifles from the saddle boots and to make sure there were no weapons in the saddlebags.

An ashen Van Horn found nothing but the rifles which he dropped beside the discarded revolvers. Cole smiled at the earnest young face that was slowly regaining color. Then he turned on the pair of cutthroats.

"Lucky for you hombres I feel generous today," Cole snapped. "Get out and you can go on living."

"That ain't much of an offer," the bearded Grimm said angrily.

"But it's the only one we got," Monk cut in. "Let's clear out while we can."

Grimm took a step toward the guns in the dirt; metal work

gleamed dully in the sunlight. Stonewall the mule seemed interested. The other mule continued to crop grass as if scornful of humans who spent most of their waking hours trying to cheat or murder each other.

"Far enough," Cole warned when Grimm took another step toward the weapons.

"You can't turn us loose without guns," Grimm protested. He cradled the bruised fingers in his left hand.

"You run into trouble, use your teeth." Cole gave them a scornful glance. "I see either one of you around here again, I guarantee you'll stay . . . permanently. Now get out!"

As the two men rode away, Van Horn picked up his money belt. "I . . . I don't know how to thank you, mister. . . ."

"I'm called Latigo."

Van Horn was finally able to introduce himself. He said he was from an Ohio village known as Caleb Crossing.

Cole swung down. "So you're heading for the goldfields."

"How did you know?" the young man asked in surprise.

"It's easy." Cole pointed at the gear beside the tent. "Your pickax and shovel and gold pan are all shiny and new. So is your confidence." Then he laughed softly. "Got to confess I overheard you talking to your mule about El Dorado Gulch."

Van Horn was cleaning his glasses on his shirt, apparently embarrassed that he had been overheard. "I guess you think I'm crazy, talking to Stonewall."

"I talk to my own horse," Cole admitted and gave Trooper an affectionate pat on the neck.

Van Horn hooked on his glasses, saying he had been about to eat. "Then those two ruffians came along. Will you join me, Latigo?"

"You won't have to ask me twice." Cole looped the reins around the saddle horn so Trooper could wander to the grass and water. Cole complimmented Van Horn on the savory stew.

"My mother taught me to cook. When she died, I was footloose. Was in Basin City when I heard about the gold strike. I listened to all the wild talk, then decided if others could get rich overnight, so could I."

"That's about it, mostly talk," Cole pointed out.

When the meal was finished, Van Horn said awkwardly, "I don't know quite how to put this . . . but would you consider traveling with me to El Dorado Gulch? I'd pay you, of course."

"You mean as a bodyguard?"

"I feel it might be wise."

"You could use one, Jeremy, that I've got to admit." Cole

163

smiled. "I'll ride with you. Free. Just in case we run into those two hornets. After all, it was me who stirred up their nest."

"Thank God you did."

As they rode toward the boom town Cole couldn't help but pity the young Van Horn with his bright dreams of making a gold strike. How easily Van Horn could be ground under the boot heels of such as the pair he had encountered today. But Cole knew he could not live a man's life for him. The least that could be done was to see him safely to El Dorado Gulch. From there on Van Horn would be on his own. The realities of life in a gold camp would become apparent all too soon.

After Cole had dropped the captured weapons into a deep canyon, Van Horn said, "How can I ever repay you for what you did today?"

Cole gave a brief account of the tragedy at Beaver Valley. Van Horn was shocked.

"You be my eyes and ears in El Dorado," Cole suggested; it would make the young man think he was repaying the favor, and could do no harm. He named the four men he had sought for so long. "Next time I come through, you can tell me if you've heard of these men."

Van Horn wanted to write the names down, but Cole didn't think that was such a good idea.

"Just remember them. It's enough." Cole looked at the eager face. "And keep the names under your hat. Also the fact that you ran into me."

"I'll do anything you ask, of course." Then Van Horn frowned. "But if I'm going to stake out a claim, will you be able to find me?"

"Don't worry about it," Cole assured him. A pilgrim wearing an abbreviated stovepipe hat, eyeglasses and a shiny black suit wouldn't be too hard to find.

Van Horn was disappointed in his first glimpse of El Dorado Gulch spread out below. Buildings of unpainted lumber had been roughly thrown together. Some of the establishments were under canvas until permanent structures could be erected.

"Everything looks so . . . so temporary," Van Horn said.

"Most of these camps last as long as the ore holds out. Then everybody moves on to the next strike . . . and the next."

Everywhere was activity as they descended to the rutted main street that was in reality the road. Carpenters scurried about, drays creaked with heavy loads. In the center of the sprawling camp was a tent larger than most. Two girls wearing too much lip rouge stood in the entrance and beckoned.

"Hey, you handsome fellas, we'll show you a time. Come on in, 'fore the rush starts . . ."

Van Horn looked back at them. "I guess those are what my mother used to call fallen women."

Cole was thinking of Helen. He had to resist an urge to go storming into the tent to see if by chance she might be there. But the chances of locating her in a boom town like this was about as likely as finding a flyspeck in a sandpile.

"Cindy Lou," Cole said under his breath, "you poor sweet fool."

"That big tent seems to depress you," said an observant Jeremy Horn.

"Didn't even notice it," Cole said with a shrug. He reined in. "I'll be leaving you now. Remember one thing, Jeremy. Everything here is temporary . . . including human life."

"Thanks to you, I still have mine. I'll be looking forward to your next visit."

Cole wished the young man well, then rode away. He wondered how long Van Horn's eagerness would survive. A shame he hadn't stayed in Ohio.

Cole hurried into the mountains, wanting to cover as much distance as possible before nightfall. Behind him, the raucous sounds of the gold camp gradually faded. How he would welcome the solitude of the high country.

24

Jeremy Van Horn was elated to have found a true friend in the big dark stranger who had chosen him to be his eyes and ears in El Dorado Gulch.

When he turned over a list of needed supplies to a bald storekeeper, he received his first shock.

The merchant read the list aloud, shaking his head. "Dried apples, potatoes, eggs, tea, tinned fruit, flour." He looked across his counter and instantly read the label of his customer, greenhorn. "I've only got a few items in stock. The rest, well . . . don't be surprised at the prices."

"I can pay for what I order," Van Horn assured him heartily.

Van Horn's jaw dropped when the storekeeper quoted prices: sugar, two dollars a pound; dried apples, a dollar a pound; tea, three dollars. "And there ain't no potatoes or eggs in town."

"A man could starve."

"The trick, my young friend, is to strike it rich *before* you starve."

Gunfire erupted out in the street. But the storekeeper barely noticed. "The boys better be careful with them bullets," he said as he went on filling Van Horn's order. "Somebody end up dead, and the vigilantes will be out."

Van Horn, shuddering, had barely recovered from all the racket and the dire threat of vigilantes when he saw a rather large animal nose around some tinned goods on a shelf. At first Van Horn thought it was a cat because of its size. But seeing the beady eyes, he realized what it was. "A rat," he cried.

"Another reason for high prices," the man said with a shrug. "Town's crawlin' with them. What they don't eat, they destroy."

When Van Horn paid his bill, looking ill at the amount, the merchant said, "I come up here like you to get rich, but in a different way. I'd almost feel sorry for you, stranger, if I wasn't so busy feelin' sorry for myself."

"I . . . I had no idea it was like this. People in Basin City said there was gold you could practically pick up off the streets."

"Too many fellas got big mouths they forget to keep shut. There's gold here, sure. Some of the boys are makin' it big. A few good claims, but damn few." He went on to explain that isolation was what made living so expensive. Everything had to be freighted in by wagon over dangerous passes that often were blocked by snow or rock slides.

After two weeks, Van Horn's disillusionment deepened. His money dwindled. Each day he prowled the creeks where men panned gold and fought their neighbors. Back in the hills other men burrowed into the ground like animals, seeking the precious ore.

But he found no claims that he could stake or buy.

Claim jumping had diminished, he learned, because town limits had been extended clear to Cougar Canyon. The word "vigilante" had a sobering effect.

On one of his futile excursions into the hills, three men saw him through a screen of bush. "That's him, all right," Petey Grimm snarled.

Monk Allenby agreed. "He cost us our guns."

Their companion was shorter, with a black mustache, rather elegantly dressed in a narrow-brimmed hat and frock coat. Pockets of a checkered vest were weighted on one side with a gold watch, on the other with a two-shot derringer. His current name was Slate Grayson, which meant nothing. He changed names whenever he and the other two moved from camp to camp.

"You say he's wearing a money belt," Grayson mused as Van Horn, looking forlorn astride a mule, rode down a canyon.

"Fulla gold coins it is," Grimm snapped. "I'm gonna get my hands on a gun . . ."

Grayson held up a hand with manicured nails. He reminded both men of the new menace in these outskirts of El Dorado Gulch. "Let a little blood flow and a man is liable to get his neck stretched."

"We can do it," said Monk Allenby with the stringy yellow hair, "then head for Arizona."

"We do it my way, not yours," Grayson said firmly. Petey and Monk were getting hard to handle; it was his last association with the murderous duo, although they were not aware of it. Trying to rob, then murder, the pale greenhorn now disappearing up the canyon, had been not only foolish, but risky. He told them so.

"I catch me that son of a bitch shot a gun outa my hand," Grimm said through his teeth, "an' I'll blow out his backbone."

Grayson calmed both men down, told them to keep out of town and remain in the vicinity of what he called their "mine."

Grayson intended to use what he considered to be his considerable talents to extract money bloodlessly from the tenderfoot. Then it was time to get out. Even the thought of vigilantes chilled the back of his neck.

Van Horn was standing before the narrow two-story building that passed for a hotel, a picture of dejection. Earlier in the week someone had stolen his tent and other gear. He soon learned that stabling his mules was almost as expensive as rent for the hotel room he had been forced to take. Today he had sold his mules.

"You look like a gold seeker, my young friend."

Van Horn turned at sound of the suave voice. "Well, I did come here with that intention."

The well-dressed gentleman introduced himself as Slate Grayson, offered a firm handshake and a warm smile. He said he was a claim agent and would be more than willing to assist in any way.

Van Horn told him how long he had been searching for a good claim. "They've all been taken and nobody wants to sell."

"This might be your lucky day, my young friend." Grayson drew Van Horn across the crowded walk and to a quiet spot

167

by a saddle shop. He spoke confidentially of how Van Horn reminded him of a favorite nephew and how much he would like to help out a young man who was finding life a hardship in the boom camp.

"I happen to know of an excellent claim," Grayson said quietly. "Came on the market just this morning."

Van Horn, remembering Latigo's advice, was on his guard. Still, the idea of working his own claim at long last quickened his heartbeat. Passersby jostled them, wagons rattled up and down the canyon. Where it was shadowed, iron wheel rims struck sparks on stones. Mule drivers cursed and shouted. Whips cracked. From the big tent across the street came sounds of a concertina accompanying a girl with a thin but rather pleasing voice, who sang of Mollie and home. One of the girls in the entrance, posted to entice customers, had tears running down her rouged cheeks.

"Why would anybody want to sell a good claim?" Van Horn asked skeptically.

Grayson explained that the seller was elderly and in poor health. "He asked me to find some upright young man as buyer."

"Poor health? In what way?"

"The altitude is too much for him. He wants to return to the Middle West."

"I'm from Ohio myself."

"Well, well, you and I used to be practically neighbors then." Grayson groped for the name of a state adjoining Ohio, but couldn't think of one. He covered it quickly by saying, "Riches mean nothing if a man hasn't got his health. That's what my elderly friend realizes, believe me. Why not have a drink with me, Jeremy?"

"I'll have a glass of beer."

At a crowded saloon Grayson mentioned that Van Horn had seemed interested in the big tent. "I happen to know the madam. I could introduce you and she'd see that you were matched with one of her proper young ladies. . . ."

Van Horn's face turned crimson. "I . . . I couldn't do that, Not unless I was married." He gulped beer to cover his confusion.

"My feelings exactly, Jeremy. But I was intrigued by that girl we heard singing. Rather plaintive, didn't you think?"

"I noticed one of the girls trying to wipe away tears."

"Ah, yes, and I rather imagine that inside there were few dry eyes among the gentlemen present. Any mention of home in such isolation as El Dorado Gulch is bound to touch the heartstrings."

"My home is here," Jeremy Van Horn said firmly. "I'll

never go back to Ohio. Tell me more about the gold claim."

Grayson didn't have to be urged. He spoke confidentially in the jam of men at the bar. Every deal table was occupied. "My elderly friend is most anxious to sell his claim, but it would take cash."

"I have a little under a thousand dollars left," Van Horn said in a dismal voice. "Money goes so fast here."

"But with a good claim, a man can recoup that quickly." Grayson snapped his fingers. "My friend is asking . . . nine hundred dollars."

"That would only leave me fifty dollars. . . ."

"Just leave the matter in my hands. And don't mention this to anyone. I can tell you, if word gets out about this claim, someone will double the price. I want you to have it because you remind me so much of my younger brother . . . my young nephew, I mean. I do consider the lad a brother."

They shook hands and agreed to meet in front of the hotel the following morning.

Grayson rode a mile out of town to what he called his diggings, a tunnel in the side of a hill. He carried a shotgun and some gold samples in a small leather bag. Petey Grimm and Monk Allenby were waiting for him impatiently.

They scattered the ore samples on the floor of the tunnel and Grayson fired the rest from a shotgun into a special section of the wall. Everything could easily be recovered once the transaction was completed.

"So the greenhorn's gonna buy this claim," Grimm said, grinning through his beard.

"How many times we sold it?" Allenby chuckled.

"That was BV, don't forget," Grayson said, cocking an eyebrow.

"What the hell's BV?" they wanted to know.

"Before vigilantes. Soon's we peddle this hole in the hill for the last time, we'll head for Arizona." Grayson's destination was north, but he didn't let on. It was time to part company with such irresponsible ruffians.

"I'd rather kill him for his money," Grimm said sourly. "Cost us some good guns, he did. . . ."

"A man's body weight at the end of a rope is said to stretch the neck three to four inches," Grayson said ominously. "Don't be so anxious to test the theory, Petey."

An hour later Grayson found Van Horn in town and gave him the good news. His elderly friend had agreed to sell for nine hundred dollars cash. "At first he insisted on a thousand, but when I explained your circumstances, he reluctantly agreed to lower his price. Naturally I assume you'll want an assay on samples taken from the mine before you make up your mind."

"I was just going to suggest that," Van Horn said, a little surprised.

Grayson beamed. "A man can't be too careful when he's investing hard-earned money."

As they rode out to the mine, Grayson again stressed the need for secrecy. In his eagerness for success at long last, Van Horn didn't think it strange, nor did he wonder why there seemed to be no other claims in the vicinity. Grayson handed Van Horn a pick and suggested he take a few samples from the tunnel wall and pick up any likely looking rubble from the stone floor.

Within the hour they were back in town. It would be two days before an assay could be run, they were told by a harrassed, overworked man. Grayson was agreeable. He had two days to kill before the eastbound stage came through.

On the second day the assayer had good news for Jeremy Van Horn. "Those samples assays out at five hundred and fifty dollars a ton," he said.

"Is that good?"

"Son, you're a rich man," the assayer assured an incredulous Van Horn. "By the way, is this your own strike, or did you purchase a claim?"

"Well, I . . . I'd rather not say."

The assayer sighed. "Just be careful, son. . . ."

But a joyful Van Horn was already bounding out to the street, anxious to conclude the transaction. Grayson was waiting nearby.

"All we need is your signature to make everything legal," Grayson said, smiling. "By the way, how much did the samples assay at?"

Van Horn was all business. "I'd rather wait until our papers are signed."

"I think you're a sly one, Jeremy," Grayson chuckled. "If it weren't for the fact that my elderly friend is so anxious to return to Illinois . . . well, his loss is your gain, as they say." He eyed the bulge of money belt at Van Horn's midriff. "All we need is your cash. Then I'll turn over a deed to the mine."

After the signing, Van Horn put the deed in his pocket. "If there's anything I can do for you, Mr. Grayson," said a grateful Van Horn, "please let me know."

Grayson rode out to the mine where he told his two partners that he wouldn't have Van Horn's money till afternoon.

170

"I suggest you clear out. Wait for me at the junction, about five miles south of Cougar Canyon." He added significantly, "It's out of the vigilante jurisdiction."

Before they could argue, he hurried back to town, threw a few belongings into a carpetbag, then sauntered toward the stagecoach being loaded with passengers. But as he stepped off the boardwalk, he was gripped by the arms and shoved rudely into a narrow passageway between two buildings. He looked up into the cold faces of Grimm and Allenby. Both men were armed.

"Pretty clever, Slate Grayson." Grimm sneered at the name. "Now we'll just take all the money."

Grayson recovered quickly, smiled up into the scowling faces. "We're supposed to meet at the junction. . . ."

"Had a hunch you might try to leave town," Monk Allenby said angrily, "with our money."

"*Your* money?" Grayson managed indignation. "I did all the work."

"Hand it over," Grimm ordered.

"Don't have it with me, boys," Grayson said smoothly. "I'm to meet Van Horn within the hour. . . ."

"Liar!" Allenby jerked the carpetbag from Grayson's grasp.

Grayson took a backward step toward the walk as both men ripped open the bag and eagerly peered inside.

At that moment Jeremy Van Horn was passing the narrow opening between the buildings. Instantly he saw what was happening to Mr. Grayson, who had been so fair in his dealings.

"Mr. Grayson, get away from them. . . ." It died on Van Horn's lips. At that instant he recognized the pair of would-be murderers who had been thwarted by Latigo.

"Help! Help!" Van Horn shouted up and down the street through cupped hands.

Grimm and Allenby spun around. Grimm, with his gun already drawn, fired out of sheer panic. Van Horn cried out, reeled, cumpled. As men, yelling, came at a run, Grayson saw his chance.

"Robbery, robbery!" he roared and at the same time pawed for the derringer in his vest pocket. Allenby's shot drove him back, his mouth sagging open in surprise. A bullet from Grimm's newly acquired pistol caught him in the side. Grayson was knocked back against a building wall. The sounds of gunshots reverberated in the narrow passageway. But by then, Grayson was past all awareness of sound, of anything.

Grimm seized the carpetbag and went pounding up the

171

passageway toward an alley, away from the commotion on the main street. Allenby sprinted after him.

Van Horn had managed to reach a sitting position on the walk. "*Stop them!*" he cried, pointing at the pair lunging away in the narrow opening.

"We'll get 'em!" shouted a man with a rifle.

"Good," Van Horn said weakly and fell back on the walk.

Grimm and Allenby were bottled up in the slot between buildings.

"Stand or you're dead!" somebody shouted. "Throw down your guns!"

Amos Burkett was in a saloon, savoring a whiskey when he heard the gunshots, the shouting. He smiled when men burst in to give him details. He puffed out his chest, finished his whiskey, then walked out with them on his stumpy legs. How rewarding, he thought, that at this moment he was the most important man in El Dorado Gulch. Burkett had held down the local office of Intermountain Stage Lines until lured by the power of a position no one else seemed to want. Heading up the vigilantes earned him a hundred dollars a month. Even more than that, it gave him the delicious right to take a life or spare it. More often than not in the men he condemned he saw some resemblance to one of his eight brothers who had treated him shamefully in his youth.

"Hello, Petey. And Monk." He spoke pleasantly as the crowd formed an aisle so he could reach the two glowering prisoners. "Didn't I warn you boys not two weeks ago what would happen if you were ever foolish enough to commit crimes within our town limits."

Grimm snarled through his beard. "Was that bastard callin' himself Grayson that tried to cheat us. . . ."

"And Mr. Grayson is deceased. Witnesses say you two were responsible." Burkett paused dramatically. "I sentence you to hang."

Grimm and Allenby threatened at first, then wailed and begged.

With their hands tied, Burkett marched them along the main street, a crowd surging in their wake. Saloons were closing up and even the big tent had suspended operations.

Allenby's complexion was a pasty yellow that nearly matched the ends of his stringy hair. "Listen, fellas, it ain't right to do this to us. . . ."

"Not right to murder Mr. Grayson either," Burkett interrupted pleasantly.

"Oh, Jeezus!" Petey Grimm screeched. "We ain't guilty!"

The crowd increased, men running in from side streets as word spread about the double hanging. Even the departure of the stagecoach was delayed so passengers could be a part of the excitement. Some of the girls from the big tent joined the throng, with much joshing from some of the men.

"Hi, Ruby, hi, Kate. You're gonna lose two customers."

Everyone laughed but the condemned who slogged along with dead white faces. As they neared a large tree with a sturdy limb scarred from rope burns, Grimm broke down. He had to be hustled along by the arms. How much the big bastard reminded Burkett of his brother Ben. Burkett's lips curled.

Two nooses dangled from the limb. Under these were two stepladders.

When the condemned were mounted on the ladders, ropes around their necks, Burkett looked up at them. "You are to be an example as to why we no longer condone violence in El Dorado Gulch."

Tears ran down Grimm's cheeks and into his beard. His mouth shook. Burkett was pleased to note a wet spot the size of a saucer at the front of Allenby's trousers.

"Who's to be first?" Burkett asked, looking up with a smile. "You, Mr. Grimm? Or shall it be Mr. Allenby?" Burkett looked around at the banks of expectant faces. How he loved the attention everyone gave him. Even the girls seemed enthralled.

"Make it the yaller-haired one, Mr. Burkett," spoke up one of the onlookers. "I think he's the son of a bitch shot a friend of mine up in the hills."

Burkett nodded. "You heard the verdict, Mr. Allenby. I think hanging you separately makes more of an impact."

Monk Allenby's body trembled so that he was in danger of tumbling from the ladder. Before he could faint dead away and spoil the performance, Burkett jerked aside the ladder. Allenby dangled. Grimm had only a few moments to stare in horror at the lurching body of his friend. A cheer went up when there was nothing under his boot heels but seven feet of space.

25

There was still a fair-sized crowd around the big cottonwood on the creek bank at the edge of town when Cole Cantrell rode in from the west. It had been an unrewarding and frustrating trip into wild country. There had been no sign of the men he sought.

Cole reined in and stared at the two men who hung by their necks from saddle ropes, the heads oddly canted as if they might be listening to what onlookers had to say about them.

Cole recognized the pair who had intended to rob, then murder, Jeremy Van Horn. He got the whole story from an onlooker; Grimm and Allenby had murdered a man named Slate Grayson. Young Van Horn, who had tried to stop them, had suffered a flesh wound.

Cole was about to ride on into town when he heard a voice with a soft Southern drawl. "Ah still don't believe in lynchin'."

Cole turned in the saddle to the well-dressed man who stood a few feet away. "Neither do I," Cole said.

"Heard you say it once before."

Cole frowned at the man, who had a long and aristocratic face, a neatly trimmed mustache and a beard that covered only the chin.

"Heard me say it where?" Cole wanted to know.

"Tag end of the war. Last day of carnage, as it turned out, though we didn't know it then."

"Your face is familiar, but I . . ."

"You saved me from havin' mah neck stretched like those two now danglin'."

Cole snapped his fingers. "Sergeant Burley Quint and his hanging party."

"We enemies blunderin' into each other an' then somebody decidin' we had to try an' blow everybody to kingdom come. Blasted most every tree on that purty slope, we all did, then tried to cut each other up with sabers. Only one tree limb left, an' your sergeant found it, damn his eyes. Ah am Duke Sateen."

Cole smiled, leaned down and shook hands. "Glad you're alive, Sateen."

"Tried to hunt you up to thank you," Sateen said. "But as you know everything was in somewhat of a tangle at war's end. Ah did hear later that you an' that same sergeant fought a bloody fist fight. Ah tell you, suh, the story of that momentous battle traveled south as well as nawth."

"It was a fight," Cole had to agree.

"Ah don't risk mah precious hands on another man's jaw. Use 'em for the cards." Sateen flashed the cynical smile that Cole remembered most about the man. "Had Quint come for me, ah'd have given him a chance to draw, then shot him in the gut."

"I'll never fist fight Quint again, if we ever meet. Hell no. I might not be so lucky next time. Maybe I won't shoot him in the gut, but I guarantee he'll use crutches for a spell."

"May ah buy you a drink, suh?"

"Not now. I heard one of those bastards," jerking a thumb at the dangling pair, "shot a friend of mine, Jeremy Van Horn."

Sateen nodded. "Out of his element in a place like this, that poor young man."

"This is tough country, for certain."

"Some of us made sure he got his money back," Sateen said and told of the salted mine.

"A tenderfoot for sure," Cole said with a shake of his head.

"Ah'm dealin' cards at the Lucky Lady. Don't know how long I'll stay, though. Ah drift around."

"So do I."

Sateen smiled. "Captain Cantrell, known as Latigo. Name's rather famous or infamous, dependin' on which side of the creek you're on. Just don't get yourself hanged over it, suh. Rather a permanent condition." He pointed at the two dead men, then with a jaunty wave of the hand, drifted away.

Cole stabled Trooper, asked questions about Van Horn and learned he was at the hotel.

"Took guts for that young fella to try an' get help," the red-faced hostler said. "Grayson was a no-good thief an' he'd just swindled the young fella."

Cole found Van Horn propped up in bed, looking wan.

"Minute I leave you alone," Cole smiled as they shook hands, "you get into trouble."

"Guess you think I'm pretty much of a fool," Van Horn said when Cole straddled a chair alongside the bed.

"We're all fools at one time or another."

"I've been told how Grayson . . . what do they call it . . . salted the mine. They say he sold it a dozen times."

"They won't sell it again."

"And now they're all dead." Van Horn stared past the bandage on his chest to the worn carpet. "Do you think it was right to hang Grimm and Allenby without a trial?"

"No. I don't believe in vigilantes. . . . But that's all in the past. The important thing now is getting you back to Ohio."

"I'm going to make it right here, Latigo. I'm not going back."

Another man caught up in the bright promise of the western boom towns was Chick Wilson, whom a Tucson newspaper had dubbed the Arizona Kid. This after he had

175

met and downed two notorious gunfighters within a single month. For six of his nineteen years, Chick Wilson had practiced the fast draw. He had a natural gift of lightning in his right hand, plus an uncanny ability for lethal accuracy with a .44. In his only job, helping move cattle from Texas to Arizona, he earned extra money by putting on fast-draw exhibitions. Most men stayed clear of him.

His first human target was a well-known gunfighter, Al Rawson. After a violent argument, they moved to the street before witnesses. Wilson shot Rawson before the latter had touched his weapon. Two weeks later a gun hand named Roy Clade, who had been hiding out in Mexico, heard of the snotty kid who claimed to be the best gun in the territory. Clade decided to end this threat to his reputation as a quick-draw artist once and for all.

Wilson beat him easily, then decided to seek new fields. He drifted north.

Cole happened to witness Wilson's arrival in El Dorado Gulch, just as he was leaving the hotel where he'd been talking with Van Horn. He saw a tall, lanky kid with long arms and slender fingers and an ugly scowl, who swaggered along the walk, forcing others to step aside. He wore a cowman's hat, a faded wool shirt and canvas pants. Seeing the tied-down gun, Cole sized him up instantly. Another cocky kid destined for an early grave. Too bad. Would his kind never learn that there was always somebody with just a shade more gun speed?

Amos Burkett also learned of the new arrival. He had just been angrily chewing over Cole Cantrell's presence in town when word was brought to him that Chick Wilson was at the Lucky Lady bragging about the two men he had killed in Arizona and implying that he had come north to do more of the same.

Burkett was not fool enough to pay an official visit without an escort. Four men were with him, one armed with a shotgun, when he entered the Lucky Lady and walked up to where the new arrival was drinking beer and talking in a loud voice.

"Welcome to El Dorado Gulch," Burkett said up into the scowling young face. "I just want to set down a few rules."

"Who the hell're you?"

In the sudden strained silence, Amos Burkett told him. Wilson shrugged, indicating vigilantes were unimportant. Then Burkett explained about the stout tree limb at the edge of town and how two men had recently jerked their lives away at the ends of ropes. Burkett casually mentioned the others before them.

His quiet, almost jovial way of discussing the details of such executions made an impression on Chick Wilson. He set down his beer bottle on the bartop and gave Burkett his full attention.

When Burkett asked about the men he claimed to have shot, Wilson courteously told him. He neglected certain vital facts, such as Rawson being over forty and with dimming eyesight. And Clade taking on a blast of forty-rod, then stepping directly into the furnace of a Tucson summer. Cheap whiskey and scorching sun reached his brain at the same instant.

"Both fights fair, Mr. Burkett. Done right in the middle of the day, in the street. With half the town lookin' on."

"I will tell you how you are to conduct yourself in this town, Wilson," Burkett said. An idea had taken shape in his mind when through a saloon window he had noticed Cole Cantrell dodging a wagon and horsemen in the street. Burkett went on to explain the conditions of Wilson's stay in El Dorado Gulch. Two men meeting in fair fight before witnesses, whether with guns, knives or whatever, would not be considered murder should one of them succumb. "If you should challenge a man, the showdown is to be in daylight and here in town. No back shooting, no gunning down a man you may be trying to rob. . . ."

"Not me, Mr. Burkett, sure as hell not me."

". . . such as happened to the last pair I personally hanged."

Wilson was relieved that he wouldn't be asked to leave town as Burkett had hinted at first. It had been a long ride through the mountains. He was keyed up and needed some relaxation before moving on. He was thinking of the girls in front of the big tent who had caught his eye. But talk of a rope had been sobering. If some gent was lucky enough to put out his lights with a bullet, bad enough . . . although he doubted that anyone alive could beat him at the draw. But a noose was a chilling alternative.

"I'll do just as you say, Mr. Burkett."

Amos Burkett found himself rather drawn to this cocky kid he had been prepared to escort to the town limits. Wilson was treating him with respect.

Cole entered the saloon and went over to speak to Duke Sateen who sat alone at a deal table in a chair tipped back against the wall, fingers laced behind his dark hair.

"Howdy, cap'n," Sateen drawled. "You come for that drink . . . and a game?"

Cole shook his head and sat down. "You said I did you a favor. Maybe you can do one for me."

"Ah would be delighted."

In a low voice Cole related the murder of his parents, his relentless pursuit of the men responsible. Sateen had read some of it in *Amison's Weekly* and in frontier newspapers. A lot of it gossip blown out of all proportion.

"In all this time, I've only been able to get one of them. Sam Stark."

He mentioned the four survivors—Cutter, Lewt, Dain and Lancer. "If you hear anything about them will you keep it under your hat till I come through here again?"

"Be glad to, cap'n, long as I'm in El Dorado Gulch."

"Jeremy Van Horn is stubborn. I'll probably look in on him again and see if I can't finally persuade him to go home. Where he belongs."

"You run out of trail with those murderers, eh?"

Cole looked grim. "I hear they're one place and when I get there they've pulled out. And nobody seems to know where they've gone. Seems Python is keeping them out of sight." He related his latest futile trip to the west where Python had a work crew, only to find no trace of the men he was after.

"Seems like most everybody in this end of the country comes through El Dorado Gulch sooner or later," said Sateen. "Ah'll be happy to give you any word I have of those scoundrels."

"I'm getting damned impatient." Cole stood up.

"Just don't get careless an' tangle with that banty rooster yonder," Santeen said, indicating Amos Burkett with several men at the bar. "He loves that hang rope."

Cole's lips curled. "I know him. . . ."

Sateen chuckled. "No love lost, eh, cap'n?"

"I'm staying around another day or so to see if I can't talk sense to Jeremy Van Horn. He stay around here and he's liable to get himself shot again."

"Another young fella liable to get himself shot." Sateen pointed at Chick Wilson who was regaling newcomers with stories of his Arizona killings. "But for different reasons. That one's got a mouth wide as El Dorado Gulch."

"I already looked him over," said Cole. "Just a blowhard."

26

Sateen played a few hands of poker with some miners. Finally the braggart voice of Chick Wilson beating on his eardrums became more than just an annoyance. He decided to shut him up, have a little fun to break the monotony of the gold camp, and perhaps at the same time collect a few dollars.

He strolled over to the bar, broke through the circle of men that surrounded Chick Wilson.

"Since you admit to being one of the greatest marksmen of all time," Sateen drawled, "as well as quick-draw artist, why not make a game of it?"

Wilson looked him over and laughed contemptuously. "*You* figure to outgun me?"

Several men joined in Wilson's laughter. Others crowded around, eager to hear what Sateen proposed.

"Come out back an' ah'll toss ten silver dollars into the air, five at a time. You hit nine of 'em, suh, an' you win." Sateen lit a cheroot and looked around at the expectant faces. "Ah say the kid can't do it. Ah'll put up a double eagle. Anybody match me?"

There were several eager takers. A barkeep handled the bets. Eagerly they trooped to a large vacant lot behind the Lucky Lady. Everyone looked forward to the promised entertainment, anything to take their minds off the dullness of hunting for gold.

The sudden influx of humans to the usually empty stretch of land disturbed several rats and families of mice in a pile of boxes and barrels. They went scampering off into the weeds. An exuberant drunk wanted to take potshots, but was cautioned that an innocent bystander might be hit. The hang tree was mentioned. The drunk put away his weapon quickly.

"Ready?" Sateen called to Chick Wilson.

Wilson didn't even bother to look around but seemed amused by the scurrying rats and mice. "Toss them dollars," he said indifferently, his right hand nowhere near the butt of the gun strapped to his thigh.

Sateen said, "Here goes, suh," and tossed the first of the five silver dollars into the air.

Wilson's hand moved so fast that no one even saw the gun clear leather. But an eyewink later it was spitting bullets at the dollars in the air that dully reflected mountain sunlight. He got all five of them. A cheer went up from those who had bet on Wilson. Groans from the losers.

Giving Sateen a cocky grin, Wilson reloaded his gun and holstered it. This time his right hand was scratching his nose when Sateen, frowning, tossed the second batch of silver dollars skyward.

Again he hit all five of the dollars.

Sateen paid off, his gambler's features showing no emotion.

Wilson strolled over. "Next time you want action, send me a man. Like that Latigo."

Sateen bit down on his cheroot. "Better not fool with him, kid."

"I've heard of Latigo. Clear down in Arizona Territory. Read all about that half-breed killer in *Amison's Weekly*."

"Somebody had to tell you. Ah doubt you can even read." Sateen glared at Amos Burkett, whose stumpy legs were just carrying him to the rear door of the Lucky Lady.

"I just might call you out, for insultin' me that way."

Sateen looked around, felt a chill, and knew in his heart he could never break this kid's circle of luck. "Don't be so anxious to kill a man."

"You a friend of that killer Latigo, I reckon."

"Only man he ever killed was in self-defense," Sateen felt obliged to say in defense of his friend.

"Same way with me," Wilson chuckled. "Man steps out into the street an' tries to gun me down. I got to perfect myself. So I blow off his goddamn head."

Sateen winced as a roar of laughter erupted from the remaining onlookers. Captain Cantrell had enough on his shoulders already, Sateen thought, without having to cope with this young idiot. For a fleeting moment he wondered if he could, after all, repay his debt to Cantrell without Burkett and the vigilantes supplying him with a rope collar at the hanging tree. He decided against even trying. After the demonstration today, he knew without a doubt he could never outdraw this young upstart. Viper mean and with an empty head, but talented all the same.

"Latigo was pointed out to me when you an' him was settin' together," Wilson said, leaning close. Most everyone had drifted back to the saloon and Sateen had gathered up his bullet-nicked silver dollars. "Mr. Burkett, he don't like him much," Wilson went on in a low voice. "Told me this here

Latigo is a troublemaker who figures he's a fast gun. Mebby he is. Like to put a little bet on your half-breed friend?"

Sateen gave him a cold look.

Wilson threw back his head and laughed. "You didn't do so good today, Sateen. Thought mebby you'd like a chance to get your money back." When Sateen made no reply but stood jiggling the handful of silver dollars, Wilson said, "Reckon I'll go see me some of them sweeties over at the big tent."

I hope you die from it, you bastard, Sateen thought as Wilson's cocky walk carried him in that direction.

That afternoon Sateen found Cole and warned him, but Cole shrugged it off. His mind was filled with the futile hour spent in trying to persuade Jeremy Van Horn to return to Ohio. Or at least settle in a place like Basin City, which was more civilized than El Dorado Gulch.

"Some men don't belong in this tough country, Sateen," Cole said, after relating his talk with Van Horn.

"Take mah warnin' seriously, cap'n," Sateen urged and went into detail concerning the gun speed of one Chick Wilson.

"Thanks for the warning, Sateen," Cole said with a tight grin, "but if I worried about every hombre who's trying to add my scalp to his belt, I'd have no time for breathing."

Sateen left him on the edge of the walk, having done his best. Several wagons were pulling into the turnaround next to the store. A stiff breeze swept the sky clear of clouds. . . .

She was just reaching into a jar of sweets when, from the store window, she saw his tall figure there on the walk. Cole Cantrell? Her knees almost buckled in surprise. It was Cole, wasn't it?

Her heart beat wildly as she leaned for a better look through the dusty pane of window glass. Yes, the same dark hat, the hawklike nose. It was that big gun at his belt that had frightened her at their first meeting in the mountains.

But Cole had turned out to be the kindest of men. But even so, she hesitated when she saw him there on the walk in El Dorado Gulch. There was so much to explain. She turned cold just thinking of her last day at the Lockwood ranch. She had started for her walk, her legs much stronger. Winnie, the youngest daughter, had wanted to come along, but first just had to get a ball of India rubber she had dropped behind a wagon in the yard.

That was when Helen froze in horror. Up on a ledge some distance beyond the house she saw a man; Newt or Lewt,

181

something like that. He emerged from a screen of brush and was pointing a rifle at the back of Winnie's head.

Helen remembered opening her mouth to scream at him: "I'm the one you want to kill . . . for God's sake, not that girl . . ." But nothing came from her throat, only the sound of her leaping heart.

In that terrible moment the would-be assasin must have realized his mistake, for he disappeared into the brush. Only the fact that she stood to one side of the house was why he had failed to see her. Later she saw him riding away. She complained of a sudden headache, telling a disappointed Winnie that she didn't feel like taking a walk after all.

That afternoon when Mr. Lockwood came in from working cattle, she asked if she could borrow one of the horses to ride into town. Both he and Emma were worried that she wasn't strong enough to handle a horse, but she insisted she felt fine.

Mrs. Lockwood had already mended her dress, furnished new underclothing. But all she had in the way of money was what Cole had given her.

In town she left the horse at the livery barn where Mr. Lockwood could pick it up, then wondered what to do next. If Newt or Lewt saw her here in town, so be it. A quick end to what they thought they had finished that morning under the trees in the mountains. But at least there would no longer be any danger to the Lockwood children or to the Lockwoods themselves, for that matter. Newt or Lewt would kill any of them, if necessary, in order to get to her and silence her.

She debated. Should she steal a horse? Bribe someone to give her a ride? But that meant parting with the two gold pieces Cole had given her, all the money she had in the world.

It was then that she saw the freight outfit just coming down the road from the mine and ready to pull out of town.

She ran out into the road and held up her hand. The freight wagon stopped; a man with a gray beard looked down and said, "What you want?"

"A ride."

"Where to?"

"Anywhere."

He hesitated a moment, then said, "Git in sister."

She stared out the store window; Cole still stood at the edge of the walk, looking grim.

How could she explain her life here, if she did go to him? Would he want to hear about her? Would he believe her?

Finally, she could stand it no longer. She *had* to see him, to thank him for everything he had done for her. She owed him her life, and whether he believed her or even cared was immaterial.

Cole was about to cross the crowded street when, above the clatter of wagons and teams, he heard the voice of a young woman.

"Cole! Cole Cantrell!"

He wheeled, stared, at first not believing what he saw hurrying in his direction, skirts flying. But there she was.

"Cindy Lou," he managed to say.

27

She rushed toward him, both hands lifting her calico skirts so they wouldn't be snagged by splinters on the walk. Out of breath, she halted and peered up at him. Not quite hidden by her thick hair was the scar left by the bullet that had nearly killed her.

She put out her hand. "Cole," she said happily.

Numbed, he took her hand, noting callouses. "Guess I was tongue-tied there for a minute. I can't believe it. You here in this place."

Something in his tone caused her to drop her eyes. "Reputations are sometimes hard to live down, Cole. But I've managed."

"Good."

She looked at him. "I'm not what I was."

"I'm glad."

"I suppose you thought I'd gone back to being Cindy Lou."

"Seeing you here in a boom town, I guess I did think that," he admitted. "Then I had a closer look and knew better."

She started to speak but his surprises for the day weren't over. Two youngsters, a girl of about four and a boy a year younger, burst from the store and shouted to get her attention.

"Mama!" they chorused, coming at a run. "Looky what Mr. Higgins give us." The girl halted and held out a sack for Helen's inspection.

"Gave," Helen corrected. There was licorice in a sack. "A reward for paying our bill promptly," she said to Cole as the two children stared solemnly up at his dark face. She introduced them as Terry and Ruth.

"Hello." Cole leaned down and held out a hand to each of them which they took shyly.

183

"Wait for me in the wagon," Helen said, and the children scampered to the clearing beside the store. They climbed to the seat of a high wagon loaded with supplies.

Helen told Cole about seeing him from the store window. "At first I wasn't going to come out, because it would bring back things I'm trying to forget. But . . . but here I am."

"I worried that you might be dead."

"A wonder I'm not," she said solemnly, and told him what had prompted her to flee the Lockwood ranch.

Along the rutted street a load of logs sagged on a dray drawn by a ten-mule team. Helen touched his wrist; for the first time he noticed a wedding band.

"You're wondering about the children calling me mama?"

"I can guess. Somebody else's kids."

"John's children. He was a widower."

"You seem happy, so he's been what you needed," Cole said, smiling. He looked toward the wagon where the children waited. "John in town with you?"

She shook her head. "We have a small claim east of here." She hesitated, then said, "This is one of those days when John feels poorly. He overworked yesterday and he knew better. But we needed things at the store, so I said I'd come in while he napped. I can tell by your face you think it's strange he'd sleep while I drove a wagon to town."

"Nothing strange at all. He's obviously in poor health. . . ." He let it hang there.

"John was shot at Anteitam. He has a bullet in the lung. He and his wife and the children came west for his health. But it was too much for her. She didn't last a year."

"Too bad for kids that age to lose a mother. But you're a good one. I'll bet on that."

"Yes, I am," she said firmly.

"Should I ride with you to make sure you get home all right?"

She shook her head. "It isn't far. And these days I'm always prepared." She patted her dress so he could note the weight of a revolver in her pocket. In the wagon was not only a rifle but a shotgun. "I'll never be at any man's mercy again, Cole."

Up the block on the opposite side of the street, a lanky figure emerged from the big tent. A girl was clinging to each of Chick Wilson's arms.

Helen looked away. Cole sensed what was going through her mind. But old and ugly memories were not reflected on her attractive face.

Cole tensed when he saw Wilson angling toward them, behind an Intermountain stage just pulling in.

"Mr. Tough Gunhand," Wilson sneered, halting at the edge of the walk where they were standing. "Introduce me to your lady friend."

"Tip your hat in the presence of a lady. . . ."

But Helen pressed his arm, shook her head, "No, Cole."

Wilson laughed. "See you, tough hombre." He sauntered away, hat on the back of his head, big gun swinging at his belt. Several men lifted a hand, called out to him. The Arizona Kid was becoming something of a local hero, Cole noted.

"Who was that?" Helen asked, eyeing the slender back with distaste.

"Somebody who probably won't live very long."

She caught her breath. "Don't you be the one to kill him. The vigilantes . . ."

"I'll be gone from this place before he decides I'm his meat." Then he leaned down and said quietly, "If anybody ever tries to give you trouble, anybody out of the past . . . get word to me. There are snakes in this world who might recognize you and run to your husband."

"John knows."

Cole looked in surprise at the calm face. "He . . . knows?"

"I wouldn't have married him without . . . without telling him everything."

Cole whistled softly. "You risked a lot."

"Not with John."

Cole hesitated, then said, "I'm glad he forgave you. Understood, I guess is better," he corrected quickly.

"John said that me marrying an ex-artilleryman with a punctured lung and two motherless children was a lot more for me to cope with than him accepting . . . whatever I might have been."

"I'm your friend and if you ever need a hand, I'll come running." He told her about Duke Sateen, gambler at the Lucky Lady. "Don't you go there. It's no place for you. Not these days. But send him a message. Give my name. He'll meet you. Sateen will know, if anybody does, where I can be found."

"I'll remember." Then a tremor touched her shoulders. "When I saw you from the store you looked so grim it was almost . . . frightening."

"I look grim a lot of the time. I'm still looking for those four men." And when her face paled, he said, "I killed the bearded one you knew as Sam."

"You . . . you're Latigo." Haltingly she spoke of seeing Sam Stark's body displayed in Scalplock. "My God, I didn't connect you with it . . . but you're Latigo. . . ."

185

"He had my mother's necklace. . . ."

"I can't believe it, Cole. . . . I'm so glad he didn't kill you." She shuddered, put both hands to her face for a moment. "One down, four to go."

"That's what I'm always telling myself."

"Just be careful. Please be careful."

"How do you think I've stayed alive this long?"

It was time for her to go; the children in the wagon were getting restless. She gave directions to their mine in Cougar Canyon. Would he drop by and take a meal with them? But he said it would have to be next time he was here.

"I'm sure John will be over his setback by then."

Cole smiled encouragement. "With you to help, he'll be fine."

He waited until he saw her drive the wagon out of the turnaround beside the store, realized she handled the team as well as a man and felt she would have no problem taking care of herself for now. The two children waved at him. He lifted a hand to wave back.

Cole watched the wagon until it was swallowed up in the miles of forest green. Only then did he start for the Lucky Lady. He would speak to Sateen, then head to Scalplock. Even though the trail was old, he hoped to pick up some word on Ed Lewt.

As he pushed along the crowded walk, a sudden prickling of nerves, a cold hollowness in the pit of the stomach made him wonder if the showdown he had sought for so long might be imminent. Such intense feelings he did not shrug aside. Several times in the war his life had been saved only because he had heeded them. He halted on the walk, believing at the moment that his danger lay somewhere in the immediate future and concerned the survivors of Sam Stark's murderous band.

But he was wrong. A cocky voice cracked like a gunshot along the street.

"Latigo! *Turn around!*"

In that instant Cole realized the flash of warning concerned the immediate present, not some future danger. There was a sudden cessation of sound along the street; rigs pulled up, horsemen reined in. Men froze, then began to scramble from one side of the street to the other, lining the walks.

Sateen's drawl was easily heard in the stillness. "Ah tried to warn the fool kid that he would overmatch himself."

The cocky voice again, this time directed at Sateen. "You

next, Mr. Gamblin' Man. If you got the guts to face up to me after I outdraw your friend Latigo."

Cole turned slowly, carefully to face a gangling youth known as Chick Wilson, alias the Arizona Kid.

28   In the tense crowd Cole spotted Amos Burkett. No guessing as to who he hoped to see smashed into oblivion in a fair gunfight. Cole's grin was hard as he stepped off the walk.

Chick Wilson stood in the center of the street some forty feet away, hat tipped back, a ropy lock of dank sandy hair hanging over his forehead. His lips were stretched tight over large teeth. His pale eyes already glittered with a kind of malicious triumph.

Cole didn't move. He let the seconds drag on. His silence only intensified the agony of the moment.

Finally he spoke. "What do you want, kid?"

It took Wilson a moment to react to the question, then he blurted testily, "What's it look like, Latigo? I'm callin' you out!"

"Why?"

"Huh? Whaddaya mean, *why?*"

"I asked a question, kid."

"I just told you. I'm callin' you out!"

"And I asked why."

Confusion twisted Wilson's face for an instant, then he uttered a bark of laughter. The crowd had increased as word spread quickly of the impending gunfight. Banks of strained faces were deep as men jammed tightly together, keeping well back from the possible line of fire. Girls in spangled skirts, clustered in the entrance of the big tent, squealed with excitement.

"Chick said he'd do it an' he *is!*" one of them cried.

"See you soon's this is over with, Ruby," Chick Wilson called over his shoulder. "Won't take a minute."

"Waitin' right here for you, Chick honey!" a blonde girl answered loudly.

One of the male onlookers gave a nervous laugh. "Wouldn't miss this show for a hundred dollars."

"Show it is, mister!" Wilson sang out with a grin. "Curtain's goin' up."

187

Chick Wilson started his walk, one foot sliding in front of the other, not looking down, testing for ruts or stones so as not to stumble. His eyes drilled Cole's face. After a few steps he halted.

"I gone far enough!" Wilson's voice rang clearly through the stillness. "Latigo, you walk the rest of the way. If you got the guts."

The sudden neighing of a horse caused many of the onlookers to jump, so tightly locked were their nerves.

Cole had not moved. He stood at ease, widespread feet rooted in the street dust. No expression showed on his dark face. Only a slight outthrust of jaw, eyes narrowed against the setting sun.

"I've got no quarrel with you, kid," he said, still in that cool voice. He might have been discussing the price of tobacco.

"You insulted me in front of that female you was talkin' to awhile ago!"

"Insulted you? How?"

"Draw your gun, Latigo. Any time. I'm ready!"

"Kid, I'm giving you this chance to walk away. *Take it!*"

"Mebby you didn't hear me, gunfighter! Fight or crawl!"

Cole said nothing. He just stood and stared for a full minute. Finally Wilson made a sudden, nervous shifting of feet. "Yaller," he sneered at the dark, implacable features. Wilson's Adam's apple jerked as he swallowed. He licked his lips.

Cole gunned him with his eyes, saw a flick of unease, and started walking slowly toward him. One step, two steps, taking his time as if he had an hour to force a showdown. Strain deepened in the faces of watchers.

An older woman moaned, "Ain't it awful . . . the suspense."

"Draw!" Chick Wilson screeched as the gap between them narrowed.

Still Cole came on unhurriedly, eyes burning into the moistening face. Sweat thickened at Wilson's hairline. Lips taut as bowstrings over large teeth, sagged for an instant, then stiffened resolutely.

The faint chiming of Latigo's spurs seemed unusually loud in the stillness. Massed onlookers stood rigid.

Chick Wilson wavered. Beads of sweat broke, making the long face slick.

A man wailed, "Oh God, oh God, git it over with, git it over with!"

Cole, still with that measured pace, closed in. *Ching, ching, ching* of spurs, boots scarcely seeming to touch the street so light was his step.

188

Wilson's voice cracked. "Hey . . . hey, that's close enough! Stop right there. . . ."

Cole's steady pace did not slacken. He made no move toward his gun. Panic began to twist Wilson's mouth.

"*Draw!*" Wilson screamed. And when Cole was within touching distance, "Stop! You're gettin' too close . . .!"

Desperation widened Wilson's eyes. He clamped a hand to the butt of his gun. Cole's right hand did not move. Wilson backed up, slightly off balance. His mouth collapsed.

"Damn you!" he cried. Whether he would ever have drawn the gun or not, no one was sure.

For at that moment Cole exploded. His fist smashed the point of Wilson's jaw. Wilson crashed to the street on his back, hand still clamped to the holstered gun. He stared up dazedly.

Cole stood over him. "If you draw when I'm not making a move toward my gun, you're a dead man. You know it. You'll hang. It's the law of this town." Cole's gaze flicked to Amos Burkett who stood openmouthed in the jam of people on the walk. "That right, Mr. Vigilante?"

"Well . . . yes . . ."

Then Cole leaned down, tore Wilson's hand away from his gun. Cole pulled the weapon free of its holster, straightened up. He unloaded it, the cartridges tumbling into the dust. Then he tossed the empty weapon to Burkett, who caught it in both hands.

"Give it back to him one day," Cole said. "I'd wait about five years till he's man enough to handle a gun. Without trying to get himself killed. Or somebody else."

After Cole's scornful speech, men began to stir. So great was the release of tension along the street that there were at first mere sputterings of laughter, then a few barks of it, which soon became a roaring near-hysteria. Tears spilled as men and even the few women in the crowd howled.

Amos Burkett felt all eyes on him. He puffed out his small chest and leveled a finger at Chick Wilson who by then was sitting up. Flesh had been ripped away from his jaw by Cole's powerful fist. His eyes still were not quite in focus.

"Get out of town, Wilson," Burkett ordered. It was the only thing he *could* do under the circumstances. After such public humiliation, Chick Wilson was the kind to drink back his nerve, borrow or steal a gun and go looking for somebody. Just anybody. Only sudden death could restore his crushed pride. Even if the target was a man's back instead of his breastbone.

Cole didn't linger. He had a few words with Duke Sateen, then rode out.

He was half a mile down the canyon before his own nerves began to unwind.

29

"She's a whore. She'll return to that life sooner or later. They all do. And she'll talk . . . something else they all do." E. J. Creed was speaking, his tone angry. He and his men were in an office on wheels. The twelve mules that moved it ever westward were in a rope corral near some empty supply wagons. Creed felt he had been demoted. He was no longer in charge of the Python office but now handled the grading crews that worked ahead of the track layers.

Here he was known to strangers as Joe Billings. He had dyed his hair and grown a beard. That he had not been fired for incompetence had amazed him at first until his shrewd mind put it all together. In certain areas Python was vulnerable. Key men who knew company secrets but could keep their mouths shut were invaluable. So he bided his time. He knew that once Claudius Max got over his pique, and the political situation once again swung in Python's favor, he would be back on top. His salary was still generous. Only his pride had suffered. But Max had explained that it was best if he kept out of sight for a time, so far as the general public was concerned. It had all started with that story and those goddmaned sketches that appeared in *Amison's Weekly*. Well, that wouldn't happen again.

Creed glared out one of the narrow windows. It was rough work, this new assignment. Everywhere dust when it didn't rain. Mud like Vesuvius lava when it did. Mules dragged scrapers for the grading, mules packed in supplies. He was sick of mules, their contrariness, their odor. But they were much more surefooted than horses for this precarious terrain.

He sat at his desk, resting his bad arm. He had never fully recovered from the wound, slight though it was, that their nemesis, Cantrell had inflicted in Basin City that long-ago day. The bullet had done something to a nerve, so the doctor said. It might recover in time.

He had just about managed to put Cole Cantrell from his

mind when Bill Cutter barged in with news of the prostitute Cutter and the others had raped after doing away with Cole Cantrell's parents. Cutter had spotted her in El Dorado Gulch. Just three days ago with her husband and two young children.

Creed's lengthy silence irritated Cutter. "It was her, sure as hell. Don't you believe me?"

"Yes . . . yes," Creed replied impatiently.

"She looked good, purty as all hell." Cutter's broad face with its scarred nose and cheek was faintly tinged from memory of a pleasant incident. "She fought an' kicked like hell that day in the mountains. Till Stark held her down so's I could get at her."

"Rape is a distasteful subject." Creed flashed Cutter a sideward glance of disgust. Not that the subject of rape itself was distasteful. It was the fact that they hadn't made sure she was dead, after foolishly going into detail about their crime in Beaver Valley.

Now Cutter sat on an edge of Creed's desk, his big Remington revolver jutting from an oiled holster. Ed Lewt and two of the new men, Whalen and Bonchard, were in tipped-back chairs near the door.

Cutter leaned down and spoke quietly to Creed who was hunched in a swivel chair, scowling at the far wall.

"Didn't want to go after Cindy Lou till I knowed for sure if you wanted me to . . ."

"Christ, can't you even speak the King's English? *Knowed*," Creed mimicked. Then he drew a deep breath and made a grudging apology. The job was tearing at his nerves. He glanced out the window again at the inevitable screen of dust churned up by mules and the scrapers they dragged. Soon the snows would come and choke the pass where they were working. He could then return to Basin City, get himself a woman and sit by a warm stove until the spring thaw made work again possible.

A dispatch Bill Cutter had brought today from Max was typical. It ordered the job to continue until the first mule froze to death and the first man was in danger of losing a limb from frostbite.

Bill Cutter rubbed his jaw and glowered down at a dollar-sized bald spot on Creed's bent head. "You told me to shoot nobody. Not 'less you gave the word. You says that Mr. Max is frothin' at the mouth, is the way you put it. . . ."

"All right, all right, Cutter. I'm trying to reach a decision." Creed waved his hands impatiently. "You did right, though.

As I said, once a whore, always one. She'll tire of that new life soon enough. Then is when she might get an idea of talking. Talking about Python. Maybe hoping to get some money out of the company."

"Givin' her money wouldn't help none. Can't trust them *putas*."

"I'm quite aware of her profession."

"I'll ride back an' take care of her?"

"Mmmmmm . . ."

"Her an' her husband's got a claim in Cougar Canyon. I found out that much by askin' questions. Won't be hard to find."

Creed flexed his bad arm. He could hardly speak the name Cantrell without choking. "Any sign of Cantrell up that way?"

"Heard he'd been through, but that was coupla months ago," Cutter said. "Want I should get started?" He stood up.

Creed made a decision. "You don't go alone. Lewt let her get away once. . . ."

"I *tried* to find her, damn it," Lewt said, thumping down his chair legs.

"Never mind that," Creed snapped. "You go along with Cutter." Creed eyed the two new men, big and tough. "Better the four of you go."

"What about her husband an' the kids?" Cutter asked, hitching up his gun rig.

Creed considered the question a moment, then said thoughtfully, "Try and get her alone if you can. If it isn't possible, then do what you have to. Make it look like Indians. You know how to do it."

Cutter grinned. "Had some experience."

"And listen to me, Cutter. You too, Lewt." Creed leaned across the desk, shaking a finger for emphasis. "Don't get any ideas about having fun with her first. Kill her. And this time make sure she's dead."

The four men trooped outside. Their tethered horses were already acquiring winter coats. Creed stood in the doorway, watching them ride out. The prospect of murdered children left a sour taste in his mouth. But this time there couldn't be any loose ends. And in the West didn't children die every day from smallpox or cholera or other diseases? Death was always death, wasn't it? He wasn't altogether sure, and returned to his desk and had a long pull at a bottle to scald his conscience. In working for Claudius Max he'd lost most of what little remained.

Creed thought about the job ahead. The four men should

192

get it done and be back by the middle of the following week. If anything went wrong this time . . . Creed's mouth dried. He had sent four tough men to kill one woman, leaving himself vulnerable if they failed. He thought longingly of Doak Lancer in New York, Al Dain in Kansas. Men he could depend on.

Creed strapped on a gun belt, loaded a double-barreled shotgun and put it under the blankets on his bunk.

30

Aspens ablaze on the fine fall day matched in vividness of color the blue of a sky that heralded the approach of winter. Flocks of geese formed Vs across the heavens in their annual southern migration. Elk, antelope and other wild things were on the move down from higher elevations. In the distance, Cole witnessed one of the truly majestic sights offered to man. A giant grizzly reared on hind legs to tremendous height, its massive head swinging first one way, then the other as it tested air for the scent of prey or an enemy.

Cole reined in Trooper and drew his Henry from the saddle boot, intending only to protect himself should the bear come charging up the wooded slope. When the grizzly came down on all fours and went loping away in the opposite direction, Cole breathed easier.

Later the high road he traveled leveled off. He kept his eyes open for a trail that would branch off the road and take him in the direction of a portable office he knew was being used by Python. An office always far ahead of the track layers. Once before he had observed it, but recognized no one. He had singled out one of the graders working behind a mule team. Cole casually mentioned the names of the four men he sought. But the workman said he had never seen nor heard of men by those names. The same applied to E. J. Creed, the man said. The grading crew was bossed by a bearded man named Billings who rarely left the office on wheels where he not only worked but lived. The description given of Billings didn't match Creed's, for sure.

That was weeks ago. But Cole decided to try again. Possible, just possible that after all this time conditions had changed and the men he wanted would be there. It was worth the gamble, for the first snows, which would lock everything in until spring, could come at any time.

He reached the old Indian trail he had been seeking, but just as he was about to turn left through a notch in an escarpment, he noticed the tracks of four horses coming from the direction he had intended going. Shod horses, not ponies. Fresh tracks, made within the hour, that moved northward along the high road he had been following.

Six miles in that direction was Apperson's, a mountain trading post. For some reason he couldn't define, he was curious about the quartet coming from the direction of Python's outpost. To follow the tracks six miles or so to Apperson's was probably a waste of time, he told himself. And Apperson might have already closed up for the winter. Just the same, there was a chance, however slim. Four men, four horses. Could it be possible?

Loosening the Henry so it would slide easily from its boot, he drew and checked his .44. Then he rode on, the tracks of the horses always before his eyes.

After a few miles he was rewarded by a smudge of distant blue-gray hanging above the trees, which no doubt meant a cook fire at Apperson's. Roy was still open.

In another mile a bend in the road revealed the familiar, squat log trading post ahead, with its corral and outbuildings. It was disappointing to see no strange horses at the hitch rail. It was empty, save for a sturdy chestnut mare he knew to be Apperson's, and two mules with bulky tarp-covered packs expertly roped. That meant Roy was about to pull out. At least Cole hoped to get some information, even meager, about the riders.

As he drew nearer, he saw the familiar cleared slope to the north that Apperson and his sons had denuded of trees to use as logs for construction. West of the trading post was a great thumb of granite thrusting from the earth that one of Apperson's boys had dubbed the Tooth of Hercules. Both of Apperson's sons had entered the army in the final year of the war. Neither of them survived. Apperson took his loss hard.

"Hey, Roy," Cole sang out. The door swung open.

"Voice sounds mighty familiar," said a big ruddy-faced man with a belly that ballooned out the front of a red shirt. "You couldn't be the fella they call Latigo Cantrell, now could you by any chance?"

"Could be and am!" Cole spoke loudly at Apperson's good ear. Grinning, he slid from the saddle, shook Apperson's calloused hand and slapped him on the back. He turned from evidence that four horses had been tethered at the far end of the hitch rack and gestured at window shutters already locked in place. "Looks like you're ready to pull out for the winter."

"Want to get below soon's I can. Air smells of snow." Apperson made a great show of sniffing the air. "You wanted somethin', Cole?"

"A meal."

"You had a belly like mine, you could live off what's underneath. Damn it, son, I just throwed out the last of the stew. Fellas ate most of it."

"Four of 'em, eh?" Cole pointed at the horse tracks. "How long ago, Roy?" Apperson cupped his ear and Cole repeated it.

"They left not ten minutes ago. Whyn't you come sooner?"

Cole followed Apperson into the small building with its short bar, two tables. Shelves usually crammed with merchandise were nearly empty. Everything that would last the winter here was covered with tarps. The rest of it Apperson was taking with him by pack mule. The stove was still warm.

"I could dig into one of the packs an' get you some pemmican," Apperson offered.

"I'll get me a pronghorn later on," Cole said, shaking his head.

"Plenty in the mountains around here," Apperson said. "Damn it, Cole, an hour ago we could've set an' beat the breeze an' talked about most everything. . . ."

Cole made himself smile. He wanted to lead easily into the subject of the four men. He mentioned the tracks of the four horses he had been following. "Riders came in from over west on that old Cheyenne trail. A trail I figured to take."

"What you gettin' at, Cole?"

"Did they drop any names while they were here?"

Apperson thoughtfully scratched a reddish stubble on his chin. "Didn't really pay no attention. Was already packed an' ready to pull out. They wanted tobacco an' a meal. I had the stew I figured to leave out for ol' Bob. But it was too much an' he'd likely eat it all an' get hisself sick like he does."

"Ol' Bob still alive." Cole smiled.

"So I fed most of it to them four fellas, but told 'em to hurry it up. They was some grumpy about it, but they ate in a hurry. I'd just dumped out the leavings for Ol' Bob when you come up."

"He'll eat well, anyhow." The old mountain lion had first appeared in late summer. He had only one eye and a bad paw. Roy Apperson had been about to shoot him because the animal could no longer hunt efficiently. Instead, Apperson had lowered his rifle and began setting out leftovers. They

195

seemed to respect each other, Apperson and Ol' Bob. Cole had heard about it on his last visit here. He liked what Apperson had done because it reflected his own philosophy; all life was worth saving.

Apperson spoke of the animal, grinning. "It'll happen to all of us, Cole, if we outlive murder an' accidents. When the teeth go an' the claws. Lame an' one-eyed. I really started feedin' him to keep him from gettin' desperate hungry an' mebby chawin' up one of my mules. But I bet he'd been kicked to pieces before he could get one bite." Apperson chuckled, then sobered. "He'll never last till spring, with me gone from here. But I just couldn't shoot him."

"I know."

Apperson squinted through his half-moon spectacles and said suddenly, "Why you interested in them four fellas that was here?"

"Curious is all."

"You after 'em?"

"Like I said, curious. What'd they look like, Roy?"

Apperson studied Cole for a moment, then spoke of the men. Two of them had used last names. The other two seemed to be in charge. "The big fella packed a Remington pistol that looked big as a cannon. I recollect he had a scar on his nose an' a deeper one on his cheek."

Cole's nerves hummed; the description might mean something at that. "Anything more, Roy?"

"The fella with the scar had a hoss he was worried about. Said he might have to swap with one of the others. So I figured he was the big boss."

But Apperson could remember nothing distinguishing about the other three. "Like most fellas around here . . . rawhide look about 'em. All packed guns. . . ."

"I'll catch up and have a close look," Cole drawled.

"They looked tough. I wouldn't go messin' with 'em, was I you, Cole. Don't forget you're one man against four."

"Fella with a Remington pistol and a scarred face doesn't mean much," Cole said, trying to sound indifferent. "I'll have a look all the same, but I'll keep my distance, Roy. So don't worry."

Apperson frowned, then said abruptly, "Come to think of it, I remember one of 'em had a gold tooth. Seen it when he laughed at somethin' the big fella said."

"They call him Ed by any chance?"

"By God, yes. The big fella did call him that." Apperson

looked grim. "You want I should go along with you, Cole?"

Cole shook his head. "I can handle it."

Apperson saw cold lights in the younger man's eyes. "By any chance, these the fellas you been huntin' for so long?"

"Gold tooth and scar face? Hell, likely means nothing." Cole tried to act indifferent. He didn't want Apperson mixing up in it. In addition to being hard of hearing, Apperson's eyesight behind his half-moon spectacles wasn't much better than that of the one-eyed mountain lion. Besides, it was a Cantrell fight.

"By the way, did you notice if one of 'em was a redhead?" Cole asked casually, thinking of Doak Lancer.

"Can't say's I noticed, Cole. They never took their hats off."

"Roy, how about me helping you finish closing up."

"You don't fool me none. Cole, you better go careful, you figure to tangle with them four."

"I'm just going to see where they're heading."

"They might cut down to Basin City," Apperson suggested as he locked the front door and hid the big brass key under a flat rock behind the building. "Whyn't you ride down with me, Cole?"

"Forget it, Roy. I'm not going to take any chances. Probably not even the men I'm after. Like I said, one with a scarred face and the other with a gold tooth sure isn't much to go on." He forced a grin. "See you, come spring." Cole mounted up.

Apperson stood watching him a minute, then with a gesture of resignation, grunted his way into the saddle, picked up the lead ropes of his pack mules and started down trail from the road.

Cole waited until Apperson was out of sight, then turned north and started following the tracks left by the mounts of the four men. Over a year had passed since the death of his parents and he'd been able to account for only one of the killers—Sam Stark. Not much of a showing, he reminded himself and squinted up at the great stand of trees beyond the clearing that Apperson and his sons had made with their axes. There the ribbon of road was swallowed up by tall pines.

31

It was two miles or so beyond Apperson's that Bill Cutter noticed his horse favoring the left foreleg even more than it had earlier in the day. Reining in, he jerked on the brim of his hat in disgust.

"We'll go back," he announced gruffly. He mentioned Apperson's chestnut horse that had been tied to the rail. "Big enough to pack my weight," Cutter finished.

Ed Lewt wasn't so sure it was a good idea. "Creed might get a burr up his butt if you steal a hoss. He said we got to go easy for a spell an' not do nothin' foolish."

Cutter gave a snort of sour laughter. "We're out to kill a female an' mebby her husband an' kids if they get in the way. Creed don't seem to mind that none." Cutter winked broadly. "But I forgot, it'll be the redskins do the job, not us."

"All the same . . ."

"I won't steal the damn chestnut, I'll buy it." Cutter was irritated. "That suit you, Ed?"

"What if he don't want to sell?"

"He get a taste of gun barrel rammed down his throat an' he'll sell."

They were riding back when Chad Whalen said, "What if Apperson's closed up an' left already?"

"We'll go after him," Cutter snapped, angry not only because of the horse that was letting him down but also the fool question from the new Python employee.

As they neared Apperson's again, voices suddenly drifted through the trees from that direction.

Cutter heard enough of what was said to widen his eyes with anticipation.

Apperson had greeted a newcomer loudly. "*Latigo!*"

Cutter reined in, grinning at a surprised Ed Lewt. "Claudius Max will pay ten thousand dollars for that bastard's head in a gunnysack."

Where they sat their horses on a hump in the road, trees were thinned enough so that the trading post could be seen clearly below. But it was situated at such an angle that they only got a glimpse of Apperson and the tall man who went inside. Smoke from the banked cook fire drifted from the chimney.

Cutter gave the order to double back up the road, away from the building and where the trees were thicker at the upper rim of the clearing. Here they would be out of sight should either Apperson or Cantrell glance out a window.

"We'll wait an' see what happens," he told the three men. "This time no mistakes."

Cutter dismounted, walked to where he could have a better view of the building, where two pack mules switched their tails and Apperson's big horse stood placidly. The powerfully

198

built black animal at the hitch rail was what interested Cutter at the moment. It would solve his problems of horseflesh.

Seeing that Bonchard and Whalen were standing together some distance away, Cutter beckoned to Ed Lewt. He spoke again of the ten thousand dollars, this time in a low voice.

"Nobody left but you an' me, Ed, after that half-breed Latigo Cantrell went on a killin' spree. We were lucky to stay alive an' kill him." He nudged Lewt. "That's the way we'll tell it."

Lewt glanced at the broad backs of the two new men who stood near their horses a dozen yards away. "Never liked them much anyhow," Lewt muttered, and flashed Cutter a tight grin. Cutter grinned back. A gust of wind brought down a pine cone. It rolled across the carpet of needles then part way down the long slope. One of the mules brayed from the front of the trading post.

"No matter which way Latigo rides, we got him," Cutter said.

"What about Apperson?" Lewt whispered.

"We'll see." Cutter let it hang there. Minutes slid away. He grew impatient.

Part of their problem was solved when they saw Apperson go riding off down the mountain, leading his pack mules. And then Latigo Cantrell, mounted on the big black horse, was coming up the road, his mount at a walk.

"So that's what Python's always callin' their nemesis," Lewt said softly.

"Not for long." Cutter cocked his rifle. "I want the bastard alive . . . for now. Owe him for all the hell he's made for us."

"Not to mention what he done to Sam Stark," Lewt put in.

Below them, Cole rode with head bent, eyes studying the hoof prints. Wind through the pines brought with it the sharp smell of winter. With the road beginning to climb, he could look to his right and down into the deep valley that by now was hidden under a layer of puffy clouds. His teeth clenched so hard the jaws ached. Let this be the day it ends, he prayed.

He had ridden another five yards or so when he felt a tightening of the short hairs at the back of his neck. There was a sudden change in the pattern of hoof prints. The set of tracks heading north had been nearly obscured by the same hoof prints coming south again. Up ahead he could see where the riders had pulled up, then climbed back up the steep road. This time hurrying. Cole tongued a dry lower lip. He did not lift his head.

Cole knew from the horse tracks that the four men had

been on their way back to Apperson's for one reason or another, perhaps had spotted him, then wheeled and headed for the trees above. To set up an ambush? What else?

His palms sweated coldly. He let Trooper continue up the steep road, maintaining pace for ten feet or so. Don't get too close, he warned himself. Tension crackled across his shoulder blades. Drawing a deep breath, he was set to rein Trooper off the road . . .

In that same instant, up in the trees, Chad Whalen was brushing back a lock of stringy black hair when the sight of a big animal gripped him with sudden terror. "Mountain lion!" he screeched. "Comin' for *us!*"

Tawny, scarred Ol' Bob froze in his limping advance downslope toward the last of the antelope stew that Apperson had left for him in a grassy hollow. In that moment he lifted his magnificent head and bared what remained of his yellowed teeth. But his warning snarl failed to compete with the crack of the rifle that whipped him in a great backward leap into the air and down, lifeless.

Experience on battlefields saved Cole's life. Instead of trying to extend his luck and reach shelter, he flung himself from the saddle of the hard-running horse. Ground leaped upward. He came down hard in a padding of pine needles, rolling and with the rifle held high to protect it. Above in the trees he glimpsed a big stranger. It was Chad Whalen spinning his aim from the dead mountain lion to Latigo.

Cole's Henry spoke first, and the side of Whalen's face was a sudden pulpy red. Whalen pitched forward in a sprawl of grotesquely twisted limbs.

Bonchard, also with battlefield experience, came downslope at a zigzag run as he sought to avenge the death of his friend. This one, also a stranger, didn't get far. Cole put a shot in one of his legs. But Bonchard wasn't through even though the bullet tumbled him. Rolling to a sitting position, the front of his gray shirt matted with pine needles, he aimed the rifle once again. But Cole drilled his breastbone. For an instant Bonchard sat staring at a jet of his own blood from a severed artery, then he fell back, mouth hanging open as what remained of his life continued to pump away.

Ed Lewt yelled at Cutter, his voice erupting thin and frantic from the thickest of the trees above. "Bill, Latigo's yonderly. Ten yards from that big rock!"

"Comin', Ed!" Cutter's answering shout was far to the right in the tall pines nearest the road. To try and cut down the odds, Cole fired twice in the direction of Cutter's voice.

One of the bullets struck a tree inches from Cutter's face, lashing him with splinters. Part of a pine knot slammed into his chin, gashing it deeply. He reeled, tried to open his mouth to yell at Ed Lewt, but his jaws seemed paralyzed. Instead of a shouted warning, only guttural sounds issued from his throat.

Lewt, unaware of Cutter's predicament, burst from the cover of forest directly above the body of Whalen. At a crouching run he tried to reach an outcropping of tooth-like rock off to the side of the road. Cole fired, missed, as Lewt flung himself headlong at the base of the monolith and on the far side, out of sight.

"Bill . . . *Bill Cutter!*" Lewt was yelling from the protection offered by the giant thrust of stone. Cole, still jarred from his fast dismount, glanced upslope just as Cutter reeled out of the trees. Cutter looked back over his shoulder, revealing the wash of blood on his chin. Then Cutter continued his floundering run toward the road. There wasn't time for Cole to aim the Henry, not with the threat of Lewt at his back. He pointed it like a pistol and fired. Sound waves churned into the pines and Cutter's hat brim twitched as he moved his head at the last minute. Then he was out of sight.

A scraping of boot heels over a spire of the monolith jerked Cole's head around. Lewt was trying to come at him from the back. But Cole, meeting him head on, squeezed the Henry's trigger. All he heard was the chilling emptiness of a hammer snap. In desperation, he flung the empty rifle in Lewt's face, swept up his .44. Lewt, off balance from the flung rifle, shot at the sky. Before Lewt could get set again, Cole picked a wide part of the target and fired an inch above a large brass belt buckle. A strangled coughing sound burst from a startled Lewt. And as his mouth worked, Cole saw the dull gleam of a gold tooth. Lewt was already collapsing as Cole spun, expecting to see Cutter aiming a weapon. But there was no sign of the big man with the scarred face.

As reverberations of the barrage became diminished echoes against a wall of mountains, Cole heard a horse being ridden northward at a furious pace.

As had happened so often after the searing tension of battle, Cole's nerves began to come undone like the frayed string of a war bow. A trembling in the knees spread up his spine as he peered up the grade through a faint haze of powder smoke. Cordite bit at his nostrils and throat. He saw part of the skull of the first man he had shot, open to the sky.

The stranger who had yelled the warning about a mountain lion.

Cole breathed deeply to clear his head and thought back on the violence that had burst so suddenly upon the tranquil mountain slope.

What had brought Ol' Bob down the mountain at just that moment when the ambush was planned, he wondered. He thought of Dark Star, who believed the unseen was at times more powerful than what could be seen.

Then he shook himself. His heartbeat slowed to normal as he reloaded his weapons. The sweat on his heated face had turned cold as had the dampness at the back of his shirt. As he thumbed in cartridges he looked at the second stranger he had shot, unmoving, the severed artery no longer active.

Ed Lewt, lying face down, made a low whine of pain.

Hearing it made him sick, not from pity because it came from one of those who had been at Beaver Valley that day. Lewt had lost his hat and for a moment Cole stared at the back of the tangled hair thinking how easily it could be finished with a bullet crashing into the skull. He shuddered, turned away, looked down at Apperson's with its shuttered windows, the smoke from the chimney now only faint against the sky. Cordite was fading and he sniffed the odor of cook smoke and dung from the corral. He looked at the great stacks of firewood piled against a building wall. His gaze swung over to Ol' Bob, finally at rest. Other predators also had caught the scent of the food offering, no doubt, those smaller and weaker ones. But even with his infirmities, they still deferred to Ol' Bob.

Cole turned Lewt over on his back, disarmed him and unloaded both guns. Cartridges he hurled in one direction, weapons in another. They made a noisy clatter in distant rocks, causing a great whirring of birds.

Lewt had the fingers of both hands laced tight as corset strings across the hole in his stomach. Redness seeped through the fingers. His mouth hung open so that Cole could again glimpse the dull gold of a tooth. Lewt's wide eyes stared up at him.

"Hell . . . Latigo . . . how'd you do it? Four of us? One of you. You kill Cutter?"

"Looks like he ran out on you." But a spasm of pain struck Lewt and Cole didn't know whether he heard him or not.

"Jeez I hurt. . . ."

"My mother hurt and my father hurt. You son of a bitch, you helped murder them."

202

Lewt's eyes seemed to clear. "You worn me thin, Latigo. Wouldn't gun down your folks if I had it to do over again." Lewt was struggling to form words. "Seems I was always lookin' over my shoulder for you. Ever time I heard a board creak, I jumped."

While Lewt clung to his miserable life, Cole hiked up to the trees where Cutter had been concealed. He saw blood on the ground and part of a pine knot and splinters that one of the bullets had sheared from a tree, leaving a fresh scar on the trunk. Now and then he looked down at Lewt who had not moved. Cole prowled the trees, saw where Cutter had run for his horse and ridden away. The three other horses were tied off, swinging their tails and looking around at him curiously.

He returned to Lewt. "Your great friend Cutter left in a hell of a hurry."

"Goddamn Bill . . ."

Cole hunkered beside him. "Lewt, do you know how to write?"

"Why?" Lewt blinked his eyes in the graying face.

"I'll try and get you some whiskey. . . ."

"What you want me to write?" Lewt asked narrowly, despite his pain.

"Tell your part in murdering my folks. Name Cutter and Dain and Lancer. And name those who paid you. I want Python much as I want you."

"Where's the whiskey?"

Colt pointed at Apperson's building.

"Looks closed up. How'll you get inside, Latigo?"

"I'll manage. Will you do it?"

Lewt closed his eyes a moment, then shook his head. "Sign my own death warrant? What it amounts to."

Cole watched Lewt sweat and twitch and whimper. "Whiskey will ease the hurting. Better think about it."

Lewt set his jaw stubbornly for three or four minutes, then grimaced as he was struck by a spasm of pain. His feverish eyes flicked to his captor's impassive features. "Get . . . whiskey."

Cole hurried down the slope, looking back occasionally to see Lewt still crumpled in the shadow of the monolith. Beyond him Ol' Bob lay stretched in a more merciful death than the one he would have suffered that winter. In his condition he had been a hunter without weapons.

Cole found Apperson's key under the rock. He knew where Apperson kept paper and pen and a small, capped inkwell. Apperson always left whiskey in the place, a spare bottle for

203

that first drink at the spring opening, in case he lost a loaded pack on the way up.

Cole returned to Lewt and set him so that his back was to the big rock. "Can you hold a pen?"

"Whiskey first."

Cole held the bottle to his lips. Lewt drank some, threw it up, the redness of his life streaked with the alcohol. Lewt asked for more and was able to keep it down.

Cole found a flat rock, slightly larger than the sheet of paper, that would serve as a writing desk. He dipped the pen in the inkwell, handed it to Lewt.

He told him what to write. "I, Ed Lewt helped kill Badger Cantrell and his wife. Python paid me to get rid of them because they wanted the land for a right-of-way. . . ." Cole named the accomplices, and Lewt laboriously wrote them down. Then he added his shaky signature. Cole folded the confession, put it in his pocket.

He gave Lewt another drink, then asked where he could find Dain and Lancer. Dain was somewhere east, doing work for Python, but should return to Basin City within the month. Lancer was in New York.

"Doing what?" Cole demanded.

"Boss sent for him."

That meant Claudius Max, the brains behind Python and the Centurion Pacific Railroad.

"Max on the gallows is what I want to see," Cole said grimly.

"Try it an' he'll laugh at you."

"I've got your confession," Cole reminded.

Lewt thought that over, then said, "Bandage me up. Don't feel so poorly like I did. Ride me to El Dorado Gulch. Must be a doc there. . . ."

"You mean you hope we'd run into Bill Cutter and he'd get you out of this."

Lewt made no reply. He did seem stronger, the eye clearer. Cole had seen it before on a battlefield, a man a whisper away from death, than rallying. He left the whiskey with Lewt, rummaged in the store for white cloth for bandage, then returned. He could hardly bring himself to touch this man who had gunned down the innocent Cantrells. But he managed, consoling himself that Lewt, should he survive the wound, would be legally hanged. As Lewt said, he had just signed what amounted to his death warrant.

He would tie Lewt to the saddle of one of the horses. It

would be slow going, but Bill Cutter would have to stop sometime between here and wherever he was heading. That's when it would end. He didn't fool himself that he'd be lucky enough to haul Cutter off to a judge and jury as he hoped to do with Lewt. It would be a gunfight, with one of them dead. Cole didn't plan to be the one.

"El Dorado Gulch," Cole said. "That where Cutter's heading?" Lewt bobbed his head.

Cole rode up to the horses and led one of them down. In the short time he had been gone Lewt's face had grayed even more and the eyes were no longer clear.

"Shoulda killed that goddamn Cindy Lou an' I wouldn't be in this fix." Lewt was babbling now.

"Thank God you didn't. How can a human being be so low that he can hire himself out to murder a woman?" Cole demanded angrily.

"She's good as dead."

Cole leaned down, teeth bared. "What the hell do you mean by that?"

For a moment Lewt said nothing. Then words tumbled out of him, words that Cole didn't want to hear, that made him shudder. The four men had been ordered to kill Cindy Lou.

Cole had to restrain an urge to smash Lewt in the face. "Hasn't that poor woman been through enough already?" He got Lewt by a shoulder, shook him. "You think Cutter will try and do the job alone?"

"Sure." Lewt's jaw sagged and he mumbled, "Run out on me, he did. Keeryst, Bill run an' left me. . . ."

"Lewt, I'll boost you in the saddle. You try and kick me in the head and I'll break your leg. . . ." But he knew it was not the way it could be. Not now. Not with Cutter on the loose and Helen in danger.

"I'll put you inside Apperson's," Cole snapped. "It'll give you shelter, but you don't deserve a damn thing. I'm going after Cutter before he can get a shot at that poor . . ."

But at that moment blood finally reached Lewt's lips; it sealed off the throat and the heart and the rest of the murderous mechanism that had served him through a violent life.

Cole, working swiftly, closed up Apperson's; he owed that to Roy, although it took time. He unsaddled the horse he had led down, turned it loose, and did likewise for the other two still up in the threes.

Then he looked down at Lewt who was tipped over on his

side. He had hoped to keep him alive for the hangman. But he was dead and that was the main thing.

He gave the distant body of Ol' Bob a two-fingered salute, ignored the two strangers sprawled in death and turned his horse north. Now that he was pulling out, the predators large and small, lurking just out of sight, would move in, some drawn by the scent of the discarded antelope stew, others by the dead. In the spring Roy Apperson would wonder about the clutter of gleaming bones in the new grass on the slope. Cole, if he survived, would ride by one day and tell him.

He started riding after Cutter, picking up his tracks on the road. One score had been settled today. Cole swore he'd finish Cutter before Helen could be harmed. Trooper settled into an easy, mile-eating run.

32 Higher in the mountains, some miles to the north, a Cheyenne hunting party of eight split up in twos. In the party was a slim boy with bright and reckless eyes, who bore the name Grey Otter. He was ten years old, and his father, Two Buffalos, was a subchief and leader of the hunting party.

A mile back they had spotted antelope, a large herd. But any move toward their grass would scatter the animals. Two Buffalos decreed they would split up. Grey Otter was to go with his uncle.

Two Buffalos and another warrior would be at the lure, the bait to trap the antelope. Two Buffalos had brought with him a piece of white cloth which he tied to the butt end of his war lance. He drove the point into the ground so that the cloth fluttered above the breeze like a white flag.

Two Buffalos and the other warrior hid behind a rock outcropping. Now it was a matter of patience. It could be an hour before the naturally curious animals drew closer to inspect the cloth flapping in the breeze. It might take longer.

The other six braves, including his headstrong young son, had ridden away in pairs. They would spread out on the downwind side of the broad valley.

Aside from obtaining meat for the camp, Two Buffalos' main purpose for the expedition was to teach his son patience, a trait the boy seemed to lack.

He had chosen to come with a small party, so that there would be only a handful of braves to witness a reprimand, should one be necessary. Two Buffalos did not wish to subject his son to ridicule before a large group.

The braves he had chosen were relatives and close friends. Not one of them would talk should Grey Otter fail the test. Two Buffalos dearly loved his only son but knew his shortcomings. And the reason Two Buffalos had not been home to personally direct his son along the path to manhood. For too long the boy had been· left with the women.

Grey Otter in his young mind believed today's test to be a waste. He was already proficient with a war lance and bow and arrow and longed to prove himself so that he could be trusted with a rifle.

And he thought of how this might be done, a way to prove himself before the day was finished.

Grey Otter smiled to himself as he rode with his uncle to the south side of the valley which was downwind from the grazing antelope. The others would be at intervals farther west. Grey Otter and his uncle hid their ponies in a grove of aspens, then crept to their hiding place in the brush and rock. From this elevation Grey Otter could look down the valley and see the fluttering white cloth that eventually, if all went well, would attract the antelope.

Already the heads of some of the animals had lifted. They stared curiously at the white cloth. What occupied Grey Otter's mind, however, were the elk tracks they had come across earlier. He intended to slip away and find an elk, the largest in the herd. His father would be proud of him when they all rode back to see the great antlered animal he had brought down. At first, of course, his father would appear angry but secretly his heart would swell with pride. It would show that his son was worthy one day of becoming a chief.

Clouds slid out from under the sun and warmed their backs. His uncle, mostly bone and with missing teeth, grunted in his contentment and settled down nearby to wait out the antelope.

Grey Otter in his young wisdom knew it was only a matter of time before his uncle dozed. His heartbeat quickened. Grey Otter was bright for his age, and could speak English, having been taught by his father who had attended a mission school.

His uncle might doze in the warm sun, but he would be ready to spring awake at the first shout. According to plan, they would swing in behind the antelope and quickly cut off those who attempted to escape back up the canyon. Most of the herd would be bunched near the white cloth. It was their curiosity that did them in, but they never learned, and the few survivors would repeat the mistake time and again. Nature had endowed them with a curiosity that could not be denied. Anything unusual would attract them. And they always inspected it at close range.

Grey Otter listened to his uncle's steady breathing, saw the eyelids drop and finally close. Holding his breath, the boy eased back from the wall of brush and rock that screened them from the antelope and slung his bow and quiver of arrows over a shoulder. Once clear of the hiding place he moved faster, at a silent, crouching run to his pony. He rode out through the aspens. Now his only problem was to remember exactly where they had seen the elk tracks. How much more sensible to hunt for elk than to teach him patience by wasting half a day with antelope.

When it became necessary, he would have patience, he told himself, as he rode down through the trees, his sharp eyes seeking the imprints left by the elk herd.

Bill Cutter's head began to clear but the pounding, uneven pace of the horse jarred him and sent a knifing pain through his skull. It was when he could think straight once again that he realized his horrible mistake. When half-out on his feet, he had blindly flung himself into a saddle. His own saddle, his own horse. The one that had been giving him trouble all day and now was going lame. He groaned, not only from the pain of the gashed chin but because of his bad luck. Why in hell couldn't he have picked one of the other horses, he asked himself.

He remembered reeling dazedly toward the horses, having had enough of that sharp-shooting half-breed Latigo. Bonchard and Whalen dead; he could tell that just from glancing at them crumpled there on the slope. And Ed Lewt was pinned down somewhere out of sight. Without thinking, Cutter had grabbed his own horse and spurred away from the furious exchange of gunfire that faded quickly behind him. And pushing the horse to extremes had worsened its lameness.

That was miles back, just how many he had no idea. All he knew was that he remained alive only because of sheer luck. For a few moments there after that smashing blow to the chin, he had been out on his feet, reacting solely from instinct. Latigo Cantrell could have come up that slope and shot him to pieces.

Cutter pulled up the limping horse and strained his ears to detect any sounds that would indicate a threat. His heart raced from the after shock of that savage encounter. When he was sure there were no sounds of pursuit, Cutter dismounted. The tired horse stood awkwardly, its weight off the bad leg. Cutter knelt by a small stream and gingerly washed the blood off his chin. At first he thought he had been grazed by a ricochet. Then he realized it was part of a pine knot that had been blasted loose by the slug.

Cutter knew Latigo was after him. It was as certain as sunrise. He was a little surprised that by now he didn't hear sounds of that big black horse Latigo rode pounding from the direction of Apperson's. How he'd love to get his hands on that animal.

Cutter decided he would try and reach El Dorado Gulch, if the damned horse held out. There he would find a replacement and proceed to the job that the four of them had been assigned. Once Cindy Lou was dispatched, Cutter intended to swing over east to Basin City. Creed should be there by then and if not, he'd wait. Then he would collect money for the four of them, not letting on to Creed that the other three were out of it; he was assuming Lewt was dead. Cutter would have all the money for his own pocket. By the time Creed learned the truth, Cutter intended to be somewhere south where winters were mild. He'd had enough of Python.

Again he listened for any sounds of movement along the road, but heard nothing. It was his misfortune that few travelers used the high road this late in the year. Not much chance to find a good horse to replace his lame one. Well, he'd have to do with what he had.

But when he mounted up, the animal balked. After much cursing and quirting and bloodying of spur rowels he managed to push it to a limping walk. Despite his brutality it would go no faster.

He had covered no more than a few miles when the bad leg suddenly collapsed. As the horse went down, Cutter was pitched into the road. The jarring fall reopened the wound. He got up, dazed and swearing. His jaws ached like fire. Blood dripped down the front of his shirt, fresh stains mingling with the old. His horse was trying unsuccessfully to regain its feet. It rolled one eye at Cutter who jerked free his rifle from the boot, feeling no pity for the animal, only a burning rage.

"You bastard, lettin' me down . . ." He shot it in the eye.

He managed to free his saddle and hide it in the thick

brush beside the road. After filling his pockets with shells from the saddlebag, he started off down the road, rifle in one hand, big Remington revolver jiggling at his belt. His shaggy hair brushed his shoulders.

Hiking in high-heeled boots soon tired Cutter's feet. He began to ache from the unnatural pitch of the heels designed for stirrups, not solid ground. He recalled a previous trip along this road and tried to remember if there were isolated ranches that could be seen from the road; he'd steal a horse, kill if necessary to get one. But he couldn't remember any ranch.

As time slipped away, what really began to concern him was Latigo. If Latigo had come out of the gunfight alive, then by now he'd surely be coming hell-bent along this road to finish the job. Latigo would find the dead horse, see fresh boot tracks in the road. From then on, Latigo would be wary and not come riding in blindly, so that meant there was damn little chance to set up an ambush. Even if he was lucky enough to catch a glimpse of him in the distance.

Cutter thought of hiding and waiting it out. But what if Latigo wasn't coming, was dead or wounded? Christ, a man afoot in these mountains could freeze to death if a sudden blizzard howled in. Which was possible this time of year. Apperson had already closed up, smelling an early winter. And wild things were certainly on the move.

Somehow he had to reach El Dorado Gulch. How many miles? He tried to think but was distracted by blisters beginning to form under the chafing leather of his boots.

Grey Otter, riding down through the flaming aspens to lower country, picked up the tracks of elk. He had hoped to find them feeding so he wouldn't have to ride so far. But they were on the move and if he hoped to bring one down he would have to cover distance. The sight of the heavier indentations left by one set of hooves spurred him on. An animal that size would provide much meat for the camp. He smiled. He might even earn a coup feather for downing such a formidable foe with a single arrow through the heart. A pleasing daydream kept him going.

Down through the trees he could see the rutted wagon road and the broad path left by the elk in crossing it. His dark eyes searched the distance, but there was no sign of the animals. They had simply disappeared below the road, under thick clouds that filled a broad valley rim to rim.

No matter, under the overcast he would find his bull elk.

But for the first time there was a nudge of apprehension. Under the cloud cover that from this elevation was impenetrable, there might be more to face than elk.

While pondering this, he saw the white man afoot on the road some twenty feet below where he sat his pony. A heavyset man with a scarred face and bloodstained clothing, he carried a rifle and wore a big pistol. From the blood and the way he was limping, Grey Otter wondered if the stranger had encountered a bear that had clawed him, killed his horse and set him afoot.

Grey Otter's pony snuffled as it caught scent of the man. Too late, the boy tried to pull back but the stranger had halted and was peering up at him. Now that the man's face was turned, Grey Otter could see the ugly wound at the point of his chin. The man started to lift his rifle, which caused Grey Otter's mouth to dry. Then the man changed his mind. He lowered the weapon and raised his right hand in the sign of peace. He smiled, although the effort made him grimace.

"How!" the man called pleasantly to Grey Otter up in the aspens. "You savvy American, kid?"

Grey Otter was proud of his limited ability with the language. "Yes . . . I . . . speak . . . English," he replied haltingly.

"Well, now, that's fine, kid," the man said, raising his voice. "Got jumped by outlaws a ways back." He jerked a thumb over his shoulder. "They shot me an' my hoss. I got away but the hoss was bad hit an' it give out on me."

The man spoke so fast the Grey Otter failed to comprehend most of it. "You . . . are . . . hurt?"

Cutter scowled. I just said so, you dumb little red belly. "Fine hoss you got there, kid. Will he carry double?"

"My pony." Grey Otter patted the animal's neck.

"Sure it's your pony, kid. Come on down to the road here. I need a little help."

Grey Otter was cautious, but Cutter cajoled and pleaded. Finally the boy urged the pony downslope to some young fir trees just above the road. There he had his first close look at the man. Something about the eyes sent a shock of warning through the boy.

Grey Otter uttered a war cry. He was reaching over his shoulder for an arrow to fit to the string of his war bow when something smashed into him. Just before the sky fell and the earth closed in he saw a faint jet of smoke at the muzzle of the stranger's rifle.

Cutter stood over him, the reins of the nervous Indian pony

211

clasped in one hand. "It's a tough world, kid. It belongs to the strong."

He thought of riding back to retrieve the saddle he had cached. But it would waste time and he might encounter Latigo. Besides, hadn't he heard that an Indian pony was not trained to accept a forty-pound stock saddle? It took a lot of patience and time before they got used to the weight. Cutter had neither. And the pony was already skittish, pulling on the reins, snorting at the scent of blood.

When he started to swing aboard, Cutter remembered at the last moment that Indians mounted differently than whites. Careful to keep a firm grip on the reins, he switched sides. Even mounted from the right, the pony made a few buck jumps, not liking the feel of him nor his strange scent. Cutter rode it down quickly and expertly.

Then he looked up at the boy who lay unmoving where he had fallen. He was sure there was no life left in the kid. A great smear of blood darkened the front of the buckskin shirt.

Clouds, ominously black, streamed in under the sun.

Cutter shivered. Clamping the pony's barrel with his knees, he lifted the rifle, aimed at the boy's skull just to make sure of him. Then he decided not to waste another shot that might be needed later on. He rode off up the trail.

33 A buildup of clouds failed to dampen Grover Kinsacker's spirits, because the contrast at higher elevations was welcome after what they had had below. He and his family had just climbed through the roof of the valley overcast. His heavy wagon, pulled by four mules, groaned on the steep grade. A tall, lean man with a flop-brimmed hat, heavy jacket and pants of homespun, he trudged beside his team, occasionally giving one of the mules a gentle poke with the end of a long pole.

He waved back to his wife who handled the reins from the high seat of the canvas-topped wagon. "Sun looks good, Martha, what we can see of it!" he shouted above the squeal of wheels.

"Doesn't it though," she called back. She was a buxom woman with a roundly pleasant face. Her mother had come

West in forty-eight in just such an outfit as this. The mother had left her children behind, Martha and a brother, intending to send for them once Oregon was reached. But cholera wiped out most of the party before their dreams could be fulfilled. Martha had been raised by an aunt. And now Martha herself was coming west with her own children.

Mark, eight, walked beside his father, the pace of the lumbering wagon slow enough to match the stride of his short legs. Behind Mark strolled Amy, tall and angular, dressed like a boy because such attire was more practical. She was strong and willing and had been a great help to her father on the long journey.

With Martha on the wagon seat were the twin babies, Trudy and Joe.

Martha felt she had been blessed. A fine husband in Grover and four handsome children.

Martha knew that their family would probably be one of the last to cross the continent in this fashion. Steam cars would soon replace the vulnerable prairie schooner. Union Pacific was pushing westward to the north of where they were now, Martha had learned. And another line, Centurion Pacific, was drilling its way through the mountains to the south.

At last they reached the high road but found it to be a little improvement over the steep one they had taken to climb out of the valley. At least it was level.

"Thank the good Lord for small favors, Grover," Martha called to her husband.

"I do indeed thank Him." He pointed at the darkening sky. "But we may be in for a storm."

"How far do you think it is to El Dorado Gulch?"

"Twenty miles, maybe." He glanced anxiously at the sky again, the brief sunlight now gone. "Half that would be best. We better hunt for a camp site."

"As you wish."

Grover had halted the outfit so as to give the mules a rest after the long pull. Martha hoped Grover would be able to stake a good claim. Mark and Amy were eager to help work it and earn their share of the gold they would find. Such fabulous tales of quick riches as they had heard in Basin City impressed Grover. She'd wait and see and hope.

If Grover's dreams weren't realized here, perhaps he could be persuaded to continue on to Oregon, as her mother had planned to do. There was still land to be taken up.

*   *   *

A grim Two Buffalos led the hunting party of seven down the mountain, following the tracks left earlier by the missing member, Grey Otter. As miles passed under the hooves of their ponies, the heart of Two Buffalos was heavy, outweighing his earlier anger at the boy's disobedience.

Below, through a screen of trees, was the wagon road at last. For some reason his blood chilled when he saw a line of vultures perched on a long tree limb. At the approach of ponies and men, the scavengers flapped great wings and took to the sky. Then suddenly Two Buffalos saw what had attracted them, a crumpled form half-hidden in a new growth of spindly fir trees.

"My son!" he cried out in his grief. One of the young trees had been snapped by the weight of Grey Otter's body.

Two Buffalos saw the blood and felt sickened. He rode close, his gaze shifting to the road. Indentations in the dust told a story. A white man afoot. Then the tracks of a pony. The white man had found a mount. Grey Otter killed for his pony.

Stoically, Two Buffalos turned to the hunting party and pointed a bronzed finger down at his son. "Take him home."

"I go with you, Two Buffalos." The boy's uncle sat his pony, eyes downcast.

"You failed him. You failed me." Two Buffalos spoke scornfully to his older brother, then dismounted. His son had fallen with his hand on his arrow and war bow.

Faint movement at the boy's bloodied chest caused Two Buffalos to stiffen, then lean down.

"He lives!" cried the uncle to the hazy sky. Tears rolled down his lined cheeks.

"Take him home," Two Buffalos repeated, but raw emotion caused his voice to shake.

Gently he unclasped his son's fingers from the war bow and the arrow. "He was going to fight for his life," Two Buffalos said, nearly choking. The boy had barely time to nock an arrow when he was shot.

Two Buffalos mounted, his son's weapons in hand. The boy's uncle insisted it was he who should be the avenger. "I fell asleep. . . ."

Others in the party also wanted to join in the hunt for the white man. Two of them could take Grey Otter back to the Cheyenne camp, the rest ride with Two Buffalos. But Two Buffalos refused to unbend. It was his right alone to settle with the white man. He rode away, not looking around. Since the coming of the rails and the singing wire there had been few white men he would trust. Now he felt an abiding hatred for them all—men, women and children. It made no difference in the blood haze that shrouded his mind, just so their skins were white.

Then after a few miles, some of the madness drained away and he pinned his eyes on the pony tracks.

He noticed something he had not seen before in his moments of blind grief. Someone had come along this road after the pony had been stolen and ridden away. Tracks made by a shod horse, which meant white man. A strong horse with a long stride, moving swiftly. Who was the rider? Probably someone on the way to the white man's folly at El Dorado Gulch? Where one in ten thousand might find riches.

Two Buffalos kept his senses attuned to possible danger. Two riders on the road, traveling in the same direction. The one he pursued riding an unshod pony. The other mounted on a powerful animal. If this man chose to interfere because of danger to a fellow white man, then he would die. Not in agony as would the other, but quickly for his foolishness.

He rode with Grey Otter's war bow clenched in his left hand, ready to nock an arrow with the right. A searing flesh wound would bring down the man he sought, a knife would finish it.

Amy Kinsacker's long-legged stride matched that of her father's. They had not yet found a camp site but there might be something suitable around the next bend in the road, her father said.

He turned his bearded face to her, pride shining in his brown eyes. "We'll find enough gold to send you to the academy."

Amy sighed. That meant St. Louis. She wanted to stay in the West. Here was excitement, a new life. On the long journey westward, she had begun to bloom. She had long arms and legs and a straight spine. Her hair was chestnut, her eyes large and green. She had an aquiline nose and a pretty mouth for smiling. Men were beginning to notice her, which was pleasing. For so long she had been without curves, having shot up too fast. But now her growth was in directions other than up. She was fourteen and in another year could be married, if she wanted it. She wasn't quite sure. Her mother had married at fifteen.

215

"How much longer, Poppa?" Her brother Mark was asking. The long climb out of the valley had tired him. He refused to ride in the wagon; if Amy could walk, so could he.

"You be our scout. Run ahead and see if there's a good camp site around the next bend," his father said.

Martha called from the wagon seat. "I hope it's beside water. I doubt if there's any dirt left on the plains. It's all on me."

Grover started to laugh, then broke off as they heard sounds of a rider coming at a pretty good clip. They looked back to see who might be catching up around a bend in the road they had just cleared.

"Don't go running off yet, Mark," Grover warned, "till I see who it is." Here the road was too narrow for a rider to squeeze by because of a high cut bank to the left, a sheer drop on the right. Grover had the wagon as close to the edge as he dared.

As the sounds of the hoof beats drew nearer, Grover waited for the wagon seat to catch up to him, then walked beside it. He slid his prodding pole into its place at the side of the wagon, then said, "Better hand me down my rifle, Martha."

Amy was staring back down the road. The hoof beats halted abruptly. "Poppa, it's a man. And he looks as if he's been hurt."

Grover took the rifle from his wife and turned to follow Amy's pointing finger, in the direction of a big man in a heavy coat spotted with blood. Grover took note of the man's pistol at the waist, the rifle gripped in his right hand.

"Howdy," Grover sang out a little nervously to the scowling stranger, whose Indian pony now stood with feet widespread, eyes sullen.

"Hoss throwed me is how I got busted up," the man called, walking the pony toward the tailgate of the slow-moving wagon. "Had to buy this pony off an injun. . . ."

"No room for you to get by," Grover called. He gestured with his rifle. "Not 'less you ride up into the trees and maybe get by us that way."

Cutter kept pace with the wagon. "Head's really hurtin," he said. "Wouldn't happen to have some whiskey, would you?"

"Never touch it," Grover told him, although he did.

"Neither do I. 'Less somethin' ails me. Like my head does now. Pain's somethin' fierce. Sometimes it's the only medicine a fella can git his hands on."

"Yes, I expect." Grover didn't like the way the stranger's eyes were making light touches over Amy's body. He licked his lips. "Should be a turnout soon. I'll pull over and let you

216

by. Amy, why don't you climb in the wagon and get those things together your mother wanted." He tried to sound casual in his attempt to get Amy under the canvas top and out of sight, but it came out squeaky with tension.

"What things, Grover?" Martha started to say, then realized what he meant. "Oh, yes, I remember. Amy, will you do it, please?" Worry flickered in her eyes.

Without a word, Amy waited for the wagon to catch up and climbed in. She crawled between the twins.

Cutter leaned over on the pony so he could see beyond the tailgate when Amy made her entry into the wagon. He enjoyed the tightness of her cotton shirt and canvas work pants.

"Strong lookin' mules you got there," Cutter called out when he saw the man looking his way.

"A good team," Grover called back.

"Any of 'em been broke to saddle?"

"They'll all take a saddle." It was the wrong thing for Grover to say.

Cutter hid his smile. Through the wagon flaps he could see Amy stirring around inside. His bloodstream heated up like a Yellowstone geyser when he thought of spending a long winter with a filly like that.

He looked to his right. It was straight down, maybe a thousand feet. Hell, how often did an outfit like this run off the road and remain undiscovered till spring? Easy to do.

"There's a turnout ahead," Grover called back, relief in his voice, "then you can be on your way."

"See it," Cutter responded good-naturedly. "Wonder if the young lady inside the wagon could hand me out a piece of bread or somethin'. Ain't had a bite since last night."

Martha hesitated for a moment. "Amy, hand the man some biscuits," she called back from the wagon seat. Her voice shook slightly.

Cutter waited for the slim arm to appear through the wagon flaps with the biscuits. He was ready to grab it when he realized someone was behind him, the approach covered by the rattle and screech of the wagon.

"Cutter, get your hands up! Don't turn around!"

Cutter flung himself off the pony and headfirst into the wagon, through the flaps. His momentum bowled over Amy who was kneeling on a pile of blankets, a pan of biscuits in her hand. Biscuits and pan went flying.

Cutter seized Amy by a wrist. "Keep your mouth shut!" he warned the terrified girl.

217

With the barrel of his gun he pushed aside the canvas flaps and peered out. He saw that his pony had swung around in the road and was trying to squeeze past a big black horse. One of the pony's hoofs slid off the edge of the sheer drop. It lost its balance, screaming and kicking air until lost from sight beneath the clouds. But it was the rider on the black horse that held Cutter's eye.

"Latigo Cantrell, by God," Cutter cried.

Amy screamed and clawed at Cutter's face. "Momma, *run!*"

Cutter ducked his head in time so that Amy nails raked his forehead instead of his eyes. The wagon was just swinging into the turnoff when Martha Kinsacker, a twin under each arm, jumped into the road.

As the wagon came to a halt, Cole shouted, "Step out, Cutter!" He reined in Trooper.

Cole lifted his Henry rifle. The girl tried to leap from the front of the wagon as the older woman had done. He glimpsed a leg, an arm, a partial, pale profile. Cutter caught her by the long hair, jerked her back. In so doing, he lost his balance, but quickly regained it and leaped from the wagon, the girl's body a shield. They crashed to the road. Army's head rolled as the man rammed a pistol into her side.

"Stand back everybody!" Cutter yelled. "Gal's dead if you don't!"

"Don't harm her. . . ." Martha began to sob. "Please don't harm her!"

Cole began to taunt him, knowing it was risky for the girl, but seeing it as his only hope. "Step out, Cutter! Fight like a man! Not behind a girl. I'll meet you halfway!"

"Go to hell!"

Cole, desperate, tried again. "Keep these people out of it, Cutter. It's not their fight, it's *ours!*"

"Throw down that rifle, Latigo. *Now!*"

Cole saw the wedge of face above the girl's shoulder. A small enough target to be sure. But directly behind her was the mother, on her feet now, frozen. And near the team the husband stood unmoving, rifle pointed at the ground. The young boy, eyes enormous in a strained white face kept crying, "What'll we do, Poppa, what'll we do?"

"Just what he tells you," Grover said shakily. "We've got to think of your mother and the twins and your sister."

34

Cutter, crouched behind the girl, turned his head slightly to yell at her father. "Throw that rifle over the edge or I'll blow out your daughter's backbone."

Grover threw his rifle away.

Cole was drained. Never had he felt so trapped. He hadn't counted on a family being mixed up in it. If Cutter could accept an assignment to murder Helen, it meant the whole family was expendable.

"You heard me, Latigo!" Cutter shouted again. "Rifle first, then throw down your pistol!" The girl cried out as Cutter rammed her in the side with the pistol. Her face was utterly drained of color.

Cole let his Henry rifle fall into the road, then inched a hand toward his gun butt.

"Careful," Cutter warned. "I'd as soon kill her as breathe. You know that, Latigo."

"Yeah, I know that." Cole hesitated, hoping for a break of some kind.

Cutter said, "You got to the count of three, Latigo. If that pistol ain't in the road by then, the gal's dead. Then the old lady . . ."

Cutter started to count. All Cole had to do was to see the terrified face of the young girl, her mother clutching the weeping twins by the hand. The young boy, trembling, the fearful father.

Cole lifted his revolver and let it fall, careful that it did not strike a stone in the road. He wanted no damage to the weapon. Somehow he would prevail. All he needed was for Cutter to let down his guard.

He stepped down from Trooper. The big horse snorted and tossed his head.

Cutter grinned. He pulled the girl harder against him. She had torn out the knee of the canvas pants in her fall from the wagon. There was blood, lacerated flesh.

"Kid," Cutter beckoned to the boy. "I want every gun out of that wagon. *Everything!*"

"Do what he says," Grover implored his son in a trembling voice.

219

In less than a minute the frightened boy deposited a rifle and two revolvers on the ground next to Cutter's feet.

"Latigo, turn your back!" Cutter seemed amused.

Cole knew that if he obeyed, he was dead. He was dead anyway, unless somebody produced a miracle. It didn't seem likely to happen, even though he'd fervently hoped otherwise. His eyes gunned not Cutter's face, but the girl's. He tried to will her to let herself fall to her knees or twist from Cutter's grasp and leap aside. Anything to make more of a target and less risk to herself.

She failed to respond, her mind and muscles paralyzed by fear.

It was the mother who abruptly shifted the balance. Screaming, she brushed the twins aside and leaped. She caught Amy by an arm and literally tore her away from Cutter. Cole flung himself at the .44 he had been forced to discard. A shot slammed into one of the road ruts. Hardened earth and bits of stone disintegrated as the bullet howled in rocochet. A peppering pain struck Cole's left eye. Seizing the gun, he cocked it and rolled, away from Trooper and perilously near the cliff edge. He sprang up, sighted the gun.

The woman, a raging lioness in defense of her family, was clawing at Cutter's face, at the bloodied furrows made earlier by her daughter's nails. Cutter swung her around so that her back was to Cole. In that infinity of time Cole had to shift his aim. He fired over their heads instead of into Martha's broad back.

Cutter's gun appeared, a black snout of muzzle between the woman's arm and her rib cage. A flash, and Cole felt the impact lift him, spin him, slam him to the road. The .44 fell out of his hand.

Powder flash had set the woman's dress on fire. She was screaming.

"Shut her up!" Cutter yelled at the man, who sprang forward to help his wife.

Then Cutter, keeping an eye on Cole, gathered up the weapons he had ordered the boy to bring him. He threw them over the drop at the edge of the road. They clattered and scraped rock, until a long breath later there was a distant crack. Evidently one of the gun hammers had struck some hard object and discharged a shell.

Cutter walked the fifteen yards to where Cole lay on his back. He studied the bloodless face, the bullet hole in the left side, the shirt heavy with blood.

220

Then he turned to the snorting, big black horse, hauled it in by the reins and tied it to a stump.

He stood over Cole. "Latigo . . . can you hear me?"

Cole's eyelids fluttered. He stared up into the face of the man he had hunted for so long. He thought of his parents and this man's part in their deaths. The thought seared through the numbness of his mind but could not connect to nerves and tendons and muscle. His arms refused to move.

Cutter was going through his pockets. He came upon the confession signed by Ed Lewt. His lips moved over each word. Then he laughed. He ripped the page into small pieces and threw them over the edge. Wind currents whirled them away.

A sound of a wagon moving, wheels squeaking, mules digging in as a whip cracked. Cutter leaped to his feet, glaring at the wagon just disappearing around a bend in the road.

"Let' 'em go," Cole whispered. "They're no part of this."

Cutter looked down at him, the thick legs widespread. "I'll catch up with 'em. That's a good hoss you got there." He smiled. "He'll get me where I want to go."

"You're pure son of a bitch, Cutter," Cole gasped.

"You ain't the only one thinks so." Cutter seemed amused. Then he scowled down at the crumpled figure in the road. "Tell me somethin', Latigo. Why the hell did you keep after us an' keep after us? Christ, you gunned down Sam Stark. You put a bullet in Creed. Didn't mind that so much 'cause I hate the bastard. But Ed Lewt was my friend."

"You ask why I . . . why I kept after you?"

"Yeah."

"My parents." The words were coming harder now, but with the ability to move his lips, he could also twitch a finger. Hope leaped in him. He concentrated on the face peering down, the eyes mocking. "In Beaver Valley. Don't you remember? Badger Cantrell and White Elk . . ."

"So long ago I most forgot them two."

"I never forgot." Cole's left hand clutched the medicine bag under the bloodstained shirt. His right moved an inch toward the revolver that still lay within reach. Cutter wasn't fooled. As Cole made a feeble stab toward the weapon, Cutter kicked it away. It spun over the cliff edge and down.

Cutter leaned down and tore Cole's hand away from the small pouch suspended from his neck by the blue cord. "What's that?" Cutter demanded.

"Medicine . . . strong medicine."

"I'll give you my kinda medicine!" Cutter pointed his big Remington revolver at Cole's face. "You gonna beg for mercy?"

Cole shook his head as he looked up at the weapon. When it was fired, which was inevitable now, he would see the flick of muzzle flash, perhaps live another second or so to see the spill of smoke from the barrel.

Something remembered from childhood struggled from a recess of his mind. It was a death chant, taught him by the Crows. In the mountain stillness the eerie sound rose from Cole's lips. But his limbs were heavy chains. Only his heart throbbed and that not for long.

"So long, Latigo," Cutter said and his big thumb drew back the hammer of the Remington.

Louder, more defiant, sounded the Crow death chant. Cole's eyes burned up into the face above. There came to him a faint, dull sound as that made by the point of a butcher's knife thrust into gristle and bone.

A strong startled look crossed Cutter's face. His legs seemed suddenly to assume a mighty weight. His knees caved and he sprawled across Cole's legs. Had Cole been able to move his arm, he could have touched the feathered shaft of an arrow buried inches deep in Cutter's back.

A voice spoke to him in Cheyenne. Cole no longer uttered the Crow death chant. He looked dazedly up at the bronzed face of a warrior, met the black and penetrating gaze. Then the face swam out of sight and there was only darkness.

In El Dorado Gulch, first drenched by rain then whitened by a light snowfall, Grover Kinsacker told his story. Excited men saddled up and asked him to lead them to the spot, more than twenty miles south, where Latigo Cantrell had last been seen. Among the riders were Duke Sateen and Jeremy Van Horn. Their mission was to retrieve the body of Latigo Cantrell and give it a decent burial in the town's ever-expanding cemetery.

But when they reached the site of the tragedy, rain had washed out all sign and the clouds had spit enough snow to whiten the roadway.

Predators had beat them to the body of Latigo Cantrell, most everyone agreed.

Duke Sateen, the gambler, wasn't so sure. "Ah got me a strong hunch that Cap'n Cantrell is still alive," he said. "Somewhere."

The others shook their heads and smiled in disbelief.

Grover Kinsacker, as the only witness, was positive. "The man called Latigo is dead, I'm sorry to say. I'm as sure of it as I am that his body is gone. I was unarmed and I had my family to consider. I got out of there fast as I could. . . ." He closed his eyes.

"Wonder Cutter didn't come after you," one of the men spoke up.

"Something must have scared him off." Grover clenched his teeth, thinking of their close call. "I hope to see such a miserable creature hang by the neck."

"If he's still on this earth, he'll hang. You can bet your britches on that."

"Latigo Cantrell saved our lives. No doubt in my mind. If any man ever died a hero, he sure did."

In a Cheyenne camp, the Indian medicine was working on Grey Otter, the boy, and Cole Cantrell, the man. A strong herb tea had reduced Cole's fever and a poultice was healing his wound. On this his first rational day, he thought of the vengeance trail. Three down, two to go: Al Dain, Doak Lancer.

He was smiling when Dark Star spoke to the Cheyenne, Two Buffalos. "I have come to take him home. . . ."

THRILLS * CHILLS * MYSTERY
from FAWCETT BOOKS

☐ THE GLOW	24333	$2.75
by Brooks Stanwood		
☐ THAT MAN GULL	04637	$1.95
by Anthony Stuart		
☐ THE GREEN RIPPER	14340	$2.50
by John D. MacDonald		
☐ MURDER IN THREE ACTS	03188	$1.75
by Agatha Christie		
☐ NINE O'CLOCK TIDE	04527	$1.95
by Mignon G. Eberhart		
☐ DEAD LOW TIDE	14166	$1.75
by John D. MacDonald		
☐ DEATH OF AN EXPERT WITNESS	04301	$2.25
by P. D. James		
☐ PRELUDE TO TERROR	24034	$2.50
by Helen MacInnes		
☐ AN UNSUITABLE JOB FOR A WOMAN	00297	$2.25
by P. D. James		
☐ FINAL CUT	14372	$1.95
by Max Perry		
☐ FALLING STAR	24347	$1.95
by Lillian O'Donnell		
☐ A CLUTCH OF VIPERS	04632	$1.95
by Jack S. Scott		